THE PROMISE

www.rbooks.co.uk

THE PROMISE

Susan Sallis

BANTAM PRESS

LONDON · TORONTO · SYDNEY · AUCKLAND · JOHANNESBURG

TRANSWORLD PUBLISHERS
61–63 Uxbridge Road, London W5 5SA
A Random House Group Company
www.rbooks.co.uk

First published in Great Britain
in 2011 by Bantam Press
an imprint of Transworld Publishers

A CIP catalogue record for this book
is available from the British Library.

ISBN 9780593067406

Addresses for Random House Group Ltd companies outside the UK
can be found at: www.randomhouse.co.uk
The Random House Group Ltd Reg. No. 954009

The Random House Group Limited supports the Forest Stewardship
Council (FSC), the leading international forest-certification organization.
All our titles that are printed on Greenpeace-approved FSC-certified paper
carry the FSC logo. Our paper procurement policy can be found at
www.rbooks.co.uk/environment

Typeset in 11½/15¼pt New Baskerville by
Kestrel Data, Exeter, Devon
Printed in the UK by
CPI Mackays, Chatham ME5 8TD

2 4 6 8 10 9 7 5 3 1

To the people who have shared
their memories with me

THE PROMISE

Prologue – Coventry

There were four of the Thorpe family in the Anderson shelter the night of the raid on Coventry. Mum and Dad, Florrie and little May. Jack was missing; properly missing. He had been one of those who did not get back from Dunkirk.

They all knew what to do; Dad was an air raid warden when he wasn't at the factory making steel plating for armoured cars. Until that night his duties had consisted of looking for chinks in blackout curtains, making sure people had their gas masks with them at all times, giving lessons on the use of stirrup pumps when dealing with incendiary bombs, being ready to light the oil drums that would create a smokescreen if 'they' actually decided to give Coventry the once-over.

That night, as the alert wailed over the ancient town, he herded people into their nearest shelters, patrolled his patch, then joined his family in their own shelter, where Mum had already mummified both girls in the grey army blankets issued with the gas masks ages ago when the prospect of another war was both out of the question and exciting.

May still thought it was exciting. She was eleven and enjoyed air raid practices at school when they sang 'We're going to hang Adolf's knickers on his Siegfried Line', and she still got the giggles when they did gas mask drill and

Miss Lemming's muffled voice said, 'Sit down, children!' sounding as if it might be saying something else entirely. She still believed Jack was alive. Jack was not only her big brother, he was a hero.

Florrie was less excited. She was seventeen and preparing to go down to Wiltshire, where in an enormous shed, inappropriately called HMS *Horatio*, space was being prepared to train new recruits in the use of charts and plotting. Now that the time for departure was almost on her, she realized that training to be a Wren meant leaving her family. As the sky outside the shelter filled with the throb of the first wave of bombers, her feeling of dread solidified into fear, then terror.

They obeyed Dad to the letter. 'Heads down, hands over heads, cover ears, crouch right over . . .'

After what seemed like hours, the chaos outside appeared to sort itself out into some kind of pattern. They lifted their heads slightly, regulated the panic breathing, registered the tense tremor in their thighs, the nausea in their throats. There was still noise but the overpowering roar of countless aircraft was . . . less.

Dad said, 'I think they call it carpet bombing. It might be over.' He waited and now they could hear screams and wails; human sounds. 'I'd better go and see what's what. Don't anyone dare poke their heads out of the opening.'

He was gone for ages. The screams sorted themselves out into cries for help, responses, directions, meaningless shouts; all against a background of other noises that could have been houses crashing down and . . . fire.

And then the second wave of planes came in. The first had been from west to east; these were from south to north.

A grid pattern. This was carpet bombing. And it was closer to their street. The sheer pulsating pressure of the roar shut out most other sounds but they could still hear the whistle of falling bombs. Close. Closer.

Dad arrived as the high-pitched squeal of a descending explosive cut right through the engine throb, like cheese wire through Leicester Red. They saw him quite clearly in the opening, silhouetted against a sheet of flame. He made no effort to drop through; he seemed to leap on to the framework, spreadeagle himself, make a human shield to absorb some of the blast. That was how it happened. Suddenly he too was a hero.

Florrie was eventually stretchered out of the hole unconscious. The other two recalled nothing until they were in the crypt of the church, waiting in a queue for tea. Above them the cacophony went on. They got tea and biscuits and sat next to two children who were crying and stank of urine. Mum told May to watch her manners. Then to stop grizzling. In answer to the girl's unanswerable questions she repeated monotonously, 'I don't know.' And varied it occasionally with a waspish 'How should I know?' In this strange way they both reached a point when they did know. Knew that there was nothing; no house, no cups and saucers and teapots, no blankets or clothes. No pictures of Grampy. No Jack. No Dad . . . no Dad . . . no Jack . . . 'Stop grizzling, our May! Others worse off than us! Florrie's going to be all right and you and me – we're fine. We're fine, d'you hear me? We're fine!'

Another bomb dropped very close and people screamed and the ceiling of the crypt snowed dust. The tarpaulin sheltering the stone steps to the surface flapped as someone arrived. May looked up just before starting to cry again and saw a man in the hairy khaki of a soldier, wearing a tin hat, blood on his face. He looked across the card tables, the tea urn and the thick white china cups and saucers and saw her and lifted a hand. She screamed once. 'Jack!' She had known. All along she had known he would come back.

They lived with Grandma Thorpe just outside the city boundary. Jack came and went; somewhere in an army records office he must have been posted as a deserter, or dead. He queued with all of them and obtained an emergency identity card but never risked applying for ration books. When the police were issued with pistols in case of riots, somehow he obtained one. Mum was terrified he would use it on himself. He accused her once of 'always calling me a coward'. She remembered using the word 'deserter'. But never 'coward'. She became as thin as a rasher of wind.

But Jack made May happy. She didn't care that he was a deserter. He had arrived when Dad had gone and he was a hero. A lot of the time he lived out in the Warwickshire countryside in a ruined barn next to a bombed-out farm-house and she would take food to him. When Florrie came home on leave, she said he was 'going funny' and they should talk to the doctor about him. Mum warned her fiercely never to say things like that again.

On VE day Florrie was home and Grandma Thorpe was in hospital and they sat around, eating chocolate biscuits from an American food parcel. Florrie had duly inherited Great-aunt Florence's house – always promised to her – married someone called Bert and had a baby girl exactly nine months later. It was her way out of the Wrens; she had not set eyes on the sea in her two years' service.

She wanted things to go back to how they had been. She knew she could not resurrect Dad or make Jack into a hero like May had, but she could help put some flesh back on her mother and she could find an office job for Jack where no one knew him. Life was kinder in the south.

She laid out her plans while she fed the baby.

'We've got to forget Coventry. Even Grandma agreed with me when I visited. She said to sell the house and move down to Devon with me. A fresh start. That's what she said. A fresh start.' The others pretended to consider it; they all knew it would not happen. The authorities would eventually catch up with Jack wherever he went. When he arrived and wolfed down the biscuits May had saved for him, they did not even mention it.

Later he took May into town to see some of the celebrations. They both said goodbye to Florrie and her baby; she was catching the seven fifteen to Brum and then an express to Exeter. It would take five hours. Like living in another country.

There was a bonfire illuminating the ruins of the cathedral. That was where it happened. It was almost dark; they had stayed too long. People were drunk and someone suddenly yelled, 'That's 'im, Sarge! He bin living rough ever since Dun-bloody-kirk! Bloody deserter!' At the same time, a man who had had his arm around May's waist, trying to get her to dance, bent her backwards, grinning and yelling, 'Tango, little lady! Tango!' and then swept her out of the light and slammed her against one of the broken walls and began to slaver over her face, sucking, biting, pushing. Like a dog. Just like a dog.

Afterwards, May was never certain which came first, Jack's

arrest or her . . . She did not like the word and forced herself to say it in her head. Rape. Arrest or rape. Rape or arrest. They happened simultaneously.

There were so many people; a band was playing; a group of women were doing a knees-up around a smaller fire. Couples were dancing and kissing and doing much more. She could see over the man's shoulder that Jack was being arrested. She screamed and the man thought she was calling for help and ripped the front of her dress from top to bottom. Jack was trying to fight off a military policeman. The man pinioned her hands above her head. She screamed again, this time for herself as well as for Jack. He could see her, he could see what was happening. He yelled and started to run towards her, dragging two men with him. She was held like one of the specimens in the biology room at school, pinned against the wall while the man sobbed frantically into her ear. And then he was gone, ripped away. And Jack was gone too, dragged backwards towards a van, shouting, 'I know you – I know you!'

It was shame that got May home safely. There was such a racket going on that no one seemed to realize about the dress. She drew it around her, pulled up her knickers and went home. And Jack got away somehow. Tracked the man who had raped her, an old neighbour of theirs. Shot him dead and then shot himself.

That night Mum started to say it. Over and over again. That same night, after the police arrived and told them about Jack and then the man, she woke May and began. The man had a name. George Hutchinson. It was vaguely familiar.

It might have been different if Florrie had not left for her train back home. She might have screamed hysterically that the man – George Hutchinson – had deserved it because he had raped her fifteen-year-old sister. But Florrie rarely changed her plans and was already on the Exeter train. She was told that Jack had been arrested and had shot himself. And that was all. She wasn't there when Mum washed May and tucked her into bed with cocoa and codeine. She was not there when Mum woke May and started to say those dreadful words.

'Promise me . . . promise me you will never tell anyone.'

Through her tears May tried to explain that Jack was a hero and people should know that. Mum said, 'Not even Florrie. You're not going to carry this load around with you all your life, my girl. Promise me . . . now.'

Eventually, exhausted, May promised.

After Mum's funeral a year later, when Florrie and she were having a quiet chat, May dropped George Hutchinson's name into the teacup conversation. A test. To see just how much Florrie knew or guessed. It meant nothing to her.

'If our Jack knew him, why on earth did he go for him?' She tutted and shook her head. 'I suppose he called him yellow-belly or something even worse. It must have been the last straw for our Jack. Poor devil.'

'He was a hero, Florrie. Living hand to mouth all that time, keeping plenty of firewood, rabbits for the pot – that's why he wanted that revolver. He was a hero.'

'I suppose he was. Yes. You have to be dead to be a hero.' Florrie spoke without cynicism. 'First Dad, then Jack.' She grinned. 'Are we going to be heroes when we die, our May?'

'Why not?' They both managed to laugh. They were at their mother's funeral and they laughed. But May had her diploma from the Commercial College, she had a good job in the Town Hall, she was not going to die for a long time. It was different for Florrie. She had not enjoyed being a Wren and she was not enjoying being a wife, though she admitted that if she hadn't first of all been a wife she could not have been a mother, and baby Carrie more than made up for that dreadful honeymoon in Wiltshire. 'Only once then?' May asked. 'You bet!' Florrie replied and tried to laugh again. She said, 'If you come and live with us it will be all right, our May. You can get a good job in Exeter – better than here prob'ly – and I can put up with Bert if I've got you for company.'

They laughed because what else could you do? But Florrie need not have worried about a second night like the first one in Wiltshire because she and Bert and the baby changed trains at Birmingham and were in the front coach when it crashed into a goods train taking china clay from Cornwall to Stoke-on-Trent. Six people died immediately and they accounted for three of those. As May's boss, Mr Partridge, said, 'They went together, Miss Thorpe. They lived together and the three of them died together.' May wished so much she had gone with them as Florrie had suggested. The four of them. Now there was just one.

But – as Mr Partridge said later – time heals all. May inherited the house in Devon and let it immediately. She was also sole owner of Grandma Thorpe's house and she had a good job. Walter Partridge was Chairman of the Council and he reminded her of Dad. He had hinted that when his secretary retired next year, she should apply for the job.

So much to be thankful for.

One

February 2009

Steve Coles looked across his desk at the two sixth-formers, Daisy Patek and Marcus Budd. Sometimes his head ached when he ran a quick eye over his tutor group; they were so vulnerable and did not seem to know it. Especially these two. Beautiful, clever, with the kind of enquiring minds that made teaching an amazing pleasure. Almost eighteen, believing themselves to be adults, certain that they would continue to be friends as they had been since the age of three. More than friends perhaps.

Daisy said, 'You OK, Steve?'

He nodded. 'Just wondering whether this is such a good idea after all.'

Daisy said, 'Sounds OK to me.'

'She's coming up to eighty. One or two spells in hospital. I know BC is keen on tying in this citizenship thing with you two taking modern history A's this summer, but if she gets upset . . .' BC was Barry Carter, head of the school.

Marcus made a face. 'You'll have to carry the can?'

Steve frowned slightly. 'I was thinking of her. Miss Thorpe. Maiden lady living in sheltered accommodation and so on.

17

And we don't know whether we're raking up memories that are . . . well, unbearable.'

Marcus considered this, glancing at Daisy, who lifted her brows and turned down her mouth at the same time. He said, 'Listen. You've written to her and she has agreed to see us and talk to us. Let's just do this first visit. We'll do the getting-to-know-you bit. Yes? That will satisfy BC. We might not even mention Coventry.'

Steve said heavily, 'I mentioned Coventry. In my introductory letter. And she replied saying she couldn't remember much but she was happy to try to answer your questions.'

Daisy turned back to the table, eyes now wide with exaggerated astonishment.

'Where's the problem then? We're keen to get the third dimension here. We've read the books, watched the history channel, googled. Now we've got the chance to talk to someone who was actually there. And she's agreed to it. So let's . . . sort of . . . like . . . go for it.'

'Daisy.' Marcus checked her impatience. 'She's on her own. Probably everyone she knew then is dead.' He hesitated. 'I mean . . . Mum and me . . . we don't often talk about Dad.'

Daisy nodded immediately. Marc's dad had been dead for two years.

'Miss Thorpe's – like – vulnerable. But we know that, so we're not going to barge in and ask her what it was like to suddenly not have a father or a brother. Anyway, it was ages ago.'

Steve winced at her brash words. The way she used that word: vulnerable. Marcus, sole carer for his mother, knew about vulnerability. But Daisy, adored only child of a professional couple . . . Steve wondered whether he was sickening for something; his body was aching.

'All I'm saying is, be aware that there might be areas that are completely out of bounds to a couple of teenagers who can barely define arse or elbow.'

'Sir!' They both laughed as he intended. After all, their vulnerability was closely bound up with innocence and you didn't want to be the person who damaged that.

'So you'd like to do it?'

'I'm keen.' Daisy looked at Marcus and he looked back; they were both grinning.

'Likewise.' Marcus levered his long length upwards. 'You worry too much, Steve. We'll be old enough to vote next year.'

Steve leaned back in his chair; for some reason he was exhausted. He said, 'You will also be old enough, young Marcus, to go to Afghanistan, fully armed, and shoot as many so-called rebels as you can.'

Daisy stood up too. Steve was reminded of a pea shooting out of its pod. She said, 'As if. That's an option Marcus will not be taking.'

'Quite. But Miss Thorpe's father and brother probably weren't offered options.' He pushed their folders across the desk. 'Take plenty of notes. Jenner House has got a good reputation. See if you agree with it. The headmaster will be especially interested in those sorts of observations. And if you get round to talking about the past, you could go on with your non-script essays, Daisy. I've given you a mark for your illustrations of the Battle of Britain but I hope you realize that the A-level history examiners will be after text rather than drawings.'

'D'you know, sir, that is almost weird. I had thought of asking Miss Thorpe about her school uniform and whether she took her gas mask to bed with her!'

'Out!'

'Yes, sir.'

'And if you want to drop by after tomorrow's interview—'

'Not interview, Steve. Meeting.'

'Tomorrow's meeting. Yes. If you want to drop by after tomorrow's meeting, feel free to do so.'

He watched them barge into each other as they went through the door. It would all start to happen soon. Marcus would get a provisional place at Leeds – his first choice – and would have to turn it down because he couldn't leave his mother, and Daisy would offer to keep an eye because she would be doing a year's art foundation course at Bristol so would continue to live at home.

He thought grimly that he loved them all and yet could not afford to care too much. Objectivity was so important. Then he wondered whether he had swine flu. If he had, then he had certainly infected them and probably the whole school would have to be quarantined.

He wondered what Julia might have prepared for supper. Her culinary range was not wide and nothing she usually cooked appealed to his imagination at the moment. But home did. And his own bed did. He locked everything up and began the long trek down corridors and round to the science block, where he could slip through to the car park. He opened up thankfully and slid into the driving seat. On the floor was the empty plastic box from yesterday's picnic in the Forest of Dean. He wrestled off the lid and was sick into the bits of tomato, cucumber and bread.

He drove carefully. He felt so sorry for himself he completely forgot Marcus and Daisy.

Two

The doorbell rang, its annoying ping-pong immediately supplemented by the bank of lights sitting on top of the bureau. Miss Thorpe began to lever herself out of the chair, muttering fiercely as the stiffness in ankles, knees, hips and shoulders crescendoed into two sharp twinges in her elbows. Before she could get herself fully upright the bell rang again and the lights dutifully flashed. 'Shut up!' she hissed at them furiously. The social worker had been the one to instigate the lights. *'No, I know you're not deaf, Miss Thorpe. But if you've got the radio on you could easily miss the doorbell. You certainly won't miss the lights.'*

She was right there. The dratted things were a peculiar shade of blue that hit the eyeball, central vision, peripheral vision, the whole lot, then went on through the brain and out the other side. She had explained to the social worker, whose name was Britney (*'Call me Britney, dear, it's easier than Mrs Longsmith.' 'No, thank you,' Miss Thorpe had replied*), that visitors had to use the key pad outside the flats before they could get inside the building. Mrs Britney Longsmith had interrupted smilingly, 'I know that, dear. But you and I both know that most people are admitted before they've even read the instructions. So it really is important for you to have a decent system in your own flat.' And the lights had arrived.

They stopped flashing just as Miss Thorpe reached the door. She opened it cautiously. Her new glasses were still unfamiliar and the blueness of the blue lights had for a moment stunned her. She was expecting to see two children so she looked down. A voice came from her own level.

'Good morning, Miss Thorpe. I am Daisy Patek and this is Marcus Budd. You are expecting us?'

The girl was beautiful. It was the eyes. Enormous dark doe-eyes. Miss Thorpe was reminded of the first time she had been to the cinema; it was to see Walt Disney's *Snow White*. Those almond eyes had taken up half Snow White's face. And here they were again, in the flesh.

For some reason Miss Thorpe could only nod. Surely she wasn't overcome by this pretty schoolgirl? Perhaps it was also the way the girl made a special rhythm from her name. Daisy P'tek. She could have said Pah-tek.

The girl said briskly, 'That's OK then. We wondered whether Steve had made one of his famous cock-ups. Told you the wrong day or something. We couldn't get you on the key pad outside. Someone let us in.'

The boy leaned forward. He was taller than the girl, somehow protective of her.

'Stephen Coles. Our personal tutor. Teacher. Who arranged this meeting for us. We're doing modern history and he rang the manager of . . .' he waved his hand, 'this place in case anyone had personal experience of the Blitz and she told him that you had been in Coventry.'

The girl glanced at him fondly as if he were a pet dog. 'Jenner House. Like you could forget that!'

Miss Thorpe nodded again, then, releasing the door,

turned round and stretched her hands out to the wall as she moved slowly and carefully down the tiny hallway. She was anxious not to stumble in front of these children.

'Close the door as you come through,' she said. Her voice emerged hoarsely. She had not spoken to anyone that day and it was two o'clock. Surely her lunch should have opened up her tubes . . . She could not remember lunch. 'I must have nodded off. I didn't hear the outer door. How fortunate that someone was around to let you in.'

'My aunty is on the cleaning team here.' The girl sat in one of the chairs Miss Thorpe had brought forward that morning . . . so she could not have forgotten that the children were coming. The boy waited to the rear and side of her own special chair. He put a hand under her arm and helped her down. She looked up at him, surprised. Weren't all these strange teenagers meant to be hooligans?

Daisy P'tek smiled that same small, fond smile. 'Marcus is a carer – he can't help himself!' She laughed, so it must be a joke. And Marcus was smiling too as he settled himself in the other chair.

'This is nice,' he commented. 'Everything is so – so – within reach.'

Miss Thorpe had to smile at him. 'You mean small and cramped,' she said.

'I didn't mean that.' He leaned back, somehow managing to smile and frown at the same time as he considered the bed-sitting-room around him. Miss Thorpe tried to remember whether she had hidden her awful old nightie and dressing gown under the duvet or whether the whole thing was a pile of bedding and clothing surmounted by her bedtime reading. Surely if she had remembered to pull out the chairs she had remembered to tidy her bed?

Daisy grew tired of the silence and said, 'He likes it just the way it is – that's what he's trying to say, only he takes, like, half an hour to utter one word.'

Marcus nodded. 'I do like it. It's very much a pad, isn't it? More than that, even – a den. It's like a den.'

Miss Thorpe did not know how she felt about living in a den like an animal. She said, 'There's a kitchen and a bathroom. And of course outside in the corridor is the library, and there's the residents' lounge downstairs and the hairdressing room, and there are chairs in the corridor inside the bay windows. They're really nice.'

'He doesn't know about the rest of the house,' Daisy said. 'I know it well because sometimes I've helped Aunty with the cleaning and she lets me explore. I know just what you mean. You don't kind of, like, *think* small, do you? Because you live in such a big house. With an important name. Did you know that Dr Jenner invented a vaccine for smallpox?'

Marcus was definitely annoyed. 'Of course Miss Thorpe knows that! She lives in a house named after him, for goodness' sake!'

'I might easily not have known it.' Miss Thorpe spoke quickly because the big almond eyes looked stricken.

Then the girl said, 'No . . . but I didn't mean to sound like a condescending bitch and I did, didn't I?'

Miss Thorpe was thoroughly taken aback by this statement and went into automatic. 'Not at all.' She cleared her throat. 'Shall we have a cup of coffee?'

Daisy beamed instantly. 'That would be great. Have you got any teabags?'

'Oh yes. But I thought you young people preferred coffee. I would prefer tea too.' She began to lever herself up and Daisy held out a restraining hand.

'Marcus will do it. He's excellent with drinks. And I'm not too bad with listening and passing on inexplicabilities.' She sat back, smiling at herself, and Miss Thorpe suddenly stopped worrying about where she had put coffee, teabags, mugs and milk and smiled too. The small bedsit was filled with winter afternoon sunshine. The fridge made its usual gasping sound as it opened and closed. Daisy's curiously lightweight voice was lowered, telling her something fairly confidential. Daisy had no idea, of course, that in spite of what Miss Thorpe had told Mrs Britney Longsmith, she was just slightly deaf. She caught that word again, spoken rather more viciously this time. 'Bitch'. Not a pretty word at all. Yet why not? Bitches were so often sweet and affectionate, yet when the term was applied to human beings . . . Same with cows. Miss Thorpe frowned and said, 'Oh dear.'

Daisy nodded vigorously and said, 'Like . . . exactly!'

Marcus came in with a tray and put it on the trolley, which already held Miss Thorpe's combined radio, tape and CD player, knitting, large-print book of an Agatha Christie murder and the letter from Mr Coles giving her the names of her visitors. The silver-plated milk jug and sugar bowl were sitting beside the big teapot; the mugs were clumped beside them. 'There's a tin of biscuits on the draining board—' Miss Thorpe began. Marcus tipped his chair on to its back legs, reached behind him and picked up the tin without having to move his feet, thus proving that everything really was 'within reach'.

He said, 'Your kitchen is so *neat*. Everything is so *there*.'

'Yours is always neat too. It's only when . . .' Daisy looked round at him, faltered and then changed her tone to neutral. 'It's only when other people try to help out.' She turned back to Miss Thorpe and grinned. 'I'm hopeless in kitchens. My mother's the same. Daddy just hates it when she wants to cook or anything.'

'Shall I pour?' Marcus spoke levelly and Daisy visibly wilted. Miss Thorpe felt a movement, a flutter, in her solar plexus; she was recognizing . . . what? An emotion? Daisy P'tek, lovely Snow White Daisy, was being chided. Very gently but very definitely she was being put in her place. And it was hurting her. Why was it hurting her? She was beautiful, vivacious, and knew full well that the tall, gangling, unusually kind boy now pouring tea was in love with her.

Miss Thorpe knew the answer. She knew too the sudden pain of empathy. She too had been chided once – more than once probably – by someone she loved more than he loved her.

She said, 'Yes, please, Marcus. I have a bad habit of pouring tea in the wrong place and there are no such things as burn dressings in modern first-aid kits.'

They both stared at her. Her voice was no longer hoarse and, apart from her description of the merits of Jenner House, these were the most words she had managed since their arrival. Best of all, Daisy realized she was being rescued.

She said, laughing suddenly, 'All they can suggest is you hold the burn beneath a cold tap. And actually it does work.'

'We used to put butter on a burn.' Miss Thorpe accepted a mug of tea and inhaled the steam appreciatively. 'The worst thing to do of course.' She inhaled again. 'Why does tea always go down better when someone else makes it?'

Marcus relaxed and removed the lid of the biscuit tin. Neat rows of biscuits revealed themselves. The children made noises of appreciation.

'I've had them since Christmas,' Miss Thorpe apologized. 'It would be good to see them go. If you didn't mind.' She glanced doubtfully at Daisy's dainty figure; she had recently heard a piece on the radio about girls starving themselves in order to get into tiny dresses.

But Daisy was smiling. 'You are so *honest*, Miss Thorpe! You go first.' She turned to Marcus. 'And please don't start, like, counting my calories for me!'

He relaxed further and grinned conspiratorially across the table. 'She's always eating sweet things. Her mum likes Indian food – it's how she and Daisy's dad met – and by the time she's got it all together for a curry she can't face making a pudding so Daisy pigs out on sweets and chocolate.'

Miss Thorpe looked at Daisy, saw that she had taken no offence at this offensive remark and shook her head.

'It doesn't seem to be doing her much harm.' She bit into her biscuit and found to her surprise that her mouth watered appreciatively. She had another tin in the cupboard, also un-opened. She had thought she did not want chocolate biscuits any longer, but perhaps she was wrong.

Daisy said through her third biscuit, 'This is heaven.'

Miss Thorpe said, surprised, 'It is. I am reminded of VE day. We had saved a tin of biscuits from an American gift parcel and we opened it for tea. My sister was home and our neighbours came in. I thought that was heaven too.'

Daisy actually stopped nibbling around the edges of a chocolate sandwich and leaned forward. 'That's the sort of thing we hoped you'd say. Like you were still half there. Like you could take us with you. Like VE day was not just a date in a book but happened like' – she waved her biscuit above her head – 'last week or the week before!'

Miss Thorpe started to laugh as if it were a joke, then saw that neither of them was even smiling. She was suddenly embarrassed; as if they had caught her only half dressed.

'But it wasn't last week, you see. It was so long ago that my memory isn't . . . correct. It's the past. It's gone.' She remembered the words the doctor had said to her, not that long ago. 'We have to move on.'

Daisy waved her biscuit dismissively. 'May I ask . . . Mr Coles said I mustn't be brash – like I'm ever brash!' She laughed, then was serious again. 'But if you didn't mind – and you can tell me to shut up if you *do* mind – how old were you when you ate that chocolate biscuit on VE day?'

Miss Thorpe stared into those liquid brown eyes; she had never been beautiful like this girl, but she had had her moments. Somebody, once, had called her the perfect English rose.

She said, 'I was fifteen.'

They both sat back in their chairs. Marcus reached into his pocket and pulled out a tissue and wiped his fingers carefully, thoughtfully.

He said, 'We're seventeen. So we are two years older. And we have something chocolatey every lunchtime. Yet, just at this moment, we could be sitting here eating our first chocolate biscuit for five years.'

Miss Thorpe frowned slightly. 'Perhaps not five years. There were these gift parcels from America. And the black market. And perhaps your parents would have used their points on chocolate biscuits rather than tinned peaches or salmon – it depends.'

'But it's still a huge treat,' he insisted.

She nodded. 'Because it was a luxury anyway. It doesn't make a meal like the fruit or fish would have done.'

28

'So there was a feeling of being wicked. Like we're feeling now?'

'Well, yes. I suppose so.'

Marcus said, 'More than that. They're a symbol. They symbolize the end of the war. The men – and women – coming home?'

Miss Thorpe closed her eyes for a moment and allowed herself to go back. She smiled slightly. 'I dare say Mum and the others thought like that. I thought it would be chocolate biscuits every day and going to bed . . . living . . . without being frightened all the time . . . and my Cambridge Certificate results coming through.' She opened her eyes, surprised. 'And something else too. Just a touch of disappointment that I would not be old enough to join the Wrens. I wanted to go to sea.' She smiled ruefully. 'I must have been very selfish.'

'Not a bit!' Daisy's palm was warm; it seemed to send a surge of energy into the back of Miss Thorpe's hand. She looked down at the two hands and just for a moment it seemed to her that the bit of her own hand visible behind Daisy P'tek's was devoid of liver blotches and knotted veins. Two smooth hands, one on top of the other. Who had likened that to a 'hand sandwich'? And then Daisy removed her hand and took another chocolate biscuit and Miss Thorpe could see her own swollen, arthritic knuckles again.

Daisy went on, 'We're all like that, surely? Nothing to do with what age we are. I bet – right at this moment – you are wondering how much longer we're going to stay and how many biscuits we'll leave in the tin!'

Miss Thorpe laughed with them but shook her head. 'No. I'm not. I am still half in our shabby old dining room, remembering Florrie in her uniform and knowing that I wouldn't be wearing one. Florrie was in the Wrens, then she got married and had a baby.'

'Florrie. That's a nice name.'

'My mother's great-aunt was called Florence. After Florence Nightingale. She was our Florrie's godmother – she promised Florrie her house in Devon when she died. So . . . when that happened, Florrie got married and had her baby so that she could get out of the Wrens. I think I simply wanted to wear the uniform!'

For the first time there was real sadness in Miss Thorpe's voice and Marcus said quickly, 'What is your first name, Miss Thorpe?' He caught Daisy's gaze and added, 'Or should I not ask that?'

Miss Thorpe looked at him steadily for a few seconds, then shook her head. 'You shouldn't really. But I know you want to take my mind off Florrie and Bert and I know you will enjoy my answer.' She had not told anyone in the house and she had no idea why these two children should be able to elicit such a secret from her. But it was turning out to be a strange afternoon. So she said, 'I am called May. But I was christened Mabel.'

They did not immediately put two and two together. Marcus got there first. He said wonderingly, 'Mabel. Mabel Thorpe. Isn't there a place called Mablethorpe?'

Daisy started to giggle. Miss Thorpe said, 'Gracie Fields made it famous for a while. I promised myself I would go there one day but I never have.'

'Your parents must have been just great – what a wonderful sense of humour. Yet they called you May. Like they were protecting you in case you didn't think it was that funny. Like it made it a private joke. Florence Nightingale and Mabel Thorpe.' Daisy could hardly speak for giggling. 'When you see the old photographs, everyone looks so grim. But you were just the same as we are now – and your jokes have lasted right up until today!'

Miss Thorpe smiled along with them. It did not seem worth telling them that her father had saved his family when he spreadeagled himself over the entrance to the air raid shelter in the garden that terrible night; that her mother would be dead exactly one year after VE day and that Florrie, Bert and their baby had been killed in the terrible train disaster of 1946. What was even worse was that she could not remember the baby's name. She could still remember the wonderful smell of her burgeoning hair, the plump hands and feet, the smooth round knees. But not her name.

Marcus was full of earnest enthusiasm. 'You see, Miss Thorpe, this is what we want to hear. We know all the text-book stuff and we've read novels around the time of Coventry. The carpet bombing – the grid system – the number of bombers and the helplessness of our anti-aircraft gunners—'

'They were called ack-ack gunners,' she put in.

'And we want to know how you felt. The chocolate biscuits. The school certificate results. And somehow to know that we are the same people. Am I making sense?'

'I think so,' she said slowly. 'But . . . we come from different worlds. We really do. And so do I, in a way. That girl eating the biscuits . . . that wasn't me as I am now.' She swallowed, seeing the sense of what the doctor had said. 'We have to move on.'

There was a small silence, sad on her side of the table, frustrated on theirs.

Then Daisy said, 'Let's start at the basics. Don't be upset. But what if you let us call you May? And what if I tell you that

I am taking my driving test before Easter and if I pass I can borrow Mum's car and take you to Mablethorpe? Would that be a start?'

Miss Thorpe had to smile. The girl was the whole of youth personified. And Marcus was her protector. It was classic.

She said, 'I won't mind. I'm almost sure I won't mind you calling me May. But not just yet because if it slips out in front of anyone here they will be . . . quite shocked. Everyone uses forenames in this place but not where children are concerned. They think it means the children don't respect them. I think – I'm afraid – that even their own grandchildren frighten them at times. And as for a trip to Mablethorpe . . . I'd prefer to stay put. If you don't mind. But I am very flattered by the invitation. Thank you, Daisy.'

'Perhaps you'll change your mind. And will you let us know when we can call you May?'

'Of course.'

'Then I'll go and wash up and you can have Marcus to yourself for five minutes.'

A whole hour later, she walked them to the lift and waited while it rose ponderously from the lower ground floor. Daisy said knowledgeably, 'The laundry is down there. And the rubbish skips. Aunty says people used to prop the door with a chair to keep the lift handy. The manager had to have a stern word!'

She and Marcus laughed but it had been a time of friction in the house and Miss Thorpe had heard both sides and decided she wanted nothing to do with either. Marcus said, 'Sounds like old BC lecturing us. Perhaps some people never get over being Terrible Teenagers.'

They laughed again and Miss Thorpe recalled Arthur

Wentworth – in his eighties – describing Mary and Cyril Smithson – both almost ninety and living on the ground floor – as 'a pair of hooligans'. She smiled and nodded.

Marcus said, 'BC is our headmaster, May. Sorry – Miss Thorpe. Barry Carter.'

Her smile widened. She liked Marcus using her name. She knew it would be easy for Daisy but not for Marcus. She said, 'A coincidence that his initials also mean Before Christ. He can't be that old.'

The lift arrived and the doors opened. Just before they closed on the two children, Daisy leaned forward and said, 'Actually, Miss Thorpe, they stand for something else much more, like, appropriate.' The outer door settled into place and the inner door followed suit. But not before Miss Thorpe had heard Daisy say through a bubble of childish giggles, 'Bum-Crack!'

She stood for a moment staring at the grey door with its single small window like an eye looking back at her. Then she pursed her lips on a smile of outrage and turned back into the hallway. It was already getting dark; a typically grey February afternoon, not quite dark enough for the ceiling lights to come on as she passed beneath them. Right at the end of the hall, where the staircase led up and down, a figure appeared. She needed spectacles to see any distance, so she could only make out that it was male. And as he was swinging around the banister to continue climbing, he must want the top floor. Suddenly the overhead lights came on. He started up the last flight of stairs two at a time.

Miss Thorpe turned right and went into the library, which she always called the book room because the word library was much too grandiose. She went to the reference shelf which contained a Gideon Bible, *Hymns Ancient and*

Modern, a psalter, a street directory and an incomplete set of encyclopaedias. The volume covering H to M was out of place but it was there. She tucked it under her arm and went back to her flat.

Before she closed and locked her door for the night, she peered back towards the stairs. Two steps in one go? No one in Jenner House was capable of that so it must have been a visitor.

She sat in her chair, switched on the reading lamp and began to search the encyclopaedia for an entry on Jenner.

Three

The check-in with Stephen Coles was a formality and Daisy would have skipped it for Marcus's sake. She knew he was always anxious to get home well before dark.

She took it on herself as usual and said, 'We mustn't get into the chat, Marc. I'm absolutely starving and you know what Steve is like.'

'One of the few who really care about us?' Marcus kicked a stone in the gutter and it narrowly missed a parked car. 'Anyway, how can you possibly be starving? You've eaten a kilo of chocolate biscuits in the last two hours.'

'Well, I somehow am. I've got this metabolism that only responds to proper meals. It's telling me I've had nothing to eat since breakfast.'

He didn't answer. They passed the line of parked cars, then the pub. From the other side of the road someone yelled at them, 'Hello, young lovers!' It was the crazy kid from year nine who reckoned he was androgynous but failed to offer a definition of the word. Daisy could stand no more silence and said, 'You should go over and kick his ass. Cheeky little sod. Who does he think he is?'

'He doesn't know, that's the point,' Marcus replied briefly. There was a silence that was not comfortable. Then Marcus said, 'He's new. Comes in on the bus from Gloucester. Trying to find a slot for himself.'

'How do you know this?'

'I talked to him one day.'

Daisy was baffled. Why were they talking about the androgynous boy?

They turned into the school gates. 'Listen.' She stopped suddenly in her tracks. 'Come and have a meal with us. Go on. Just for once think of yourself before your mother. Please, Marc. Dad will walk home with you after and smooth things over.'

'There's nothing to "smooth over", for Pete's sake. Why do you have to make a drama of everything?' He made his voice light but then added seriously, 'It's OK. Just that Uncle Ted came round last night and wanted her to go round there and have a day with him and Aunty Gertie.' He made a face. 'He doesn't believe in agoraphobia and thinks depression just means being a bit fed-up!' Another pause, then he said, 'He wants her to go back into hospital when the A-levels come up. Respite care, it's called.'

Daisy said nothing. Marcus's father, Stanley, had been very much in the background of the family, commuting to Bristol every day to a job in a bank, and Aunty Alison had been fine . . . kept the cottage spick and span, worked for the women's group who called themselves the Village Vixens, chatted to Daisy after school . . . until Stan died two years ago.

They went past the caretaker, who asked how it was going. Then another of Daisy's aunties waved a mop at them. They arrived at the door of the staff room.

Daisy said quietly, 'Wouldn't hospital be the answer, Marc? Like . . . for her as well as you?'

He opened the door and whispered fiercely, 'She hates hospitals. Scared stiff of them.'

She came back desperately, 'But if it helps her—'

He almost shoved her through the doorway.

'You don't get it, do you? She's my mother. I love her!'

She looked up at him. Her enormous eyes seemed liquid in the flat fluorescent light. She said, 'Oh . . . shit, Marc! Of course I get it! I'm just so . . . sorry.'

Stephen Coles was nowhere to be seen. The French exchange woman spread her hands helplessly. 'He has not arrived. Perhaps he is ill? Said he must dash. We all have problems, yes?'

'Yes, indeedie,' Daisy said and piloted Marcus back to the door. 'We'll see him tomorrow.'

Suddenly Marcus had forgotten the lovely leisurely afternoon with Miss Thorpe, the sense of belonging to all time instead of simply now. Suddenly he was in a panic to get home.

'Damn Steve bloody Coles,' he said untypically as they went back through corridors that now smelled of disinfectant. 'If anything has happened, it will be his fault!'

She stared at him. He was always reasonable; this was worse than unreasonable, it was simply illogical. She was about to point this out, when Aunty Mitzie waved her mop again and called out, 'Pictures. Tonight. Romantic. In Mumbai.' That was so nice and normal. Aunty Vera, who worked at Jenner House, had already told her the two of them were going and she had assumed it was a Bollywood. Now, she suddenly realized it was *Slumdog Millionaire* and forgot to tell Marcus how illogical he was being. He pushed through the outer doors and let them swing back almost in her face. She skipped through, angry, confused. She understood about his mother – of course she did – but did his concern – his love – mean he had no time at all for their friendship?

They almost ran back the way they had come. Outside, the darkness seemed to be rising from the damp ground; it was chest high. The lights from the pub cut a swathe through it and she could see that his face was streaked. Oh God. Was he crying? She panted, 'I'll come back with you. It'll be all right.'

'No.'

'But—'

'No. Please don't argue, Daisy. I . . . don't . . . want . . . you.'

She was suddenly furious. Like the French exchange woman had said, we all have problems, for God's sake. Her mother was a barrister and had married her clerk, who had left Mother India because he had been over-Anglicized at his posh school – and how unfair was that? Her mother had said to her once – and once only – that the words mixed and race meant that Daisy had a huge pot of genes to choose from and if ever she complained again about the way certain people used those two words, she should just remember the genes and be grateful to her parents for supplying them! Daisy had lived by that ever since. Even so, didn't Marcus realize the enormous problems caused by that amazing gene pot?

She tightened muscles against her own pain and said airily, 'That's OK. I'll, like, peel off here, then. See you tomorrow.'

She turned right and took the steep rise to Nob Hill as if demons were chasing her. By the time she reached the top she had the sort of stitch in her side that obviously came from both sides of her gene pool. And she needed her father with such intensity, tears were streaming down her face. She took the steps at the side of the house and the security lights came on and illuminated them, and there was the start of the garden with its skeleton winter trees and shrubs and the archway and the pond and the stone mermaid and the light disappearing into the invisible river. She ran down the steps and the dark breeze dried her tears but failed to give her back herself.

Nehru Patek was alone in the basement kitchen. The pillars supporting the house above cast their shadows over the enormous table that so often was surrounded by his sisters and their husbands and children. Tonight he had laid just three places on the corner facing the television. They would have English soup and watch the news, then they would switch off the set and tell each other about their day. He might mention the family from Gloucester. Though a great deal of his work for the Commission for Equality and Human Rights was strictly confidential, he would appreciate the sheer logic that would come from his wife and the imaginative leaps that Daisy would contribute. A general discussion perhaps.

When Daisy came in with a streaked face and swimming eyes he thought at first she had one of her lightning-strike colds. She closed the door on the early darkness and stood in the fluorescent brightness, dropping her bag, gloves, scarf and coat where she stood. He held aloft the long-handled spoon and said, 'Aww, bubba. Sit by the radiator and cook your poor bones and I will make hot tea.'

She said, 'No. I've had pots of tea this afternoon.'

'Then, what?'

'Cuddles. Please, Daddy.'

She began to cry in earnest and he dropped the spoon and swept her off her feet and sat in the tubular chair next to the radiator. As it swung to and fro, he rocked her and said things in Hindi and then changed them to 'There, there, my baby.' Phrases he had learned from Marietta and from English books.

It was when Marietta had discovered him reading *What Katy Did* interspersed with the file on a baby-battering case that their amazing love affair had been born. She had asked him where she could get a decent curry and he had offered to take her to where his sister worked and they had gone to Ruby Murray's and looked at each other across the table and recognized fate. Marietta cut through everything and said, 'You know we'll have to be married.'

He had smiled enormously and said, 'Your church or mine?' Which was mildly funny because Marietta had long since declared her religious disbeliefs and he had left India because he had gone to a missionary school and was a Christian.

He used Marietta's commonsensical phrase now. 'It will all seem better in the morning, bubba.'

She lifted her head. 'I know it will, Daddy. Marc will manage. As usual. It was just that we'd had such a good afternoon with Miss Thorpe. May Thorpe. And then it got dark quickly and I said I wanted to get home and Marc didn't argue. He was sort of, kind of, like, desperate. And it was awful. He said I didn't understand. He loves her. She does dreadful things, hides his shoes, locks him out. But he loves her.'

He cuddled her again. 'Of course. He loved her when she used to take him to playgroup fifteen years ago and when she made picnics for him in midwinter – for you too, bubba. She was so good at dreaming up little treats. But he would have loved her anyway. Why would he stop now?'

'I don't mean he should stop loving her. But . . . she's not that person any more. She hates him. She told him once that she wished he had died instead of his father.'

'If he told you that she spoke those words, bubba, they could not have hurt him deeply. He knew she was like an angry child hitting out wildly. And think why she must have said those words.'

She was no longer crying. She sniffed loudly and said, 'Because he won't let her have any alcohol.'

'I do not believe Alison Budd is an alcoholic. And sometimes I wonder whether a drink is better than pills. And if a drink . . . yes, or two or three . . . made her feel better able to cope, of course she hated anyone who denied her that. And he – poor Marc – is denying her the alcohol because he loves her and she never used to drink and it frightens him.' He kissed the top of her head. 'You understood this all the time. He thought you did not but it is obvious he was wrong.'

'Oh Daddy!' She managed a small laugh into his shoulder. 'I am not surprised Mummy wants you to go on with your exams! You have more coils than a snake!'

He too laughed. 'The really unfair thing about this is that later on this evening, after dinner, it is you who must telephone and apologize.' He pulled her upright so that he could look into those wonderful eyes. 'You do know that, bubba, do you not?'

For a moment mutinous words hovered around her head like bees. Then she nodded silently.

Ten minutes later, when Daisy had washed her hands and face and was setting out bowls, Marietta Patek came in from the garden steps, stood where Daisy had stood and divested herself of bag and outer garments on to the floor just as her daughter had done.

Daisy went to her and hugged her and they both made a joke about the gene pot and then laughed and Daisy picked up her mother's stuff and took it through into the lower hall. When she came back her parents were clasped together as usual, rocking back and forth, talking about a local solicitor who had an enormous belief in his client but no evidence to back it up. Daisy tried to remember Marc's father and could not. His parents must have loved each other like this, otherwise why had his death wrecked Alison so completely? Was it possible for married couples to love each other too much, she wondered. Was it better to keep a little bit of yourself separate and strong so that . . . so that . . . She thought of Miss Thorpe, who had been alone all her life. And had . . . moved on. To Jenner House.

She shivered and said loudly, 'I'm starving!' and they broke apart and Daddy lifted his spoon and said, 'English Windsor soup!'

They watched the six o'clock news and there had been another bomb in India and more bodies and injured people than they could cope with. Hillary Clinton made a speech declaring America's support for the Indian government. Daddy stopped eating and stared at the television screen, stricken. 'Eat up, darling. This is delicious,' Mummy said, putting her head between his and Hillary Clinton's.

'How can I eat?' He stared at her now. 'How can I sit here so safely and eat?'

'Because you need strength to continue to bring your family here and then to look after them like you do.' Mummy leaned right forward now and said very sternly, 'Eat, Nerrie Patek. Those terrorists are not going to win. Eat.'

Daisy got up and crossed the kitchen to switch off the television. She resumed her seat and said, 'I saw Aunty Vera today. It was our day for Jenner House and Miss Thorpe had gone to sleep and didn't hear us at the outer door. Aunty Vera was doing the flowers in the hall and let us in. She said that Aunty Mitzie is taking her to the pictures tonight.'

Mummy picked up, smiling. 'What are they going to see?'

Daisy opened her mouth to tell her that it was *Slumdog Millionaire*, then changed it slurringly. 'Not sure. Something about football, I think.'

That definitely brought Daddy back to the present. '*Football?*' he asked incredulously. Vera and Mitzie were interested in one thing only and it was not football. Someone must have told them that *Slumdog* was about a love that survived through torture and terrorism. Daisy wondered whether indeed they would survive through the two hours of it.

'Perhaps it was ballroom dancing,' she amended vaguely. 'Shall I make coffee? I want to phone Marc, like, asap.'

'You've been with him all afternoon!' Mummy looked affronted.

'We had . . . words. I want to apologize.'

Daddy said, 'Go on. I'll tell Mummy, yes?'

'Course. No big deal.' But it was.

She went into the lower hall, picked up the phone and sat on the stairs while she pushed at numbers. Engaged. And again. Then half a ring-tone and Marc picked up.

'Oh God. Daisy, I've been trying to get you. I watched you going up the hill like a bat out of hell and tried you on your mobile and you'd switched off. Don't know what got into me—'

'Shut up. What got into you was my total insensitivity. I had all the facts but I still didn't feel it. Bit like Coventry. We knew about carpet bombing and the grid system of strafing

43

and the cathedral and . . . like . . . everything. Miss Thorpe filled in how it actually *was*.' She gave a little sob. 'Marc, I'm sorry.'

'Shut up, yourself. I was a pain. Leave it at that.'

'I was a pain – a worse pain. So leave it like that. OK?' He started to protest and she overrode him. 'Listen, how were things? When you got home.'

He hesitated then puffed a sigh down the phone, nearly blowing her ear out, and said, 'I wasn't going to tell you because it's so far away.' He stopped and there was another puff. She held the receiver away from her ear. 'I've got in. It's so great.' Another puff and she screwed up her face, about to ask him what the hell was going on, then for once in her life kept her mouth closed. 'Mum was fine. Sleepy. She'd had a ham sandwich at midday and we had a Cup-a-Soup and cheese on toast and a yog and she said I was a good boy and produced a letter from Leeds.' His voice escalated ecstatically. 'I'm in, Dais! I've got a place. Modern history . . . European.'

'Leeds. I thought you said it had to be Bristol. Because of—'

'I know. But she was over the moon about it. Said she would get Ted to keep an eye on things. I'll be home every week-end, I promise. Daisy, this is what I wanted all the time and I didn't know it until I knew . . . read the letter. You know.' He paused. 'You're not saying anything. D'you think it's too far?'

She became fully conscious of his joy when she heard it trickling away. She said quickly, 'Absolutely not! I'm just flabbergasted. She sounds pretty . . . well, marvellous about it.'

'She'd opened the letter. Had all day to get used to it. And she hadn't found anything to drink, I can always tell.'

Desperate for his joy to bubble again, she said, 'It's the best news for ages. Seriously, Marc. You'll have all week for your work. You wouldn't get that at Bristol. My God, the more I think about it the better it gets! Oh Marc, congratulations. This makes everything just . . . like . . . perfect.'

'I know. That's what I thought. Here's Mum for a word.'

She only spoke to Daisy when she was sober and unhappy; this time she was sober and almost as joyous as Marc.

'Darling Daisy, isn't this great? I was dying for him to come home and hear the news.' Daisy thought how strange it was that Marc had suddenly known he was needed . . . She tried to tell Mrs Budd about it but she already knew. 'Darling, it happens all the time – you know what he's like – wired into all of us. But usually it's because I'm . . . ill. And this time—'

'I know,' Daisy interrupted. She wanted to stop the conversation right there and then. It was as if the terrible truth was lurking behind her halfway up the stairs. She even glanced round for it but knew she was being silly. It was the other end of the phone, it was inside Mrs Budd and she hadn't seen it until Mrs Budd spoke about Marcus's internal 'wiring'. Of course he wouldn't go all the way up to Leeds. The wiring wouldn't stretch that far.

She replaced the phone carefully; it was a wall phone and often fell to the carpet, always when Daisy was using it. Mummy had said only last week, 'Daisy, I know you are always in a hurry but you can train yourself out of that and into being much more careful with . . . things, objects.' Had she meant that it was possible to bypass the gene pot and make yourself a separate person?

The kitchen door opened and her parents came through. Her mother looked at her, paused, then said cheerfully, 'We thought we'd have coffee upstairs. You know, pretend we're not the sort of people who live and die in their kitchen!'

There was a small galley off the sitting room anyway, where they could make drinks and dole out biscuits to callers. She told them about Marcus's offer of a place at Leeds. And his mother's determination that he would go and she would stop being 'ill'. It sounded less awful when she put it so succinctly. She shook her head. 'Why am I so . . . like . . . doom-laden tonight?'

Mummy said prosaically, 'You're tired.' Then she grinned. 'All those hormones rushing around – like – you know – sort of—' She ducked as Daisy picked up a cushion.

Daddy said, 'Stop it, you two. Drink your coffee as ladies should. Etta, you will have work to do in the office later and Daisy must write up her interview at Jenner House and I have some reading to do.'

That sobered them all right. Mummy sighed gustily and Daisy said, 'It wasn't actually an interview. It was a chat.' She recalled the afternoon with Miss Thorpe and how easy it had been. 'We drank two pots of tea and Marcus said I ate a kilo of chocolate biscuits!'

They were appalled. 'Probably your Miss Thorpe will have starved herself to provide a whole tin of chocolate biscuits!' Mummy was prone to exaggeration lately; probably caught it from Aunty Vera.

Daisy explained that the biscuits had been left over from Christmas. 'It was still in date though. I looked at the tin.'

'She must be a very nice woman,' Daddy said.

'Not exactly. Nice – of course – but more than nice. Sort of . . . real. She was sort of distant until she talked about the Coventry raid. She remembered the king visiting them a couple of days after it happened.'

Mummy was on to her like a ton of bricks. 'What do you mean by not exactly nice? What did she say? Was the place clean?'

'Of course. You know it must be clean with Aunty Vera around. Honestly! All I meant was she's not just a "nice old lady". She's a bit different from the usual . . . I'm not sure. I think she's a dreamer and apparently everyone tells her she has to move on.'

'Lives too much in the past – not surprised after an experience like Coventry. How old was she when it happened?'

'Eleven, I think. But she's not . . . like . . . *morbid* or anything. She remembers the good things more than the bad ones, I think.' Daisy frowned. 'Do you think we might be stirring up bad memories for her?'

'Who knows?' Mummy stared into the electric fire. 'Remembering bad times makes you grateful for what you have now. But we don't know. Human beings rarely know about each other. They live and eat and sleep together and then they get a shock.'

Nehru and Daisy exchanged glances. They both knew that Marietta got much too involved with her work. Next week she would be defending a woman who had stabbed her husband.

Nehru put his hand over his wife's. 'Perhaps no work tonight, Etta? You and Daisy . . . you are both tired.'

Daisy sighed theatrically. 'Those bloody genes!' she said. But she went up to her room as soon as her coffee had gone. She could hear her parents talking underneath her and knew that they were discussing next week's case. Mummy would be saying, 'All she needs are good character references. The husband's disappeared and her friends say she's got a temper.' And Daddy would remind her that the woman had pleaded guilty, her children had been removed by Social Services and it was an awful thing to have done.

Daisy said to her reflection, 'Thank God for visual art!' and then wondered just when she had stopped calling Marc's mother 'Aunty Alison' and gone all formal with 'Mrs Budd'.

She thought that tomorrow she could make a joke to Marcus about her family life, then thought better of it. He had said once that he hoped his mother's addiction wasn't infectious and that's what genes were in a way.

She kept staring into the mirror. She said defiantly, 'Well, I couldn't have done law. And I couldn't be a nurse like Mitzie used to be. At least art is dealing with objects, not people. So I have got out of that gene pot.'

She went to the door and leaned over the banisters to say goodnight to her parents. There was silence from below. Then suddenly her mother's voice said, 'How did I live without you, my love?'

And Daddy must have kissed her because there was a lot of snuffling and giggling, then he said, 'Thank God you did!'

She called down, 'I can hear everything you're saying, you know!'

And Daddy said, 'Fortunately you cannot see us!' He was laughing his head off. Mummy told him to shut up.

'Goodnight, young lovers,' Daisy yelled down like that androgynous kid from year nine.

Mummy yelled back, 'Goodnight, precocious daughter!'

'Sleep well.' They all spoke together.

Daisy went to bed.

Four

For the first time since she had come to Jenner House, May Thorpe overslept. The strident intercom bell woke her at 9.15am and kept going hysterically until she had got both legs on the floor, pulled herself upright by the grab rail on the wall and reached around the corner for the receiver. Mrs Ballinger's voice had an edge of anxiety to it as she said, 'Zoe here, Miss Thorpe. Are you all right?'

'Yes. Overslept.' Of course none of them were 'all right'. But then there were degrees of 'all right'. She straightened her body and took a deep breath. 'Such a good night, that's all.' She paused then said, 'Zoe.'

'Oh . . . oh . . .' Mrs Ballinger had always been Mrs Ballinger as far as Miss Thorpe was concerned. 'I'm so glad . . . May.' There was a waiting pause, then she went on in her usual brisk voice intended to bring energy into each of the bedsits. 'Don't forget it's the coffee morning today, dear. And a bring-and-buy table. It will be a good chance for you all to meet the new financial adviser. His name is Toby Marsh and he's rather dishy.'

May closed her eyes. Zoe had almost won her over for a moment, but May was not anyone's 'dear' and where on earth did the word 'dishy' come from? Especially in connection with a financial adviser who had obviously been sent by head office to tell them the rents must go up next year.

She muttered something, replaced the receiver and worked her way around the wall towards the bathroom. It was then, as she recalled her wonderful sleep and yesterday's children and the struggles of Dr Jenner, that she realized Toby Marsh must have been the man taking the stairs two at a time last night. She felt a pang of disappointment. How very . . . ordinary. Just when life had taken a rather unusual turn.

At ten thirty, when she was wading through a bowl of something unpronounceable that should be called dust with raisins, Arthur Wentworth rang the bell.

'Thought I'd better walk you down to the lounge,' he said jovially, smoothing his tie into his buttoned sports jacket. 'Can't risk any muggings in the lift!' He chuckled at this joke which he used every time he saw her.

'The lounge?'

She got her tongue around the silly modern word and wondered how a verb could have become a noun and then how the letters 'o' and 'u' could have rolled into an 'ow' sound and if 'lounge' had ever sounded like 'lozenge'. Sort of. Like. She smiled as she recalled Daisy P'tek's funny vernacular. Mr Wentworth thought the smile was for him.

'Lounge. Coffee morning. Bring-and-buy. The accountant chappie . . . whatever-his-name-is.'

'Toby Marsh.' For some reason she remembered the name but she had forgotten the coffee morning and explained she had overslept.

'But Zoe should have opened up your flat the moment you didn't reply to the wake-up call!' He was appalled that the system had apparently broken down.

'She did. I mean, I did.'

'Didn't she remind you about the coffee morning?' He was unwilling to relinquish a possible complaint. He had a roguish relationship with the manager and often opened a conversation with the words, 'Now, dear lady, I am not complaining but I feel I must bring your attention to . . .' Once it had been a cat in the eucalyptus tree and that alert had been much appreciated by its frantic owner as well as most of the residents, who had gathered along the terrace to watch the firemen rescue the 'poor dear moggie', as Zoe had put it. But another time it had been the state of the newspapers ranged along the table in the entrance hall. Zoe explained it had been raining when they arrived and he had had to be satisfied with that, but he often asked her whether there was anyone who might iron his *Times* for him of a morning.

May managed to smile at him.

'Yes. I forgot, I'm afraid. It's rather late to think about it now.'

'You forgot? Dear lady, you're in a world of your own – we all know that. What on earth were you thinking about this morning?'

'Well, actually Dr Jenner. You know, the one who discovered a vaccine that would work against smallpox.'

He stared, then said, 'We have to move on, May.'

Those words. And the use of her name. He was such an old buffer. Yet he wore his RAF tie and 'jollied the old ladies'. Just as he had probably done as a young airman.

She said, 'I really don't think I can manage to socialize this morning—' She hesitated to call him Arthur and he plunged in, unexpectedly embarrassed.

'That's the very time you should push yourself. I saw those two youngsters from the school who came to interview you yesterday. Probably drained you dry, that's why you overslept.'

He took a breath and dropped righteous indignation in favour of sweet reason. 'Listen, dear lady. I will go on down to the lounge, find us a table and get in the coffee. You change into your glad rags and join me for a spot of decent ordinary socializing. It's not right the way they use us as historic specimens these days. Tell them to read the books or do whatever they do on this internet arrangement. It's all documented, they just can't be bothered to read any more!' The lift pinged and he moved off smartly, calling back, 'See you in ten minutes!'

She stood where she was for a moment, looking down at her clothes. She was wearing her usual tweed skirt and a brown jumper. She had no gladder rags. Alternative jumpers of course, and the pleated grey skirt that had to be pressed after each wearing. Perhaps he meant her slippers. Obviously she should not be wearing those outside the bedsit. And she did not want to go down and drink coffee and smile and then come back to her cereal dish and a cold teapot. Damn Arthur Wentworth. Everyone knew she did not attend this sort of a do. He knew. Silly old buffer. But the thought of him sitting at one of the small tables with two cups of coffee . . .

She said, 'Damn him!' then picked up her cereal dish and put it on the draining board next to the teapot, which was already cold. Then went to the sliding doors of the cupboard, hung on to the grab rail and looked at her clothes. Ten minutes later – 'Spot-on,' said Arthur Wentworth – she went into the lounge wearing black shoes and jumper with the grey pleated skirt. And her cultured pearls. She took her walking stick so that she could stand upright. Arthur stood up – almost to attention – smoothed his tie into his sports jacket and drew out a chair. He had reversed the usual placing of cup and saucer so that her saucer was on top of the cup.

'To keep the contents nice and hot,' he told her gallantly. It reminded her so much of the canteen back in 'those days', when the helpers had got ahead of themselves pouring the tea and had lidded each cup with its saucer.

She settled herself, let him take her stick and felt the others surrounding her. Somebody's family was visiting and a child ran past, closely followed by an older one. The smaller child fell and cried piteously. It was incredibly like that canteen underneath the church . . . yes, it had been underneath the church at the end of their road. There had been tables, card tables with green baize tops. If you so much as coughed they would collapse. 'Sit still!' Mum had said over and over again. Like a mantra. Like she had said earlier, 'Help us, God . . . oh, God help us.' And there had been children crying. Always. Children crying. Screaming. Wailing. 'Drink your tea,' Mum said. 'It's shock. Just drink your tea.'

She took the cup and saucer that was being offered and sipped obediently. 'Nice and hot,' she said. Then, 'It's not tea.'

Arthur guffawed a Father Christmas laugh. 'Right on the nose!' He leaned forward and said in a stage whisper, 'Coffee morning. It's where you drink coffee.'

'But we can have tea, surely?'

His patience was wearing thin but he looked at her pearls and forced a smile. 'Of course you can, dear lady. I'll go and get you tea.'

'Not for me, Mr Wentworth. But if you'd prefer a cup . . .'

He relapsed on to his chair. 'I thought you said you wanted tea!'

'Did I? No, I'm sure I didn't. Coffee in the morning, tea in the afternoon.' She smiled at him. 'I was surprised by those children from the local school, you know. I'd got the coffee jar at the ready in the kitchen, but they chose tea. We drank our way through two pots of it and very good it was too. The boy made it. Things change, don't they?'

He stared at her, bemused and confused. 'I thought . . .' he began, then stopped and changed tack. 'You're looking particularly good today, dear lady.'

This was typical Arthurian legend but she played along with it for some reason and smiled tightly, which still revealed dimples in her lined face. She practised it sometimes, look-ing in the bathroom mirror; she always ended up laughing at herself because how a man could be charmed by two dents in a woman's face was quite beyond her. Yet they had been. Oh yes, they had been. And believe it or not, this one was.

She stopped smiling and ducked her head demurely. 'Oh, Mr Wentworth—'

'I wish you'd call me Arthur. Everyone does.'

'Well, I wish you wouldn't call me dear lady because that's what you call all the women here and probably down in the shops too.'

'I'll call you May. Such a pretty name. My sister was called Mary and everyone called her May.'

'Ne'er cast a clout till May is out,' she said as if it was sig-nificant, or even relevant.

'Indeed, indeed. People imagine that advice refers to the month of May. But of course it's the flower that's meant. The beautiful, white, virginal flower. Oh May, beautiful, waxen almost, and—'

She said tartly, 'I am not a virgin, Mr Wentworth. Not by any means!'

He was so shocked he nearly fell off his chair. She must remember to tell Marcus and Daisy to moderate their language if they met him in the hallway or the lift. And she should have known better, upsetting an old man who as a young man had been among the first of the few. That was what Mrs Ballinger had said when she introduced her. 'Be kind to him, Miss Thorpe. He was among the first of the few.' Or had she meant the First of the Few?

She leaned across the table. 'Arthur, I do apologize. I cannot think what is the matter with me today. All this talk of the war is not good for me.'

'You have to move on,' he said in a strangulated voice. 'I myself, unmarried, but . . . well, obviously . . . a man of the world and all that.'

She tried hard to smile coyly and produce another dimpled face.

'You must have been a handsome man, Arthur. And in your uniform completely irresistible.'

She saw he was looking past her at the doorway. 'Here cometh our Zoe with the new man.'

'Toby Marsh,' she said.

'Yes.' He lifted a hand in salute and she said quickly, 'Why don't you go and have a word, Arthur? Give him a personal welcome.'

'Good idea, dear lady. Excuse me for a moment then.'

He stood up and almost immediately someone slid into his seat and lumped two little boys on to the other two chairs. The little one was still crying and the woman bent over him and massaged his tiny scarred kneecap. 'Mummy make it better, Bobby.' The other one sat in sullen silence.

May said, 'Would you like a biscuit? Those round ones are very nice.'

She addressed the sullen boy but the mother smiled upwards briefly and put a biscuit into the smaller boy's hand. He stopped crying and stuffed the biscuit into his mouth. May pushed the plate towards the sullen boy. He said angrily, 'That was the only Jammie Dodger. Don't like those fingers.'

Luckily Zoe was calling for attention, which meant silence. The hush was instant, everyone wanting to know about Toby Marsh.

'Before I declare the table sale open . . .' A trestle table stood just by the door, covered in an embroidered cloth. It held a medley of useless objects, including a pipe rack which everyone knew belonged to Arthur. He was the sole pipe smoker in the place. Zoe looked at the pipe rack indulgently and then whipped back to the non-smokers as Bobby demanded another biscuit. Even Bobby was quelled by her steely grey eyes, though his mother thrust a biscuit at him to make doubly sure of silence.

'As I was saying . . .' Zoe had lost her thread, 'I would like to introduce a new member of the team. Toby Marsh.' She turned slightly, smiled hugely, held her hand out palm upwards towards the young man sitting next to her. Everybody murmured and Arthur led an uncertain round of applause. May noticed he was sitting on the other side of Toby Marsh. Zoe swept on, 'Mr Marsh comes to us as the Trust's accountant, but he is multi-talented and I believe has degrees in law as well as sociology and – and . . .' She looked at him again rather wildly; she had once more lost her thread. May felt sorry for her, it was the sort of thing that happened all the time in old age.

Mr Marsh stood up, laughing gently. 'Mrs Ballinger would make a wonderful public relations officer as well as being such an excellent manager of Jenner House – thank you, Zoe, for your introduction.'

It was all rather trite but there was something about this

tall, sandy-haired young man that was making the harassed young mother smile and a huge grin was spreading across Arthur's face. Miss Thorpe put a finger to her cheek and felt a dimple invert itself. It was at that precise moment, when the appreciative ripple was still resonating around the room, before the inevitable statistics were 'wheeled out', as Arthur put it later, when Miss Thorpe's finger was actually indicating her dimple; it was then that Toby Marsh looked across the room, acknowledging his welcome, and . . . saw her. Afterwards, when she remembered it and admitted to herself that it was no silly-old-woman thingie, there was no other way she could identify it other than by simply saying those words. He saw her.

It was just a moment and it passed immediately; nothing of it lingered except inside her head. But there was a sense of urgency about that moment; a frantic determination not to let it go; not to let it drown in the spiel that Toby Marsh uttered so convincingly but so familiarly too about how 'every resident could help with the overall necessity to keep the charges down' and 'to invest far more than money in their communal home'. A pause, then a rich tone of jolly fun in his voice: 'Any gardeners here present, don't hold back,' and, worse still, 'What about vacuum addicts? This is just the place for you . . . long corridors all beautifully carpeted . . . cutting down on outside contractors.' Hadn't Daisy P'tek got relatives who might be put out of work if residents took to vacuuming the long corridors? Miss Thorpe squeezed her eyes tightly shut for a moment to block out all extraneous thoughts and was suddenly back in the crypt of their old church and there was Jack seeing her from the gaping hole that had been a doorway and grinning and putting up his thumb and coming across between all the people and the

trestle tables and saying, 'You don't have to point it out, May
– I'd recognize that dimple anywhere!'

It must have been the shock of seeing him so vividly, after
all those years of not seeing him; of associating him with
the new accountant-cum-lawyer-cum sociologist; of the sheer
coincidence of putting her finger just below her dimple as
she had then . . . Whatever it was, she felt a jarring inside
her head as if the left-hand side of her brain scraped hard
against the right-hand side. And the very next instant she was
opening her eyes on the familiar landscape of her room and
Mrs Ballinger's face hovering in front of the open cupboard
– how could she have forgotten to slide the door back into
place? – and Arthur Wentworth holding a whisky bottle over
one of her mugs.

'She's coming round!' Mrs Ballinger's voice was wobbly
with relief. It hardened irritably as Miss Thorpe tried to sit
up. 'For goodness' sake, stay where you are, May! The doctor
is on his way and he said—'

'Just a funny turn,' May said, still struggling to sit up. 'I
had my stick – I could have managed quite well—'

'I brought the stick up!' Arthur Wentworth sounded as if
he was ordering an attack on the enemy. He put the bottle
and mug on the chest of drawers. 'Here it is, dear lady, let
me—'

Mrs Ballinger brushed him away and he got his heel caught
on the stick and almost fell.

'For goodness' sake, Arthur! Haven't we got problems
enough without you constantly trying to be gallant? And
we cannot give her any alcohol until she has seen Dr
Makepeace!'

May at last got her legs over the edge of the bed and her
feet on the floor. She forced some strength into her voice.

'Actually, I wouldn't mind . . . Why didn't I come up in the lift?'

'You did.' Mrs Ballinger now sounded tired. The coffee morning had been a fiasco. 'You fainted, May. As you know, we are not allowed to pick you up in case we hurt ourselves. Mr Marsh didn't know about that rule, though of course with his legal training he should have. Anyway, he picked you up as if you were a feather and brought you back to your room in the lift.'

'How did he know which room . . .' Silly question but Mrs Ballinger – Zoe – replied, still in her tired voice.

'We came with him of course. I used the master key and Mr Wentworth refused to leave you. I telephoned the doctor en route. Toby made sure you were breathing properly – he took your pulse, a first-aider as well as everything else – and then he went back downstairs to carry on with the meeting and the table sale.'

'Marvellous chap. Make an absolutely spiffing tail gunner. Eyes everywhere.' Arthur Wentworth sucked in air till his cheeks almost popped, then expelled it appreciatively.

May felt her eyes begin to fill. She took Mrs Ballinger's hand. 'You are marvellous. You rise to every occasion. I am so grateful. And I feel such a fool. Making a scene . . . spoiling the coffee morning and Mr Marsh's speech and you two . . . you could be enjoying it right now. You must. You must go back down and tell people I am absolutely fine and – look – seriously now, take these and have a raffle! No, I insist. Really. I never wear them and I have left all my bits and bobs to be sold and the proceeds to go to the residents' association, so—' She at last undid the clasp of her pearls and handed them to Mrs Ballinger, who closed long fingers over them. 'Don't argue, Zoe. You'll make quite a bit of money probably and perhaps we could start saving for – for – a greenhouse!' It came to her as she spoke, what an asset a greenhouse would be. She herself could bring on seedlings and prick them out so that perhaps Arthur could eventually put them in the front border . . . Wasn't that what Toby Marsh was meaning when he made his turgid plea for economies?

'Please go. Both of you. You're needed down there. And the doctor knows where I am.'

Eventually Arthur left. He didn't like it, not any of it. The pearls were probably the only thing of value May possessed and she was in no fit state to make such a wildly extravagant gift to something so trivial as a table sale! But Zoe, unlikely though it might be, seemed to understand. She held May's hand over her own and looked at her steadily for a second or two, then nodded and said, 'If you are sure,' and May nodded too and said, yes, she was sure. And Zoe put a mug into her hand. And May drank the whisky.

Five

The next day, when May's lunch arrived, a familiar face was lurking behind the dinner lady's bulk. May had made space on her trolley and wrapped cutlery in a napkin next to the cruet. She wasn't happy with the day so far; the aftermath of the fainting business meant that half the residents seemed to think it their duty to ring her bell and 'just enquire'. Some of them handed over get well cards too. One was actually homemade and the verse read, 'When you get this little letter, Hope you're feeling much much better.' May had glanced incredulously at her reflection in the cupboard looking glass but then said, 'It was well meant.'

She had to admit Zoe had been wonderful. She had ushered Arthur out and stood by the bed making notes while the doctor took blood samples for analysis. She had insisted on 'complete bed rest', and then she had talked May into letting her order meals on wheels.

'I know how it is when I'm on my own. I can't fancy any of the things that would do me good and end up with a boiled egg. Have a cooked meal delivered tomorrow – no, it's not too late, I will order it for you. If you like it you could have two or three every week. I'm sure your diet is partly to blame for this little upset. Until the test results come through let's go for a few old-fashioned cooked meals.'

May couldn't stand out against such unexpected kindness. 'Just one,' she stipulated reluctantly. 'I'm afraid I've got such odd tastes these days and if I have to waste it . . . well, I hate waste.'

'Of course you do! You're that generation. But these people have a very good reputation. Now you're sure you'll be all right? Pull the cord the moment you feel at all shaky – promise?'

'Promise.'

Zoe smiled as if congratulating her on winning Wimbledon. She left and the next minute it seemed – May had not slept so well for ages – the visitors started arriving. By the time the famous meal was delivered, May was exhausted yet strangely anxious. Not about the fainting fit any more, but the absence of Arthur Wentworth. It wasn't that she particularly wanted to see him with his RAF tie and his cavalry twills, but where on earth was he? He had hovered about for a while yesterday until Zoe had assured him that all Miss Thorpe needed was rest. But he had not been among the 'enquirers' this morning. She wondered whether her brash – brazen – announcement during Wednesday's coffee morning had disgusted him.

The dinner lady was twittering about it being poached salmon and treacle pudding today and she hoped Miss Thorpe would enjoy it. And the figure still hovering behind her suddenly spoke. 'I am the aunty of Daisy Patek, Miss Thorpe. How are you today?'

May was surprised. She knew Vera by sight of course and remembered that Daisy had said her aunt worked as a cleaner, but she had not expected her to take a personal interest in the goings-on of yesterday.

She said, 'I am perfectly well, thank you. How kind . . . Is Daisy all right?'

'She is well. Yes. But she wishes to call and see you after lunch and is asking if you are better enough.'

May felt better instantly. 'Certainly. I would like that. Is she outside now?'

'No.' Vera produced a mobile phone from beneath her overall. 'She telephoned me. Just. To ask about the pictures.' Vera's voice became tragic. 'We had to leave the cinema, Miss Thorpe.'

The dinner lady said firmly, 'It's better to eat the salmon while it is still hot. And if this lady's niece is to call on you this afternoon you will need a rest. So we will leave you in peace.' She moved into the narrow hallway and breasted Aunty Vera out of the door. May had time to call, 'Thank you – thank you both!' and they were gone. She looked at her meal with sudden interest. Poached salmon and a sauce. Could it be hollandaise? It was. And the potatoes were small and new and there were tiny sprigs of broccoli and the orange of carrots. And in an hour or two Daisy P'tek, who reminded her so much of Snow White, would be sharing her world again.

Daisy on her own? What about Marcus who made the tea and cleared it all up so beautifully? Where was Marcus? And where on earth was Arthur Wentworth?

Marcus was not waiting for Daisy outside the pub and he was not at school. He had phoned to say that the doctor was calling to see his mother and it might make him late for school, in which case would she tell Steve Coles about the place at Leeds.

He was always early, so she knew immediately that he was going to be late, but she hung about outside the pub watching the mist creep along the valley, then she hung about outside the school gates. The kid from year nine appeared and went past her singing some horrible song about someone called Mildred who was jilted by someone called Walter at the altar. She ignored him – obviously – but she didn't linger any more.

Perhaps Marcus had gone on ahead so that he could talk to Steve Coles about the acceptance from Leeds. And Steve would remind him that any offers were subject to the A-level results and the exams had not even been taken yet. As if Marc couldn't sit all the exams in the world with his hands tied behind his back. She conjured up a vision of his dark head bent over an exam paper, a biro between his teeth and five-hundred-word essays appearing on the blank page below his face. The Industrial Revolution. The causes of the First World War: never mind poor old Archduke Ferdie, what about the Russian Bear and the Turkish Scimitar? She grinned as she went through the series of doors to the staff area. Marc had not chattered at poor Miss Thorpe on Tuesday like she had, but she had felt him soaking it up. Blotting paper, that was Marcus . . . She had watched him blotting away at Miss Thorpe's occasional words, sorting them into a picture. She had done it herself; it was one of the things they did together. That telepathy thing that Aunty Alison had mentioned so glibly on the phone.

She paused outside Mr Coles's door, surprised that in her head she had called Marcus's mum 'Aunty Alison'. There had been a time when she had loved Aunty Alison. That had been when Aunty Alison met her from nursery school and took her home to play with Marcus until Daddy finished work and picked her up.

She knocked on the door. No reply. She tried the handle. Locked.

She went back to the stairs. They would be in the library probably. But they weren't. Mrs Arbuthnot, the librarian, had not seen Mr Coles since Monday.

'I heard he'd got this flu bug. She doesn't feed him properly. He's much too thin.'

Daisy was surprised. Mr Coles was like anaglypta wallpaper; unnoticeable but always there.

She said, 'D'you need help? I can't get into the art room until after assembly.'

Mrs Arbuthnot was gushingly grateful. 'You angel! That pile there. All reference books. Watch the serial numbers.'

Daisy nodded. Mrs A knew that her thoughts might be as random as a butterfly but when given a practical task she was more reliable than Mrs A herself. So that was all right. She definitely did not want to go on Mrs A's worry list underneath the head, whose wife was suddenly interested in a hypnotherapist, and Mr Coles, whose wife apparently fed him a diet of junk food. Why was it always down to wives? Was that their role in life – to feel guilty for . . . for everything? For being alive? Daisy shivered. Aunty Alison was alive and her husband was not. Did she feel guilty about that?

She finished relocating the books and sat by the window, where she could watch everyone going into assembly. Not quite everyone, however, because a voice from the other side of the magazine rack said almost in her ear, 'Still waiting at the church then, Mildred?'

She would have killed him if she could have grabbed him but there was no way she was going to chase him past Mrs Arbuthnot's counter so she did the ignoring bit again, and two minutes later saw him join the queue outside the hall.

He was small, as small as she was herself. But she was nearly always with people; Marcus usually, of course, but if he was somewhere else, then the other art students. Anyway, because she never minded being on her own – like now – she did not appear isolated. This kid was in the middle of a crowd but he was alone. Had he arrived just this term? And was it really true that he had announced during his first English lesson that he was androgynous?

He reached the double doors and suddenly looked up at the window. She was about to lean away and then did not. He lifted a hand in salute. There was something about him. Seen from this angle . . . he was mixed race.

She lifted her own hand and waved to him. He grinned. He was pale, almost yellow in the winter light, and his mother had used henna on his hair but she couldn't do anything about the smile. His family had come from Kashmir.

And then her mobile phone vibrated urgently against her thigh.

Aunty Mitzie said, '*I* wasn't too bad. I mean, I could see it was going to have a happy ending. But Vera . . . oh Daisy dear, your aunty Vera was – was – well, we had to leave. Her sobs were disturbing others.'

'I'm so sorry, Aunty. I should have warned you.'

'It was *Vera*. Vera is soft. I am hard. I would like to have watched the ending and then all would have been well.'

'When you come to supper next, I will tell you the story. It is so wonderful at the end. Good triumphs over evil. All that sort of thing.'

'That will be this evening, then. I will look forward to it.' Aunty's mobile suddenly chimed and she fished it out from her overall pocket. 'It is your aunty Vera,' she mouthed and tucked her head into her shoulder.

Daisy was halted in her tracks. She had been making plans all morning and they relied on Daddy being able to drive her to Gloucester General. Of course Daddy would cancel the aunties and their husbands because . . . because he would. But, but, but . . . Daddy and Mummy, they did so much, worked so hard. He would be assembling the ingredients for one of his enormous curries during the lunch hour and then there was that case they were discussing on Tuesday night. Was that coming to court soon? She hadn't paid attention because she had been so smart-alecky about their lovey-doveyness. At their age too!

She grinned to herself but she was still feeling . . . well, frantic really. Marc had been so . . . so brief on the phone; less than brief, actually: so *terse*. The ambulance was taking him and his mother from the local hospital to Gloucester and Aunty Alison was going to be all right. He told her that and then . . . was gone. No time for questions. She tried to ring him back during mid-morning break and again at the start of the lunch hour but he had switched off. Her brain felt addled. She needed Daddy to sort her out just as he had sorted her out on Tuesday and if the aunties were coming to supper there would be no chance of that. And just why did she want to drive to Gloucester anyway? The emergency, whatever it had been, was being dealt with and hadn't Marc made it crystal clear that he would prefer to handle it on his own anyway?

She bit her bottom lip furiously. She needed to do something. She remembered the trip to Hampton Court maze. Every bloody turning had proved to be the wrong one, but it had been fun because Marc was with her. She needed someone with her to go through this maze. And everyone was otherwise engaged.

Aunty Mitzie tucked her phone away. 'That lady you went to see at Jenner House. Vera says she collapsed yesterday morning right in the middle of a very important meeting in the lounge!'

'Collapsed? Miss Thorpe? What happened? Is she in hospital? I'll go to see her – that's what I should do—'

Aunty Mitzie opened her eyes so wide they nudged at her headscarf.

'What has got into you, child? You sound like your aunty Vera! They should teach you how to be calm. I notice all the time, children running, bashing doors open. This would not happen in India.'

'Aunty, you went to a convent and this is a comprehensive.' But Daisy took a deep breath and slowed down. 'Is . . . Miss Thorpe . . . in the cottage hospital?'

Mitzie's eyes became normal, which meant exasperated. Her constant exasperation was usually to do with the State of the World, but for now it was equally divided between Vera who was too soft and Daisy who was too quick. After she had explained this she said, 'Miss Thorpe is in her room at Jenner House as usual. No ill effects. Apparently.'

'Good. I'll go and see her. Now.'

Mitzie's hand clamped on her arm. 'You will do no such thing. The lady will be having her lunch. And it is possible she will rest after it.'

'I need to see her—'

'Yet there is a slight chance that she does not need to see you, Miss Daisy Patek!' Mitzie looked at the tiny, beautiful face and visibly melted. 'So . . . you will telephone your aunty Vera and enquire whether visitors are permitted.'

'Of course! You are an angel, Aunty. Yet your feet are always on the ground!'

'Perhaps my wings have been damaged by people like Vera and you!'

'Daddy will mend them.' Daisy flashed her aunty Mitzie an enormous smile and went with the others into the cafeteria. She stood in the queue and fished out her phone and broke a school rule by punching up Vera's number and pressing 'go'. And Vera would be only too pleased to go up to Miss Thorpe's room and make enquiries, and, yes, she would ring Daisy back asap. 'Over and out,' she said crisply and was on her way before Daisy could pocket her phone and ask for black coffee and a baked potato.

Daisy took her food to the window where there were high counters and stools overlooking the playing fields and stared out at another foggy February day. The village had grown – probably literally grown out of the ground – because it was in a basin of the hills. A natural gathering place for selling and hiring. Walk just a little way up any of the hills and there were views, often sunlit, of the Severn Sea and Welsh hills. But in the village itself the mist and cloud so often settled as if exhausted after all the climbing and the views were constantly changing as it breathed gently among the pubs and cottages and the ancient church . . . and the playing fields.

Daisy watched some girls at netball practice, running and shouting and bashing. Aunty Mitzie was right, there was a lot of that at school. The cafeteria was a prime example; behind her, voices were raised to incredible volume as some of the more strident year-sevens conversed from one end of the room to the other. And something was going on in the far corner; she twisted on her stool, praying that Marcus was somehow miraculously back. But it was the young ones. Boys, three or four of them, mucking about with someone else's food. A lump of mashed potato went flying. The androgynous kid grabbed his plate and held it defensively. Daisy got up and wandered over. The boys sat down and ate assiduously. She might be small but they had heard rumours about Daisy Patek. Some of her group called her Daisy the Dervish and though these twelve-year-olds had no idea what a dervish was, they still understood that nobody messed with Daisy Patek.

She stood there staring at them as if they needed hoovering up by her aunty.

Then she directed her gaze at the boy from Kashmir. 'Dennis, I thought I told you to meet me at lunchtime.'

The boys sniggered. 'Dennis!' one of them repeated jeeringly. 'His name's Zack!'

She swept them with her darkest gaze. 'We've got names for all of you. Yours is Pinhead. Zack's is Dennis the Menace. Got it?'

'What's mine, Daisy?' asked the largest specimen.

She said, 'Larry the Lamb.' She jerked her head towards the window. 'Don't hang about, Dennis – I'm pushed for time. Bring your food.' He was still clutching his plate and scraped his chair back to follow her.

She waited till he had settled himself on the stool next to her, then said, 'For Pete's sake, why d'you even *sit* with the Gorms?'

'They're OK. Why d'you call them Gorms?'

'Because they're gormless of course. Eat your . . . stuff.'

He eyed his wet rice unenthusiastically and she exploded again. 'School cooks can't manage rice. You should have baked potatoes with a different filling every day. And always look at the veggie options. And never, *never* tell the Gorms that you are androgynous.'

He spooned in the rice and made a face as he chewed it. 'I did. That's why they let me sit with them.' He swallowed with difficulty. 'D'you know what it means?'

'Yeah. It's not unknown in plants and . . . and nature generally. But the Gorms won't get further than the plant section so they'll call you pansy or something equally trite. Dennis is much better, I assure you. They will have vaguely heard about Dennis the Menace.'

'Who is he?'

'A cartoon character. Never mind. Another thing you mustn't do in this school is stalk people.'

'I can't help it. I get off the bus at the pub so that I don't have to go into school with the . . . Gorms. And there you are.' He pushed away his plate. 'You see, I'm in love with you.'

'Oh, for God's sake, Dennis. You're a kid!'

'I'm almost thirteen! And I've got a high IQ. That's why my parents wanted me to come to this school, cos it's got a high standard.'

'But the Gorms haven't, you idiot! And I'm almost eighteen by the way.'

He made a comic face. 'Another generation.'

She eyed him sternly. 'Quite. Absolutely.' She finished her black coffee, which was cold, and squashed the poly-cup on to the skin of the baked potato, ready to bin it all on her way out.

'So you come in on the school bus from Gloucester and that's why you got involved with the Gorms. Now listen to me. You get yourself a pair of glasses – clear lenses of course – and you carry a book.' She dug around in her bag and came up with a slim volume on the Impressionists. 'You can borrow this. And you get your nose into it the minute you get on the bus. There will be a certain amount of scoffing but then they will lose interest and the arty-farties will pick you up. By all means tell *them* you are androgynous: makes you more interesting. What's your religion?'

He hesitated, then ducked his head and blurted, 'Presbyterian.'

'Brilliant. Get a life of John Knox from Mrs Arbuthnot. Carry that about too. See what happens.'

He grinned. 'This is a bit like *Pygmalion*, isn't it? Only you're Professor Higgins and I'm Eliza Dolittle.'

She gave him another look. 'Got to go. Things to do. Go to the library. Now.'

She slid off her stool, shouldered her bag, clutched her cardboard plate and left the canteen. When she walked down the drive ten minutes later she looked back at the windows of the cafeteria and saw he was not there and he was not behind her. Well . . . it had stopped her thinking about Marcus and Aunty Alison for half an hour. In love indeed! It was pathetic. Pitiful. But she grinned as the school disappeared into the fog. Just past the pub there was a little newsagent's and often they had bunches of flowers. There wouldn't be much choice this weather but . . . maybe a tiny bunch of snowdrops for Miss Thorpe? Mabel Thorpe. May. They had done funny things with names even in those days . . . Perhaps nothing much changed really.

Six

Daisy had no doubts about her welcome. Miss Thorpe had been diffident, cautious, almost wary on Tuesday but when she had melted, her smile had been like today's, wide and almost excited. Daisy had thought of it as a Christmas smile. It was on her face when she opened the door that Thursday afternoon. Cautious and wary she certainly was not.

Daisy followed her into the narrow hallway, turned and closed the door and then followed again into the bedsit – because that was what it was and the word studio which implied space and light was entirely euphemistic.

She noted the bent spine beneath Miss Thorpe's wrap-around-three-times cardigan and thought it had not been so bent the day before yesterday.

She said brightly, 'You look OK, Miss Thorpe, but . . . are you sure you're up to this? Aunty Vera says everyone is worried about you and you've been drowned in visitors and . . . I can go away if it's too much.' She held the snowdrops out and wished so much she'd splashed out on one of the hothouse bunches in the back of the shop. But Miss Thorpe was so delighted she had to sit down with a plump.

'Daisy, how lovely! How simply lovely! They look freshly picked – you haven't been out looking for them, surely?'

'No . . . though I should've done that. It would have been a good thing to do. I'm such an *idiot*.' She could have wept her frustration then and there but controlled it all somehow. 'Do they actually grow wild? Like daffodils? I haven't seen any and actually Marcus and I often ramble. That's what he calls it – rambling. When we just aim for the nearest hilltop and go for it.'

Miss Thorpe laughed. 'Probably not. So much of my childhood was spent gathering flowers and fruit. They tell me you can't find a cowslip these days, nor a mushroom. The best time for mushrooms was early morning; they gleamed then with the dew on them. Easy to spot. But thank you for the snowdrops wherever you found them and do sit down, Daisy dear. I am so pleased to see you.'

'Me too.' Daisy laughed. 'I don't mean I'm glad to see *me*! You know what I mean. Of course you do. You are so like Daddy. You know what people mean when they say good afternoon or what a nice day.' Miss Thorpe opened her eyes wide at this and Daisy hurried on. 'I won't sit down for a mo. I'll put these in water and make some tea if you don't mind me turning your kitchen upside down.'

'I don't mind one bit. But where is Marcus?'

Daisy spoke over her shoulder. 'I'll tell you all but is this glass all right for the flowers?'

May looked at the glass into which her teeth nestled so comfortably most nights and nodded. 'It will be perfect.'

Daisy brought the glass in and put it right in front of Miss Thorpe, who sniffed appreciatively and said incomprehensibly, 'Like the Bisto Kids.'

'I've brought some biscuits too. Marc and I call them crunchies and if you dip them in your tea they're just heaven.'

Daisy busied herself with kettle and caddy, found milk in the tiny fridge, put teabags in mugs and produced the biscuits from her bag. 'Don't let's bother with plates.' She fished out the soggy teabags and hurled them into the sink, added milk, brought the mugs to the table and began to fiddle with the wrapping on the biscuits. Smilingly Miss Thorpe passed a pair of scissors.

'They're never far away from me,' she confided. 'I can't even hack my way through an envelope these days.' She laughed. 'I've never known anyone produce afternoon tea so quickly before.'

'Aunty Mitzie says I'm in too much of a hurry.' Daisy hugged her mug and took a sip of the tea. It didn't taste like Marcus's and she made a face. 'Sorry, I haven't waited for infusion to happen, have I?'

Miss Thorpe sipped too. 'It's wonderful, just how I like it, not too strong and not too weak. I like tea ceremonies of course, they are occasions in themselves – like Tuesday when I met you and Marcus for the first time. But this sort of tea, this is when other things happen.' She smiled her Christmas smile through the steam from her mug. 'I think you have come to tell me something special.'

'Yes. But it's not something good and it will not cheer you up and I am being very selfish to – to . . .' Daisy put down her cup abruptly, fished a Kleenex from her bag and blew into it very loudly. Then she said, 'I am an only child, you see. Mummy and Daddy spoil me because of that. They wanted me so desperately but they also didn't want others just in case it became too difficult. For the children. Being mixed race and all.'

Miss Thorpe's Christmas smile held but she also frowned slightly; Daisy held her breath because if Miss Thorpe could not take this, their burgeoning relationship would have to end here.

Then Miss Thorpe said, 'They must be wonderful people, Daisy. You are so lucky and if you recognize that then you are not spoilt in the sense the world means. You are cherished.'

Daisy blew again into the Kleenex, scrubbed her eyes with her knuckles, picked up her mug and took a huge gulp of tea, then spluttered because it was too hot. Miss Thorpe said anxiously, 'Are you all right?' Daisy nodded vigorously and spluttered more scalding tea. Miss Thorpe held out her water glass and said urgently, 'Spit it out in here.' Daisy did so, covered her mouth with another Kleenex and groaned through it, 'Oh Miss Thorpe!' And Miss Thorpe said, 'It's all right, Daisy, really. Really and truly.'

Daisy breathed carefully. 'It was the way . . . well, I wondered whether you'd be able to take it. And I watched you processing the information and coming up with the only thing that mattered. Daddy and Mummy.'

The Christmas smile was there full beam. 'It shines out, Daisy. It's so wonderful that you know how important it is.'

Daisy made a hideous face. 'It's just that – they're so embarrassing at times. When there's an open evening at school, they just sort of, like, catch each other's gaze and don't look away! It's like you can feel the connection between them. I grabbed a pair of scissors once and chopped at the air and they stopped it and laughed their heads off. I'm always having words with them about it, but they can't, like, help themselves!'

Miss Thorpe's pale face seemed to be glowing. She said simply, 'How marvellous.'

'Yes. And I'm part of it too. I never feel outside. And when I was a kid I – took advantage of it. I don't mean *stuff*. I could have had stuff – I *did* have stuff – a scooter and then a bike. And ice skates – and I hate the cold . . . but I always liked the boxes better than what was inside them.' Daisy looked beyond Miss Thorpe into the dim and distant past of eight years before, when she had been the same age as Dennis the Menace, well, only three years younger.

'I wanted to do things. I wanted to go to the pantomime at Christmas. In Bristol. The Hippodrome. I loved the roof there – it can open and close, did you know? I thought it was like a fairy palace . . . I just liked being there. And Daddy wasn't well and Mummy wanted to cancel and I deliberately cried and Daddy insisted on going and afterwards he had to go to hospital and have his gall bladder removed.'

Miss Thorpe was silent again, processing this latest burst of information. Then she said, 'Surely this is the way we learn about ourselves? The fact that you remember something so clearly . . . Nothing like that has happened since?'

'No. But I still burden them. All the time. With my . . . *woes*!' Daisy spoke the old-fashioned word as if it were a curse. And then she gave a short laugh. 'And now, because I'm trying to spare them this . . . I've come to burden you!' She began to gather up her bag. 'Honestly. What am I thinking of! I am so sorry, Miss Thorpe. I'll come and see you when I'm sane. Does that sound all right?' She was laughing properly now and at herself.

Miss Thorpe's smile suddenly disappeared and re-appeared as a frown and Daisy snatched at a fleeting idea of a frown as an upside-down smile.

'Stay put, please, Daisy. Please. I mean it. To listen to the problems of others can be very therapeutic – this is something you must learn. You have come to share a problem and I am ready for that. It will be very bad for my health if you leave without—' She stopped speaking because Daisy was laughing so much she could not possibly hear the pearls of wisdom being cast before her.

When she calmed down she said breathlessly, 'I think I must have spilled some of my beans already . . . but the basic problem is that Marcus has got a place at Leeds University to read modern history and it's almost bound to go wrong because his mother is . . . unwell. And the top problem is that she – Marc's mother – had to be taken to Gloucester hospital this morning and there's no way I can go there to help out because we've got Daddy's family coming to supper tonight.'

She watched as Miss Thorpe processed this information too and was unsurprised when she said, 'Your father would of course cancel supper and drive you there if you asked him.'

Daisy nodded once.

'So you do not ask him.' Miss Thorpe nodded, satisfied on one point. Then she said, 'Back to Marcus. Is there no father?'

'He died. Cancer. Awful.'

'And Marcus has taken on certain responsibilities.' Daisy nodded. 'And his mother . . . she is . . . not well. And now – this morning – was very unwell. Sufficiently so to be taken into hospital. And you want to help – your first reaction is that you have to go to her.'

'Yes.'

'Or Marcus?'

Daisy hesitated. 'Well, yes. But of course . . . I mean . . . I sort of, like, must be *fond* of her. I used to call her Aunty Alison.'

'And now? What do you call her now?'

Daisy bit her bottom lip. 'I never see her. Hardly. I don't call her anything.'

'She demands too much of Marcus? Yes? He nurses her? He would be good at that of course. Probably too good. Perhaps she resents it at times. It is not an easy relationship. Perhaps she is frightened that he might give up his university place to look after her?'

Daisy frowned, thinking back. 'She spoke on the phone. Tuesday evening. She was delighted about it. She had it all worked out . . .'

Miss Thorpe picked up her mug and stared into it. She said in a low voice, 'Has she taken an overdose, Daisy? Is that what has happened?'

Daisy was aghast. She put one hand to her throat. She knew immediately that this was exactly what had happened. She held her breath, staring at Miss Thorpe and doing her own processing. Then she let her breath go and whispered, 'I hadn't thought . . . oh – oh – poor Aunty Alison. Everything she does – or tries to do – goes wrong.'

Miss Thorpe shook her head, shocked herself. 'I'm so sorry, Daisy. I thought you must already know and not be able to speak of it. It's probably not the case at all – I can't think what possessed me to blurt out something like that.'

'Because it's obvious. You realized . . . she lost her husband and has never been the same. She's an alcoholic . . . she's given up trying to be anything else. Of course she doesn't want to stand in Marc's way. Of course, of course. Why didn't we both see that? He believed her when she said she could cope with Uncle Ted's help. And so did I when she phoned. Oh Miss Thorpe!'

'My dear child . . .' Miss Thorpe reached across the table and took one of Daisy's hands. 'This is the time you must have faith. In Marcus. In yourself. In the future.' She looked into Daisy's drowning face and shook the hand slightly. 'And in the meantime, we will telephone the Gloucester hospital and enquire for Marcus's mother.'

Daisy clutched at the hand shaking hers. 'I've only got Marcus's mobile number.' She heard her own voice, ridiculously tragic.

Miss Thorpe released the hand and reached for the phone, pressed something or other and then asked for the number of Gloucester hospital. With her free hand she picked up a biro and pad from beside the telephone and wrote carefully. Then she replaced the receiver and smiled at Daisy. 'You or me? Neither of us is related to Marcus's mother but I think I could pass myself off as an aged aunt if you did not object.'

Daisy was suddenly without words. She nodded. Then watched, eyes enormous, as Miss Thorpe pressed digits then spoke. She was enquiring for Mrs Alison Budd who had been admitted as an emergency just this morning. Yes, well, she probably was related, Mrs Budd's mother had been a cousin once removed. Yes, she quite understood that certain information could not be passed on without the patient's consent ... There was a long pause during which Miss Thorpe made small sounds. Then she said, 'And she is going to be all right? I understand – yes, I do realize – ongoing process. Of course. Thank you, thank you so much. When she is able to talk will you give her my love? Tell her Daisy. Just Daisy. Thank you.' She replaced the receiver and said immediately, 'She is going to be all right, Daisy. The – the *procedures* have been carried out and she is now on a saline drip and fairly comfortable.'

'That means her stomach has been pumped out?' Daisy's voice was small.

'I take it so. The word "procedure" can cover a great many kinds of treatment. But she *is* going to be all right, Daisy. So, perhaps later today you can telephone Marcus and he can tell you more.'

'Yes. Though it will be awful for him. To tell me. He says I don't understand.' Daisy was chewing her lip again.

Miss Thorpe smiled. 'Not if you tell him that you wanted to ask your father to drive you to Gloucester yet you did not ask because he would have done it.'

For just a moment Daisy was confused, then she said, 'Is that how I talk? And you still understood?' And when Miss Thorpe nodded she said, 'Well then. Shall we have another mug of tea? Then I can tell you something that might well cheer you up.'

And Miss Thorpe nodded, and Daisy told her about Zack being renamed Dennis the Menace. And she did indeed laugh. They chatted on until the crunchies were all dipped and eaten and Miss Thorpe had decided that Zack probably was indeed Presbyterian because many of the nineteenth-century missionaries had gone to India from Scotland. 'I'll look it up in a day or two,' she promised. 'I've been jotting down notes about Dr Jenner and I've still got one of the encyclopaedias from the book room but we'll need the PQR volume, of course. It might be the one that's missing. People take them out to prop up wobbly chairs and so on. Nobody ever thinks that anyone could actually want to look things up – not at our age!'

'I can help there. When the aunties go home tonight I'll get on the computer.'

'Ah, yes. One of the residents was asking me why you hadn't done your Coventry research on the computer.'

Daisy made a face. 'Everyone thinks that the computer comes up with all the answers. And it is pretty amazing. But it's got no soul. The other afternoon – Tuesday – that was when we learned about the soul of Coventry. It's what Steve calls the "oral tradition" and he says that if only we'd kept it up from the beginning then we'd understand every soul who had ever put on flesh and lived among us!' She giggled. 'That's the sort of thing he says.'

Miss Thorpe said, 'Who is Steve?'

'Oh. Stephen Coles. Our personal tutor at school. We haven't seen him since we visited you because he's been ill. Mrs Arbuthnot says his wife doesn't give him proper meals.' Daisy giggled again. 'Mrs Arbuthnot is the school librarian.'

Miss Thorpe processed this then said thoughtfully, 'And Mrs Arbuthnot cares about him. One forgets things like that about schools. Yet it must have always been so.'

Daisy nodded. 'Like here, really. You care about each other.'

Another long pause. Daisy waited; she knew now that she must wait. Then Miss Thorpe nodded too and took a deep breath.

'Daisy, would you do something for me? Would you ask your aunt Vera about another of the residents? His name is Arthur Wentworth and he's a bit of a silly old buffer but he cares. And he seems to have disappeared.'

Daisy was on to it immediately. Miss Thorpe had an admirer. She reined in her avid interest with a conscious effort and nodded.

Miss Thorpe was suddenly embarrassed. 'He – and the manager – lots of people think I should . . .' she made her voice sonorous, '"move on"! As if thinking and talking about one's childhood is a bad thing! So, sometimes, well, only once actually, I said something rather shocking to poor Mr Wentworth and I am afraid he must have cast me off. That is acceptable – of course. However, I am also anxious that he

might be ill. No one would tell me in case it upset me, you
see. And I would like to know.'

Daisy nodded so vigorously she burped. Then laughed.
'Leave it with me, Miss Thorpe. You've come to the right
person!' She could not help herself from asking curiously,
'What was it you said to him – aren't you going to tell me
that?'

For a moment she thought Miss Thorpe was going to
tell her. Then her mouth stretched tightly and she shook
her head. 'You would probably find it highly amusing – as
I suppose I did when I said it. But if you didn't . . . our
friendship might not continue to flower, Daisy. And that
would be a pity.'

Daisy said for the umpteenth time, 'Oh, Miss Thorpe!' But
she did not argue and covered her own pleasure by standing
up and taking the mugs into the kitchen and as she swilled
them and put them on the draining rack she knew quite
suddenly that in spite of the awfulness of Marcus's mum
– Aunty Alison – and having to hold back and be terribly
sensible, she felt OK. She stood and looked out of the small
kitchen window at the car park, which was dreary, then at
the trees beyond all speckled with the new shoots of green
and she thought that once the gift of life had been given
there wasn't much you could do about it, except live. How on
earth had Aunty Alison forgotten that?

Miss Thorpe said goodbye and wished her well, and then
– as if it might be an afterthought, which Daisy knew darned
well it wasn't – she added, 'Daisy, on second thoughts, forget
asking your aunt about Mr Wentworth. He'll probably turn
up tomorrow. And if not, I shall hear. Gossip is absolutely
rife in Jenner House!'

Daisy smiled and nodded with fingers crossed. Then she

said, 'Thank you for sorting me out. Aunty Alison. And Mummy and Daddy. And I really don't see that you have to make a choice about moving on or back. For goodness' sake, you can do both in the space of a nano-sec!'

She took the lift past the ground floor and into the basement, where the laundry room and the rubbish skip offered mixed smells. Aunty Vera had what was called the 'cleaners' office' in a broom cupboard down on this level. But it was locked and the floor newly washed. She had gone home early to get ready for this evening's supper.

Daisy went out of the garden door and climbed the steps to the car park and was really glad to discover that there was no resentment about tonight's family gathering. She examined her thoughts meticulously. No. Nothing. Perhaps she was coming to terms with being a spoilt only child. Cherished. She loved that word. She turned out of the car park and started up the last part of the hill to home. 'Cherished,' she said aloud and experimentally. Yes, it sounded great.

Seven

The trouble with the family suppers was that half the members lapsed into Hindi when the gossip became too much for the slower and inadequate English. The uncles especially, though they were Birmingham-born, were even prouder of being Indian than their parents. Nehru and his sisters bridged the gaps between the two languages but it meant that every anecdote took a long time to become comprehensible to everyone and some of the hilarious double meanings made Daisy laugh so much she was quite unable to complete her narration of *Slumdog* until it was almost time for bed.

'This I do not understand,' Aunty Mitzie said, frowning prodigiously. 'They danced? Everybody danced? On the platform of Mumbai railway station? How could that be?'

'It was symbolic, Aunty.' Daisy flapped her hands helplessly. 'Symbolic of the triumph of the underdog. All those terrible, awful things provided the right answers and – and—'

'But it was *dangerous*! The platform edges – everyone knows that to dance on a railway platform is not allowed!'

Aunty Vera shrugged her enormous donkey jacket over the delicate silver and blue of her best sari. 'That is why I had to leave the cinema. I have been in Mumbai. All good work goes to Hindu. Muslim. You know what they tell us? Too much qualification. Which means it is because Mitzie and I go to Anglican church. I leave the cinema as I left Mumbai. As I left my Mother India. Because she wanted me no more.' She wore her tragic face. Daisy hugged her huge shoulders and led her into the lower hallway.

She asked her quietly about Arthur Wentworth; it was an excellent way to change the subject. 'This has to be discreet, Aunty. And I know,' crossed fingers, 'that you can be totally discreet. When necessary.'

Aunty Vera was on the case immediately. 'I do not know nothing—'

'Double negative, Aunty.'

'I do not know anything!' Pause for thought. 'He is in his room, that is certain, because Mrs Watkins cleans for him and she does not like it when he stays put as he tells her how to do her work. Which is necessary as she is not a good cleaner. She cleaned yesterday . . . she said he was very quiet, in fact did not speak a word except good morning and goodbye.' She frowned. 'He must be ill. I will enquire.' She noted Daisy's face and said, 'With the utmost discretion. The meals-on-wheels lady will tell me.'

'Better not, Aunty. If he's not very well, that is that.'

'I have your phone number. If he is taken into hospital I will telephone.'

Daisy nodded; she could not bear to dampen Aunty Vera's enthusiasm completely but this would be enough information for Miss Thorpe. Aunty Vera said sadly, 'Often the residents will have a day in bed, child. It is better than the sudden take-off. They are waiting for the bus, you see.'

'The bus?'

'To take them to heaven, my darling. When our father

died back home, my teacher told this to us – Mitzie and me. It has always stayed with me and given me comfort.'

'Oh Aunty . . .' This time, for some ridiculous reason, Daisy could not stop her tears. She clasped Vera around the waist and even through the thickness of her donkey jacket could feel Vera's heart against her own school shirt. Vera was shocked.

'Dearest girl. It is your age of course. Lots of tears, but happiness just around the corner.'

'Aunty, I am *almost eighteen* – that all happened when I was thirteen and went through *puberty*, for goodness' sake!' She grinned into the dark, fathomless eyes. 'It's just that I love you so much.'

This declaration was dismissed. 'Of course you do, child! We are family together!' This was hastily delivered as the door to the kitchen was flapping with the others coming through. One of the uncles had a car called a people carrier that could accommodate the parents and the two children – supposedly asleep in the spare bedroom – together with many sealed dishes of korma; he went on up the stairs to the front door, where it was parked on the road 'at the ready', as he put it. Daisy joined in with finding scarves and gloves and thought how strange it was that the uncles featured so little in her imagination. They were younger than Daddy of course and they had been born in Birmingham so their memories of India were second-hand, but stronger and fiercer than the Pateks'. Arranged marriages were not for Christians, yet they belonged to a church that boasted a predominantly Indian congregation and when Nehru was looking for husbands for his sisters he had arranged an introduction through the church. The two brothers had immediately agreed to meet the Patek girls, and had been instantly attracted to these traditional young women whose memories of Mother India were not all bad.

Daisy smiled at them warmly as she passed Uncle Matthew his balaclava. 'Drive carefully,' she said. 'I am so glad everything is working out.' Both uncles worked at Frenchay Hospital and Matthew had been made up to charge nurse just before Christmas. Saul was content to remain an orderly but Matthew was ambitious. She smiled as Matthew's face appeared through the opening of the balaclava; perhaps he was the tiniest bit like Marcus?

He said, 'I hate this hat thing. Mitzie makes me wear it.'

No, he was not like Marcus. She said, 'I'm not surprised. It's warm and she knitted it for you and you look really cute in it.'

He frowned. 'You are becoming extremely cheeky, Daisy.'

She nodded. 'I am half Indian, you know. I cannot help it.'

He cuffed her affectionately and was gone. The three of them went back to the kitchen and began to load the dishwasher. Daisy put stuff in the fridge, found a spectacle case embossed with Mitzie's name, listened to her parents talking and thought about Aunty Alison and Marcus. She had telephoned Marcus before supper and again when she went to the bathroom.

Mummy said, 'How was school, flower? Was Marcus back in circulation? Is he still over the moon about his university place?'

'School was fine.' She thought of the androgynous boy and grinned. Then she sighed, accepted a bundle of cutlery to be put away and told them about Aunty Alison. They turned and pressed their backs against the counter, staring at her, horrified.

'Why didn't you—?' 'We could have cancelled—' they went on, both talking together. She held up a hand.

'She's all right. They must have pumped out her stomach . . . I should have asked Uncle Mattie, shouldn't I? And Marcus is with her. They will sort it out.'

They were silenced, still staring at her. Then Mummy said, 'I'll telephone Ted Budd. He's Stan's brother. He'll have some news.'

Daddy chewed his lip in a way Daisy recognized. He said, 'We hardly know him. Might it be seen as . . .'

Mummy said, 'Intrusion. Perhaps. But . . .'

Daisy said, 'You could try the hospital. Miss Thorpe gave me the number.'

Daddy said, 'Hang on. When did you last ring Marcus? When you went to the bathroom? What did he say?'

'Not very much. I think . . .' Suddenly there was a lump in her throat. 'I think he is ashamed. He said it was an accident and she forgot that she had already taken her night-time pills. And we must believe that, Daddy.'

There was a long silence, then, synchronized to perfection, they both nodded. Even so, Mummy made for the phone and Daddy did not object. Daisy said, 'They won't tell you anything. Miss Thorpe had to pretend to be a distant cousin or something. Her voice is old – that probably helped.'

For the first time they picked up on Miss Thorpe and there had to be more explanations. They were exchanging glances at such regular intervals they looked like Wimbledon spectators following a fierce rally.

Daddy said slowly, 'A lot has been happening.'

'Not to me. To Marcus and Aunty Alison.'

'To you also. To Miss Thorpe also.'

'Yes.'

Mummy said in a wailing sort of voice, 'We think we are so clever with our tight little timetable and our oh-so-well-organized life. And we thought Alison accepted this . . . She accepted it because she had to! She must have felt so lonely – isolated. But to get to this . . . to try to kill herself—'

Daisy interrupted quickly. 'We don't think it was like that, either. We think . . .' She choked on the lump, swallowed and went on. 'We think she was sort of clearing the way for Marcus. Leeds. You know.'

'Oh my God.' Mummy lowered her head. 'If it had succeeded it would have wrecked Marcus.'

Daddy put out a hand and covered hers. 'There is no blame anywhere. Phone the hospital, Etta. That is all we can do. Tell them we are very old friends.' He took Miss Thorpe's piece of paper from Daisy's hand and led Mummy to the phone as if she did not know where it was. Then he came to Daisy and put his arms right round her and as Mummy started to speak he whispered in her ear, 'Well done, my flower. Very well done.' And of course that was when she started to cry.

The next day was Friday and Marcus rang early to say that they would be coming home. Uncle Ted was fetching them and bringing clothes and things and Aunty Gert would be in the house and would bring bread and milk and a stew she had made for them. On Monday they had a social worker calling to assess their needs. Everything was being taken care of and he hoped he would see her next Tuesday in time for the visit to Miss Thorpe. She relayed all this across the breakfast table and her mother made a face and said, 'I can almost see the signs saying keep off the grass.'

'Too many cooks already. She needs peace and quiet.' Daddy bit into toast glumly. 'Family are all very well but

Ted looks like Stan and he's not in the least like Stan. And Gertrude . . .' Words failed him and he rolled his dark eyes to the ceiling.

'You should hear what Miss Thorpe says about her social worker,' Daisy added.

Mummy said, 'I think we should meet this Miss Thorpe. She sounds as if she has been a very good friend to you, Daisy love.'

'Yes. She's great. Not a bit miserable or mournful.' Daisy nodded. 'I'll pop in on my way home this afternoon. She would like to know about Alison.'

'Will you give her our thanks? For being so kind to you yesterday?'

'Oh yes. She would like that too. I told her that when I pass my driving test I'll take her to Mablethorpe. That's her name, Mabel Thorpe.'

They were both tickled by this. She knew they were probably visualizing a kind of cheerful Cockney sparrow type. 'But test or no test, you are certainly not going to drive anyone right up to Manchester,' Mummy said, straightening her face suddenly.

'Mablethorpe. And anyway she wouldn't go. I don't think she wants to go very far at all.'

'Perhaps she's done all the travelling she wants. I wonder how far she had to come from Coventry to end up between Gloucester and Bristol. Now that there are no cattle markets or hirings, it's an odd place to be.'

'We're here,' Daisy pointed out.

'It suits us to be within reach of two cities. And the school had a good reputation.' Mummy was clearing the table as she spoke. She held up a cereal box. 'Dead?' she queried.

'Yes. Can I have something without bran next time?'

'Come with me tomorrow and you can choose your own.'

Daisy had none of the Indian love of the marketplace but Marcus was out of it until next Tuesday – it would be a whole week of not seeing him – and the enormous supermarket at Cribbs Causeway sold clothes. She nodded. One of the art students was wearing a skirt that had waistbands above and below the bum and Daisy coveted it. 'OK,' she said off-handedly. Her mother caught her eye and grinned at her until Daisy gave in and grinned back.

She was surprised by her own feelings. She was still desperate about Alison and even more desperate about Marcus, but she was in control. All right, she had collapsed on Daddy last night but it had been momentary. Since Miss Thorpe had sorted it all out, she no longer felt embroiled and hopeless. She accepted that she had to wait now. Be there. But just outside the door instead of inside. Somehow they had to find out what to do between them; perhaps Ted and Gertie could help, perhaps the social worker, but until they decided they must simply know that the Pateks were around, waiting.

So Daisy went into school almost blithely, hoping Mr Coles would be there, hoping that the androgynous kid had coped on the bus, already looking forward to ringing Miss Thorpe's doorbell in the afternoon. It was a bit of a let-down when Zack/Dennis was not outside the pub or inside the school gate. No sign of him as she went upstairs to Steve Coles's room either. And Steve's door was still locked.

Mrs Arbuthnot said, 'Perhaps it's swine flu? Have you got any time this morning, dear? I'm snowed under. The new intake have no idea how to use a library.'

Daisy slotted the returns in as quickly as she could. She wanted to get to the sixth form common room asap for a word with Shirley Gray about the tulip skirt and where it had come from. She kept an eye on the interior window overlooking the hall doors as kids came in for assembly; no sign of Zack. The little gang he'd been with yesterday did not look guilty; they filed in respectably enough, indeed they could have been sleepwalking. But Zack had been missing for too long; she had been the last to see him; she might even be responsible for whatever had happened to him . . . might have happened to him. Daisy suddenly felt sick.

She skipped off to the common room when she could; no sign of Shirley. It was going to be one of those days obviously. The big room smelled horribly of feet as usual; there had probably been a soccer match yesterday afternoon. If Marcus were here he would know. She went to the so-called bar, which was a jumble of glasses, mugs and milk souring in bottles. She was starting to restore order when the door flew open and Shirley came in.

'What are you *doing*?' she asked – rhetorically because it was obvious that Daisy was clearing up. 'Didn't you get my message? I left it on the door of your locker. Here it is – look!' She pulled off a yellow sticker and held it out. 'He was here when I arrived nearly an hour ago. Already in a foul mood because of the mess – reckoned none of us ever went to assembly and he wanted you and me in the back row to keep an eye on the Gloucester contingent – yes, that was the word he used – then he wanted to see you in his study pronto. You weren't even at assembly and you look as if you're in your dream world again. And where the hell is Marcus?'

'Who wants me in his study?' Daisy knew it must be the head. Barry Carter. BC. 'And I was in assembly on Monday and Tuesday. We should not agree to act as traffic wardens. And Marcus's mother is in hospital in Gloucester.'

'Oh God. He wants you both. In person. What's going on?'

'I haven't got the faintest.' Daisy told herself sternly that she did not feel sick. 'But actually I wanted to see you. Where did you get your skirt? I'm going to Cribbs Causeway tomorrow – can I get one there?'

'Don't know. Made mine. Everyone's wearing them at the club – you should come now and then if you want to keep up.' She thrust the note on to the bar. 'For Pete's sake get your head into gear! Assembly's over and he's been waiting for about ten minutes – probably drumming his fingers like he does!'

Daisy swilled then dried her hands. 'No problem. Didn't know you could sew, actually.'

'For God's sake, Daisy, I've opted for fashion – you must have noticed?'

'Yes. But sewing . . .'

'Just go!' Shirley practically shoved her out. 'Good luck!' she called.

Daisy found herself hurrying downstairs. She had nothing on her conscience, had she? Something wrong with Zack? She was suddenly frightened and scooted round a corner where the carpet began and knocked on the door before she had really gathered herself together.

He was not a big man. Perhaps that was why he always remained seated; it was a measure of his emotions that he was up and walking as she went into his room after hearing his curt 'Come!' There was sufficient space behind his desk for him to make four paces to his right and four paces to his left and he used those paces to the full, swinging himself round at the window and again at the filing cabinet as if he'd reached a summit of some kind.

He glanced to his left, ascertained it was Daisy Patek and said, 'Sit down,' then swung himself into his own chair, put his hands palm down on his desk and bent his head.

Daisy was terrified. He was getting his breath of course, but he was also getting himself together. This was what he did. He waited, assembling his facts. He knew that Daisy had talked to Zack . . . there were witnesses . . . something terrible had happened to Zack and it must be all her fault. She clenched her hands into fists on her lap. Daddy said Barry Carter was a wonderful administrator, Mummy said he had a clear and logical mind; Daisy could only see a detached and chilly man who probably identified his students by numbers. And still he waited and she could stand it no longer. He wanted her to blurt it out. She should resist. She could not.

She said, 'I liked him. All that androgynous stuff was because he wanted to – to make himself visible . . . And all it did was to get him more and more . . . not exactly bullied, I suppose, but . . . picked on. He needed an ally. Perhaps that was why he stalked Marcus and me.' She swallowed. BC's expression had not changed. She blurted, 'What's happened to him? Have they hurt him?'

BC pushed himself back in his chair. He made chewing motions with his mouth and jaw. Then he said, 'Go on.'

She rarely needed encouragement to 'go on' but this time was different. She seemed unable to form a sentence and made several starts which included people like Mrs Arbuthnot and Stephen Coles and at one point Shirley Gray and her tulip skirt. Still, he waited. She had to admire that waiting.

She took a deep breath and started again.

'I was eating lunch in the cafeteria and the boys who come in from Gloucester were over the other side and they were teasing Zack, throwing his food around, that sort of thing. So I went over and acted as if Zack and I knew each other – which we did of course – but I didn't know his name so I called him Dennis the Menace and when they, like, scoffed at that I gave them silly names too. Then I took Zack off and told him how he should cope. On the bus. And . . . it obviously didn't work.' She swallowed again and said in the sort of voice she had heard Mummy use in court, 'I take full responsibility.' And then, desperately, 'What has happened to him?'

BC took his time, then swivelled his chair slightly and picked up the phone. 'Attendance? Year eight. Gloucester boy. Forename Zack. Is he in?' A pause during which the woman in reception would be looking at her computer screen, probably terrified because it was the headmaster speaking. Daisy wondered whether she might be about to throw up. Then BC said, 'No? Ah. Good.' He looked over the receiver at Daisy and obviously repeated what he was hearing. 'Text from mother to say flu symptoms.' He looked down, picked up a pen, shifted a notepad closer and wrote something. 'Thank you, Mrs Blackdown.' He replaced the receiver. He seemed better. More cheerful somehow. He looked up.

'In answer to your question, Miss Patek, nothing has happened to him except a slight cold.'

He really was impossible. 'Miss Patek' indeed! And 'slight cold' when Zack's mother was reporting flu symptoms. She wanted to weep with relief but played his game and waited for an apology.

He put his pencil close to his notebook and looked up. He had grey eyes and they looked steely again. 'Now it is my turn, I think.' He took a breath. 'Yesterday, late afternoon when you had already left the building, I had a caller. A gentleman from Jenner House. He called me several names. The least offensive one was "an upstart opportunist who battened on the flesh of elderly people in order to satisfy a salacious appetite for some kind of fame in the world of education".' BC consulted his notepad. 'Yes, those were his words. I made notes immediately he had left, in case the whole thing came to court.' He glanced up. 'He threatened legal action.'

Daisy stared into the grey eyes. 'Was his name Arthur Wentworth?'

'It was. He was a flying officer back in the Battle of Britain. He gave me some statistics but suffice it to say he was one of the First of the Few.'

Daisy continued to stare for another three seconds while she pictured what might have happened, then she put her head on the edge of the desk and literally collapsed beneath a gale of giggles. BC's words – 'suffice it to say' – were the final straw. The relief of knowing that Zack Whatever was all right and then the mental picture of the unknown Arthur Wentworth storming in on poor old BC were just too much. She managed to control herself fairly quickly, knowing from previous experience that such mirth could easily dissolve into tears and be dismissed as hysteria. She was not hysterical, of that she was certain. She was seeing things – life perhaps – really clearly and very differently.

As soon as she stopped giggling, BC said, 'Please pull yourself together, Miss Patek. I realize that Mr Wentworth was referring to the assignment arranged for you by Mr Coles, but given that it has provoked such a furious reaction I need more information. Mr Coles is unavailable, as you doubtless know. Mr Budd is with his mother . . . I cannot believe that he would countenance any of the cannibalism – yes, Mr Wentworth referred to your interview as an act of spiritual cannibalism – but I have to go into the whole thing with great care. The man was slandering not only myself but the school and should he decide to seek publicity by going through legal channels, then . . .'

Daisy started to splutter again. 'I'm sorry – really sorry, sir. It's just that . . . the day after Marcus and I met Miss Thorpe for the first time, she went to a meeting in their communal lounge and had a fainting fit. I think she doesn't eat properly, sir, and the manager has arranged for her to have meals on wheels, which is an excellent thing . . . Anyway, I popped in yesterday to tell her about Marcus – she was just wonderful, sir. And she asked me to make enquiries about Mr Wentworth because she hadn't seen him since her . . . collapse. She didn't want him to know that she was making enquiries. And she knew I could help because my aunty is a cleaner at Jenner House. And my aunty said he was probably having a day in bed or something. But he must have been working himself up to this. And it's obvious why, isn't it?'

She giggled again and looked at BC with raised brows. He played the waiting game and she exploded. 'He fancies her, sir! He's probably desperately in love with her! And he had to blame someone for her being ill and it was us! Marcus and me. And he didn't know where we lived or anything so he came to have a go at you! It's as plain as the nose on your face. I bet you, now he's got that off his chest, he went to see her at last and they had a nice chat and – and – everything is all right again!'

She sat back in her chair, grinning like a Cheshire Cat. And when he didn't speak, she said, 'I really admire the way you kept very quiet, sir . . . so that I spilled whatever beans I had. That was clever. But please don't worry any more. I was planning to go in to see Miss Thorpe after school to give her an update on Marcus and his mother, so I can report back to you tomorrow.'

He lifted his hands and crashed them down on his desk and she sat up with a jerk.

'Miss Patek. Your assignment is at an end. You do not set foot in Jenner House again – do I make myself clear?' She could not speak and he went on without his customary wait. 'You have no idea what an unnecessary fuss this could cause. We are in the running to become a school with specialist facilities in sciences and something like this could finish our hopes in that direction.' He took a breath. 'I have received a complaint and I have dealt with it. Jenner House is now out of bounds to you and Mr Budd. Is that absolutely understood?'

She should have protested, put her case, explained that she and Miss Thorpe were now personal friends and he had no jurisdiction over . . . She said nothing.

Eight

May had always enjoyed Fridays and this one was no exception. She slept well; the doctor had assured her he was not prescribing any sleeping tablets but since her little 'fuss' on Wednesday, when he had been called in, she had slept like a top. Surely that could not be pure coincidence? And there was something else just beyond the reach of memory; something happy; something she was anticipating with a pleasure that was close to excitement.

She rolled carefully on to her back. No pain and only the slightest bit of dizziness. There must be something in those pills and whatever it was she didn't care. For a stupid instant she wondered whether to start a rumour that Miss Thorpe was on heroin and she giggled at the thought of Arthur Wentworth's face. He would most definitely strike her off his visiting list. And he would probably blame the beautiful Daisy and the tall good-looking Marcus. But he could hardly advise her to move on, could he? Taking to hard drugs at her age would be moving on at a gallop.

She stopped giggling because she remembered that her name had probably been removed from Arthur's visiting list ever since she had practically boasted about the number of lovers she had notched up in her day. How dreadful it sounded now. How could she have said such a thing? Tasteless. Utterly brash and tasteless.

And then she wondered why it should matter to her. Why should she care if she had offended a silly old buffer like Arthur Wentworth? Flying Officer Kyte. A radio comedy character. Arthur could have been a model for FO Kyte; insensitive, inaccurately pedantic, fussy . . . a complete parody. Yet kind too. Yes, very kind. If she had offended him, it did matter to her. It mattered a lot.

She frowned prodigiously and tried to claw her way back to this Friday and why it was a good day. For one thing, February was nearly done, the last day tomorrow. She never liked February Fill-Dyke, dripping umbrellas and macks and wet, stringy hair. March often offered sunshine and brisk breezes and primroses. And hadn't Daisy mentioned that they were off school next week for half-term?

She smiled, glad to have found the source of her anticipation. Daisy was popping in this evening to update her on Marcus and his mother and there was a feeling of having helped in some way. She had helped Daisy cope with the maelstrom of her emotions.

She had known from the first five minutes of Daisy and Marcus entering her flat that Daisy was a joy. It was not only her intense beauty – not by any means. Daisy Patek was clever, she was sensitive, she was infinitely caring and she was in love. What more could anyone ask? She was too quick perhaps for her own good; May was willing to bet that many of her teachers would say she had a butterfly mind. But that wasn't right. May frowned, trying to pin down something unpinnable. She smiled: unpinnable, that was a word Daisy would relish. Her butterfly mind was infectious then? But butterflies were much too fluttery . . . so what was the quality and how did you define it?

May moved her head on the pillow, smiling at herself. And then it came to her. Daisy's mind was a spark, leaping and igniting here and there. And . . . she was coming here after school. And perhaps if she had time she would come during half-term and Marcus would be with her and his mother would be home and safe. How could she be otherwise with a son like Marcus? Just for a moment May almost dropped into a hole of self-pity. If only there had been someone like Marcus around for her . . . She rolled over and sat up on the edge of her bed, bracing herself with her arms.

Sometimes, looking back objectively, seeing herself in the third person, she was appalled by the sheer loneliness of that time. She could have done with a Britney Longsmith then, or – better still – a Zoe Ballinger. But still, she had survived somehow, half knowing even in the midst of loneliness and loss that there would be other friends and, perhaps, lovers. And there had been. And she had cheapened them all by boasting about them to Arthur Wentworth!

The intercom shrilled and Zoe's voice came through stridently.

'All right, May?'

May relaxed her rigid arms and smiled. 'Good morning, Zoe. I'm very well. How are you?'

'Well . . . I'm all right, I suppose.'

May had never heard such uncertainty in Zoe Ballinger's voice before. Obviously it had occurred to none of the residents, herself included, to ask after the manager's health before.

'You don't sound all right.' May heard her own voice, un-expectedly anxious.

Zoe laughed. 'I'm fine. Honestly. It's just a date. February the twenty-seventh. An anniversary I don't enjoy. Anyway, don't forget I'm coming to escort you downstairs for lunch.'

May was surprised again. 'Lunch? I have the meals on wheels now.'

'Not today. I told you it was our fish-and-chip Friday and you thought you might try it, so I cancelled meals on wheels – everyone cancels on Fridays. Don't you feel up to it?'

May paused then said, 'Yes. I feel well up to it. I'd forgotten – strange, I knew something special was happening today. That's what it must be!' She laughed and Zoe laughed with her.

'See you at twelve thirty then,' she trilled. And was gone.

It hadn't been a complete lie . . . May told herself that as she rummaged in the wardrobe for her grey pleated skirt and black jumper. She couldn't find her pearls, then remembered she had donated them for a raffle.

'Silly old fool,' she said to herself but she was smiling. If Arthur Wentworth was having the fish-and-chip lunch she might find the opportunity to apologize to him. Put things right. Then she could tell Daisy everything was back to normal.

Zoe rang the bell at 12.25pm, admired May's outfit and with one sweeping, practised glance checked that the electrical stuff was switched off, then held out her arm for May. That meant they had to walk sideways through the tiny hall to the front door, which made them both laugh. Zoe let May lock her own front door and ring for the lift. May smiled, recognizing that Zoe was making an enormous effort. She said, 'It's really good of you to come for me. What about the fish-and-chip delivery – don't you have to sign for it or something?'

'The Smithsons offered. They're on the ground floor and can see who is arriving at the front door. And considering they're both nearly ninety they're amazingly spry.' Zoe pulled down the folding seat in the lift and when May shook her head she sat down herself with a sigh. 'Of course there are two of them. One can help the other. It makes such a difference.'

May nodded. She looked down at the strong face beneath the greying brown hair; Zoe Ballinger couldn't be far into her forties but her 'professional' look and manner normally made her seem ten years older at least. Not today, however. Not 27 February. An anniversary evidently. An anniversary that somehow or other was making her vulnerable. But she had certainly relaxed with May in these last two days. She had told her she was seeing the doctor, that she was having meals on wheels, that she was going to rest . . . there had been no arguing with that. But she had looked at her with grey eyes that were concerned rather than just stern. Somehow, even over the tannoy system, their relationship had changed. Perhaps they were friends?

The lift stopped at the ground floor and the outer doors slid open. Zoe stood up with an obvious effort and pushed the inner door so that May could walk through into the hall, before she crooked her arm ready for May's tentative hand. Behind the glass doors of the lounge people were milling about, settling themselves at the tables while the more able-bodied went back and forth to the hatch to collect plates of bread and butter and hand them around.

May said suddenly, 'Zoe . . . make this a day for treats. Fish and chips first. And then the hairdresser this afternoon.

Have a haircut. You could take one of these very short styles, your hair is so thick and springy.'

Zoe looked at her, face wide open in total surprise, but before May could make any further suggestions the lounge doors opened and there was . . . She searched for his name and found it just in time. 'Toby Marsh!' May exclaimed and noted that she sounded pleased. More than pleased. Delighted.

He reached out a hand and literally took her from Zoe's arm. 'Miss Thorpe! How are you? You look well! I cannot believe that two days ago you were so ill!'

Zoe caught them up and said uncertainly, 'Where would you like to sit?'

May could not stop smiling. She had no idea where she wanted to sit. Toby Marsh gathered Zoe to his free side and said, 'We've booked a table. Arthur actually booked it and suggested that the three of us should join him. It's in the quiet corner away from the hatch and the doors. He's gone to see if there's any tomato sauce. He's under the impression that no one eats fish and chips without vinegar and tomato sauce.' He laughed. The two women laughed. Cyril and Mary Smithson waved from their table and then laughed too. Three of the able-bodied ones came and kissed May on the cheek and said how pleased they were to see her up and about. For a moment the noise level crescendoed as people called across the room.

Toby Marsh settled May into her seat and Zoe left them to help with the serving and things calmed down.

He said, 'I'm seriously glad you're able to be here, Miss Thorpe. May I slip this into your bag? I'd rather no one else knew.'

He leaned over and dropped a slim oblong packet into

the small eco bag hanging from her chair. She was disturbed from her euphoria long enough to ask what on earth was he doing and why must it be a secret?

'It's personal. And we're not supposed to get personal with residents.' He grinned. 'I mucked that up when I carried you upstairs on Wednesday, didn't I?'

'I suppose so. I don't actually remember it of course.'

'No. But I think you already knew that we could never be *im*personal. Or is the sense of a past relationship on my side only?' He was suddenly cautious, sitting back from her, watching her with his brown eyes, intent.

She began to slip back into the past again, was conscious of it, checked it quickly. Was it something to do with sitting here, at a table in the lounge, with lots of people? Or was it him? Toby Marsh. But she could see her mother's face, as plain as day. She could hear her words. 'Promise me. Swear to me . . .'

Toby Marsh said quickly, 'Come back – don't do it again – you're here, in the lounge at Jenner House!'

And she snapped out of it just like that, as if he were some stupid hypnotist, and said, 'Actually, Mr Marsh, I think I saw you before you saw me. Tuesday evening. I'd been to the book room and was crossing the landing to my flat when you were going up the stairs. Am I right?'

He relaxed instantly. 'You are indeed. I was going to the top floor to inspect a possible leak in the bathroom. Why didn't I see you?'

'The automatic lights hadn't come on at my end of the corridor.' She wanted to ask him what he meant by a 'past relationship' and searched for words that weren't embarrassing. Could he possibly be flirting with her? A man half her age? What would that make him?

He said, 'As you know, Mrs Ballinger is hot on the impersonal approach – they emphasize it in the sociology courses too. Apparently we can be of much more use to you all if we keep you at arm's length. Is that true?'

His eyes were snappingly humorous now. She smiled back, feeling herself drawn again into the strange happiness that had been with her when she woke.

'Mrs Ballinger can be personal when she needs to be,' she said in what she hoped was an enigmatic voice. 'And I must tell you quickly that today is a rather sad anniversary for her. So . . . be gentle.'

He was surprised. 'I didn't realize I was anything else.'

She could be honest about this. 'You are . . . slightly dismissive. Perhaps.'

He looked beyond her, thinking then nodding. 'Perhaps. I have thought of her as rather . . . unimaginative, I have to admit.'

'Today she needs respect.'

He nodded again. 'Oh yes. Of course. It's a couple of years since that rotter of a husband walked out, I suppose.' He could see she was shocked and said quickly, 'I thought that was what you meant about the anniversary. Sorry.'

'I've always assumed . . . She seemed like a widow.' May closed her eyes for a moment. 'Poor Zoe. Oh dear, oh dear. I have misjudged her badly.'

'Look, if she's keeping it quiet, I shouldn't have said – these places are so full of gossip I thought you must all know.'

'Probably the others do. I have never listened to gossip.' May was genuinely upset. 'No. Please don't apologize, Mr Marsh. I am glad to know. It makes things . . . easier to understand.'

They sat silently for a while. Then he said tentatively, 'You do know that Arthur Wentworth was a pilot officer and involved in the destruction of Dresden? And holds you in such high regard that he went to see the headmaster of the local comprehensive yesterday and complained about him allowing his pupils to upset you to such an extent that you collapsed?'

She put a hand to her throat. 'Oh my God!' She looked at him tragically. 'The silly idiot! They will stop Daisy and Marcus visiting me! Oh, I could kill him!' He made some remark about that being impossible but she hardly heard him. Her mind was going round and round. He had hidden himself away because he was angry. Nothing to do with her childish boasting. The whole thing . . . he had connected her sudden collapse with the school's pupils reviving memories of Coventry. And he had memories too. Scorching memories like she had. Dresden. Coventry's revenge. Oh God, oh God . . . And he let everyone believe he was in Fighter Command . . . one of the First of the Few.

Toby Marsh's hand was warm on hers. 'You obviously didn't know. You will find him sheepish, embarrassed. He regrets storming into the head's office like he did. He's coming now.'

He did not tell her to pull herself together but someone did. Probably her mother. Or, more likely, herself. She was always saying aloud to the mirror, 'Pull yourself together, Mabel Thorpe! Right now! D'you hear me?'

Arthur Wentworth arrived, puffing. She looked up at his watery eyes and smiled widely. 'Oh Arthur, thank you so much! I really can't face fish and chips without tomato sauce. Do you feel the same?'

And his face, almost purple with a mixture of emotions he could not begin to decipher, turned a healthier red. He sat down with a plump.

'I do indeed, dear lady. Yet another thing we have in common.'

She could not think that they had anything in common except their age and perhaps the need to 'move on', but she nodded and then leaned well back in her chair. The fish and chips were arriving and the plates were very hot.

Afterwards many of them lingered, talking about the outing next week to a garden centre in Somerset. The Smithsons were planning to buy bedding plants for the flower bed just outside their ground-floor window. Zoe suggested – tentatively for her – that they might also look at the price of small greenhouses. May wanted to ask her how much her pearls had fetched but obviously could not. Surely not enough to buy a greenhouse outright, even a small one?

Zoe said they did a very nice cream tea in the adjoining café if anyone was interested. Someone from the top floor mentioned that there was also an excellent dress shop nearby. 'Seconds. From Harrods,' the woman said, her eyes sparkling.

'I hardly think Harrods,' Zoe said in her usual brisk voice. 'But we can investigate of course.' She came round to May's chair. 'I think it's time for your rest and as I have quite a stack of paperwork, shall we go?'

'Let me do it on my own, Zoe. Please. I am perfectly able.' She smiled. 'And I was serious about your hair.'

May suddenly wanted to get back to her flat and her bed and wait for Daisy to arrive. Arthur was nowhere to be seen, probably had to dash to the ground-floor toilets, and she did not wish to give him the opportunity to tell her about his interview with the headmaster at Daisy's school. She pushed herself upright and let Zoe walk with her into the hall. They waited by the lift while she thanked Zoe for a very pleasant time.

'I haven't said goodbye to Mr Marsh.' She looked round. He had not been involved in the conversation about the garden centre.

The lift arrived and Zoe held the door open. 'He had to slip away. It's his little girl's birthday. Now do lie down, May. It's important.'

May nodded but she hardly heard the words. Toby Marsh had a proper family. A wife and a little girl who was having a birthday. She had no idea why the glow that had been with her since getting up this morning was blossoming throughout her body . . . She could feel it in her toes and fingertips. It was wonderful. It was perfect. And she did not know why.

She let herself into the flat and sat on the edge of the bed and then lay down without taking off her skirt, which would crumple hopelessly under the duvet. She slept like a child for a whole hour and woke to the instant knowledge of that small family.

When she eventually sat up and put her feet to the carpet she found herself staring down into her hessian eco bag. There was a brown-paper packet lying on top of her spare glasses next to a sachet of paper handkerchiefs. For a moment she could not think what it was and then remembered Mr Marsh putting it there rather furtively. Was it something to do with the birthday party? But no, surely he said it was for her?

Very slowly she unwrapped it, took a lid from a long box and laid it aside. Her string of pearls lay, as if new, in a cream-velvet-lined bed. She stared at them, not knowing what to think. Very carefully she replaced the top and put the box into her underwear drawer. Then she stood up and went to make tea.

It was four thirty and she knew that Daisy was not coming.

Nine

Daisy was determined not to cry again so she said nothing at all until they had finished their meal and watched the news, decided that they would take Alison and Marcus some flowers on Saturday, then go to the arboretum to see the pussy willows and have lunch at Tetbury. She knew her parents weren't only doing it to take her mind off the whole business of Aunty Alison; they had almost stumbled on the arboretum this time last year on a detour from the office in Bath. They had thought it a magical place and had made a pact to come again next year. She nodded solemnly at both proposals. She wanted to get away from the village and the school; even from Marcus.

She waited until they had their coffee and the fire had taken hold and the last of the grey light had gone from the window, then she told them in a bleak voice about her interview with Mr Carter. No snide comments, no justifications for herself or for him. Simply that Mr Wentworth lived in Jenner House and thought that she and Marcus had been the cause of Miss Thorpe's sudden collapse and had complained to the headmaster.

She paused and thought about it then concluded, 'Of course Mr Wentworth wrong-footed poor old BC completely and shouted at him apparently . . .' She half smiled at the thought of them, both apoplectic probably. 'And Mr Carter didn't know what on earth it was all about. Anyway, the upshot is that I can't go and see Miss Thorpe and I didn't want to have to tell her why so I haven't even phoned her. Marcus won't be well pleased. He was getting a lot from her actually. But *he* didn't make any promises so he can go – maybe on Monday – and smooth everything over.'

Daisy stopped staring into the fire and lifted her eyes. She hadn't seen her news as being much of a bombshell; after all, there had been complaints about her 'confrontational attitude' all through her school life. But there was Mummy sitting absolutely, completely, totally . . . still. That meant she was holding every fibre of her body against explosion. And Daddy had the confused and helpless look that Daisy hated more than Mummy's rage.

And then the rage burst from the stillness like one of those fireworks – a jumping jack – that spat out fire and brimstone in short bursts.

'How dare he!' It was not a question. 'How *dare* he! I thought Barry Carter had more about him than this. We'll make an appointment to see him – very officially – Nerrie. Yes, that's what we'll do – let me do it, Nerrie darling. I can be more forceful than you—'

Daddy's hand was on her arm. 'Marietta, please stop. Your anger is taking away your common sense. Daisy has to live through this and she is happy at the local school—'

'Making her promise never to see the woman again? Nerrie, he has no right – they are friends. He'll be trying to cut out Marcus next!'

Daisy's heart contracted painfully. Would BC try to stop Marcus from seeing her? Marcus had been different lately and she had put it down to Aunty Alison but perhaps he was already being oh-so-gently counselled . . . 'Too close a relationship at this stage of your academic career could be inhibiting . . .' She hung on to her objectivity like mad.

Daddy's hand gripped Mummy's arm more tightly; he stopped looking bewildered.

'Come on, Etta. You're not trying. Molehills or mountains? It's obvious to me that this is a molehill. Look at it as if it were a film. Barry Carter, self-important head of very successful comp, suddenly confronted by the archetypal Colonel Blimp bristling with righteous indignation, wanting to take it out on someone. Can't very well tackle the kids but the organizer of such an outrage, a young man who has never seen so-called active service . . .' His voice mimicked the comic old soldier perfectly and Daisy started to grin.

Mummy interrupted furiously, 'And for that man to take it out on our daughter, Nerrie! It's not on, it's just *not on!*'

Daisy's grin widened. 'You're making me feel sorry for old BC and *that's* not on!' She went over and sat on the arm of Mummy's chair. 'Listen, I saved poor Mr Coles from a bollocking' – cries came from both parents which Daisy ignored because they had heard it before – 'Mrs Arbuthnot says he's ill because his wife doesn't feed him properly – I should have thought he was quite capable of feeding himself, but there you go, typical man – except for Daddy and Marcus of course – so he's been off for most of this week. Marcus was in Gloucester with his mum. And I was the only one left!' She slid an arm beneath her mother's neck and put her mouth to her ear. 'D'you know what we call Barry? No, not Before Christ – that's the obvious one. We call him Bum-Crack.'

They were appalled all over again, but after a very short time they started to laugh. Then Mummy said seriously,

'Listen, Daisy Patek. That promise was extorted from you. We've annulled it. Here and now. OK? You can go and see Miss Thorpe at Jenner House whenever you like. In fact if you have her phone number I think you should ring her right now and apologize for breaking your promise to her. But if you think she's gone to bed or wouldn't welcome a phone call, then leave it till tomorrow.'

Daddy leaned over and kissed Daisy. 'Half-term next week, bubba. It will all have blown over by the time you get back to school.'

Daisy looked up Miss Thorpe's number and punched it into the phone in the lower hall. There was no reply. She cancelled the call and tried Marcus's mobile. He picked up immediately.

'Daisy. We're home. We're fine. Ma had a reaction to some of her pills and it was a bit hairy for a while. But they emptied her out and someone came and talked to her about them. Now they've given me a typed list with instructions so we can't go wrong.'

He spoke quickly as if he might be afraid he'd forget some of it. She frowned. Could it in fact be true? It was so much better than an overdose. She must tell the parents.

She said, 'Give her our love. We're calling with some flowers tomorrow. Then going on to the arboretum.' She paused then said, 'Hey! Why don't you and your mum come with us? Not much walking . . . you can see loads from the coffee place. All the catkins will be out, and still some snowdrops. What do you think?'

'She left hospital just this morning, Daisy. Needs to settle in. But what a lovely thought. Say thanks to your parents. I have to go. Uncle Ted's with her and telling her how to live her life – honestly, he's a pain! School OK?'

'Fine. Loads to tell you.'

'If Ted is still around on Monday, d'you fancy an hour or two on the tops?'

Of course. It was half-term. She kept forgetting. How marvellous. 'Sure. Ring me.'

He was gone and she went to tell her parents about Aunty Alison and saw that they thought it was a cover-up. Her heart ached.

'Can we have the flowers delivered? I don't think we should visit just yet. It might be a bit too much for Aunty Alison.'

They looked at her then nodded in unison.

It was marvellous at the arboretum; Daisy found herself both blown away by the tentative beauty of emerging spring and drawn into it as if she herself could put down roots alongside the last of the snowdrops and revel in earth below and sky above. The pussy willows were so Victorian, pendulous with catkins yet modest too. The silver birch so confidently elegant. The conker trees showing green promise of the candles they would soon put forth. Daisy tried to remember the poem about them, clicking her fingers helplessly. Her father quoted sonorously, 'This is the weather the cuckoo likes, when showers betumble the chestnut spikes.' And Daisy crowed, 'Don't you just love the verb "betumble"?' And her mother said, 'It describes your hair perfectly, Daisy!' She swung Daisy's hand. 'Let's try to come again when the chestnut spikes are out.'

Lunch was enormous, four courses counting the cheese board. Even Daisy had to give up before then and save her chocolate mint for later. She said blissfully, 'This means we can have a Sunday tea upstairs when it gets dark.'

Her mother nodded. She always cooked a traditional Sunday lunch and English tea. 'Boiled eggs? With the egg cosies? And Welsh cakes?' she enquired and Daisy gave a big grin.

And then, just for a moment, in the midst of such rich contentment, Daisy thought – not even thought, perhaps felt – Aunty Alison's depth of despair, the bottomless well of emptiness, the knowledge that she was a burden . . . Daisy shivered. Her father said, 'It is cold. Let's get back home now, shall we?' And Mummy said, 'Yes, let's.' She pulled Daisy close. 'It's been great, but we don't want to catch cold.'

The moment passed. They bundled into the car; Daisy unwrapped her mint and nibbled around its edges. Mummy held out her hand for the silver paper and put it in a bag already half full of tissues. She said, apparently irrelevantly, 'We have a life. We do the best we can. It's OK to be happy just as it's OK to be sad sometimes. Today has been very happy. Yes?'

Daisy put all the chocolate into her mouth and nodded vigorously. 'Definitely. Absolutely. Totally.'

Daddy ground the gears horribly as he edged out of the car park. 'That signifies my complete agreement,' he said.

May had a peaceful night and woke to find herself in exactly the same position as when she put out her light, hardly a wrinkle in the duvet. She lay for a moment, identifying the room, then sat up, turned and put her legs to the ground in one movement. She had worked out that she could use her own body weight to accomplish various movements and it gave her pleasure to do them. She reached across to her chest of drawers, opened the top one and took out the package. The pearls were still inside; she had not dreamed the whole thing. They had fetched enough money to put a deposit on a greenhouse! She held them in her hands, reluctantly admitting that she was pleased to have them back. But . . . what on earth did it mean? Chivalry taken to a ridiculous degree? After all, he had bought them, so they were a gift. Should she accept such a gift from a man who, after all, familiar though he seemed, was still a complete stranger?

The tannoy squealed and it was Zoe, who so recently had been Mrs Ballinger. Events, if you could call them events, were moving rather quickly.

Zoe's voice, less brisk than usual, said, 'Are you all right, May?' That would have been 'Miss Thorpe' four days ago.

'I'm fine. How are you?'

'I managed to get my hair cut at that new place in Dursley. I don't know what to think. I'm wearing a hat.'

May laughed and then stopped as she realized it could have nearly blown Zoe's eardrum to pieces. She said, 'You sound much better, actually.'

'Yes. I am always glad when the twenty-seventh is over. Stupid. I'll pop up before I go home. See what you think.'

'Go home?'

'It's Saturday. I'm seeing my sister.'

May had forgotten it was the weekend. Zoe was on duty for the morning calls only. No hope of seeing Daisy either. May decided she would read some more about Jenner.

She said, 'Oh, it would be nice to see you if you've got time.'

'I'll make time. I need to show myself to someone!'

She clicked off and May went into the ensuite for a shower. She was dressed and having her first cup of tea when Zoe arrived. As she opened the door and was confronted by Zoe's stern face topped off with a skiing hat, she had to smile.

Zoe said, 'You wait. You haven't seen it yet.' They sashayed through the tiny hall and May sat down. Zoe went on, 'Sorry to be such ages. I've called the doctor for Mary Smithson. She slipped . . . hasn't fallen but thinks she might pass out like you did. Cyril is making her tea. I'll go back and be there for the doctor.' She smiled apprehensively. 'Meanwhile . . . ta-raa!' She whipped off her hat and her very short hair sprang with it and stood on end, crackling with electricity, then seemed to settle like a bird's feathers.

May clasped her hands. 'Oh Zoe! She's got it just right!'

'It was a he, actually. He couldn't get over how thick my hair was! Guess what – he asked me whether I would model for him in some competition or other. I said no of course.'

'Oh Zoe – why? It would be such fun. Please change your mind.'

'Too late now. But do you really like it? Can I leave off my hat? I feel so naked and peculiar. He said that longer hair drew my face down and it's already quite long enough, cheeky chappie, and that having the hairline on my ears would compensate – oh you know, lots of sales talk! Haven't been to a proper hairdresser for years; my sister gives me a snip now and then just to keep it tidy.'

This was the longest, chattiest speech May had ever heard from the house manager and she found herself delighted by it. After Zoe had dashed off she sat for some time, sipping her cold tea, thinking about the recent 'Mrs Ballinger' in quite a new light. Someone who had been hurt, someone who had a sister close enough to stand in for a hairdresser, someone who took her job very seriously – perhaps too seriously. But underneath the officious manner someone who really cared.

May gave up on her tea and took the cup into the tiny kitchen to be swilled and used for coffee later. Then she found a pen and wrote on her pad, 'Telephone Mrs

Smithson.' She studied the other notes. Last night or early this morning she had scribbled 'Jenner'. The relevant encyclopaedia was on the shelf next to her chair and she started to reach out for it and then stopped halfway. She frowned; what had Jenner to do with Zoe Ballinger or the necklace or Daisy Patek and Marcus Budd or indeed Arthur Wentworth who wanted her to move on?

She put a line through 'Jenner', nibbled her lip, frowned prodigiously, and eventually wrote, 'Arthur Wentworth'. She sat back in her chair with a sigh; she would have to let him tell her about his row. Her ebullience yesterday had swept all before it, but she could not keep it up. She could let the whole thing go, of course. But that might well mean he avoided her for the rest of their lives. Was that what he wanted? She decided to wait and see. If he really wanted to get it off his chest then he would eventually arrive at her door. She needed to know how serious the row had been and whether it meant the end of her visitors.

She reached for the telephone directory and turned to the back. There must have been a hundred Smiths and quite a few Smithsons but as she couldn't see any of them it was all a bit pointless. She flopped the unwieldy book shut and replaced it with some difficulty. A box of greeting cards fell out of the same shelf; they were all labelled 'left blank for your own message'. She leafed through them and found one decorated with small nosegays of flowers – crocus, snowdrops, aconites, bluebells. She squinted horribly, forcing her memory to come up with names, and at last was able to address an envelope 'to Cyril and Mary Smithson' and then begin a message with 'Dear Mary'. After all, everyone used forenames in Jenner House. She was definitely moving on.

By the time she had finished, signing herself 'May' and

120

then putting 'Thorpe' in brackets just in case, it was time for a mug of coffee, her favourite moment of the day. She sipped gently at the instant mixture and glanced at her notepad again. She saw a scrawl that she must have made in the middle of the night as she had no recollection of it now. Eventually she deciphered it as the name of a village not very far from here. Berkeley. Why on earth had she written that? She sipped again then murmured, 'Berkeley . . . what about it? Berkeley Castle? Edward's torture and death?' Another sip and then the squint and coercing of the memory cells. Berkeley. Of course. She opened her eyes wide and smiled. Even in her sleep she had recalled that Jenner House was called Jenner House because Jenner had been born and lived at Berkeley, just across the M5. She put her mug down and reached again for the encyclopaedia.

The entry was short; she worked out he had lived seventy-four years, 1749 until 1823, and had developed his famous smallpox vaccine after observing that the local farmers who caught cowpox from milking their cows were immune from the deadly smallpox. There were details of his training and of his rewards much later in life, but nothing about a wife or children or parents or whether he had a favourite colour, flower, meat or vegetable. Before he trained did he go into the fields and help with the harvest? Did he spend autumn afternoons picking blackberries with someone who wore a high-waisted muslin dress? Did they kiss and stain each other's mouths with blackberry juice? And if he did any or all of these things, were they gone for ever – lost – as if they had not happened at all? And was that why Daisy and Marcus should know about life in Coventry all those years ago – not because she was an important person, quite the opposite:

because she was a person behaving as people behaved then. They wanted to keep that . . . all of it.

Something dropped on to the thin paper of the encyclopaedia. She scrubbed her eyes angrily and closed it with a snap. She said, fairly loudly, 'I haven't broken my promise, Mother, so you don't have to keep reminding me!' She swallowed anything else she might have been going to say, took a breath, finished the coffee and stood up. She would deliver the card to the Smithsons' ground-floor flat and stop this constant nostalgia. Ridiculous nonsense. Long gone. And a good job too.

Waiting for the lift to come up from the lower ground floor seemed more tedious than usual and the dim reflection of herself in the silvered fire door was not reassuring. She straightened and ran a flat hand over her hair. After smartening herself up yesterday her everyday tweed skirt and twinset looked decidedly drab and of course her mother was right, you should not leave your bedroom still wearing slippers. She almost went back for her stick so that she could at least stand to her full height, but then the lift arrived and she needed both hands to open the door. There was a grab rail all round the tiny space, so no need for a stick.

The foyer was blessedly empty and beautifully clean, with fresh flowers on the table and a message on the board in Zoe's neat capitals telling everyone to have a nice weekend and she would be back on Monday. May found it reassuring; she smiled and stood for a moment by the enormous glass doors leading to the front garden and the quiet road beyond, the same view as from her window upstairs but a different perspective. It was a grey, calm day; the trees on the other side of the road hardly stirring. Waiting for spring? Her smile widened as she went to the first door on her right and gently pushed the card through the letter box. It was immediately pulled from her and then the door opened and there was Mary Smithson in her dressing gown, her tiny dormouse face as bright and inquisitive as always.

'I knew you would come down. When Zoe said how sorry you were to hear I had an attack just like you, I thought – Miss Thorpe will bring us a card later. I said to Cyril, Miss Thorpe will bring us a card later, that's for sure. Do come in – really – please do. Cyril will be so glad to see you.'

May said, 'Really I shouldn't, I'm still in my slippers. Just a moment then. Are you feeling better? Is Mr Smithson unwell too?'

'The doctor says we are both suffering from shock. Nothing happened of course but it could have been catastrophic. Completely catastrophic. Had I gone down in the shower I would most certainly have broken some bones. And how would Cyril manage without me?'

Cyril Smithson was sitting in the window, his newspaper open on his lap. The coffee table nudging his knees bore two glasses. He lifted one and saluted May. 'Good morning, Miss Thorpe. Mary said you would be down before lunch. The doctor left no prescription but told us to have a small glass of brandy. We always keep brandy in the house. Medicinal purposes only of course. We had a shock. The even tenure of our lives was disturbed by a near accident. Will you join us?'

'Of course she will.' Mary Smithson was already pouring from a small flat bottle. 'I said to Cyril, if Miss Thorpe comes down before lunch we will all have a drop of brandy and when I saw you looking through the doors at such a sad grey day, I knew you would be only too glad . . .'

May tried to protest but still found herself sitting at the coffee table with a glass in front of her. In spite of her wild hair and bedroom slippers she found herself interested in the layout of this double flat. The kitchen door was open and she could see through its window, which looked on to the outside of the entrance doors. How foolish she must have looked standing there aimlessly, staring out. On the other hand, Mrs Smithson was still in her dressing gown and they were both wearing slippers. She lifted her glass.

'Thank you. Both of you. I am very glad to find you recovering so pleasantly!'

They all smiled and sipped and May felt the warmth of the brandy spreading throughout her body. It reminded her of Norman. He had kept going on little sips of brandy towards the end. It was Norman who had given her the pearls. She was glad to have them back.

She finished her drink and stood up with more difficulty than usual; she was used to her own chair, which was higher than this one. And of course with the separate bedroom on the other side of the kitchen, the hall was very much wider and she could not hold the walls on either side as she made her way to the door. Mary Smithson gave a silly giggle – a very silly giggle – and said, 'The brandy has gone to your legs, Miss Thorpe!' May forced a laugh but made herself walk properly and wished again she had brought her stick.

Once in the wide foyer she felt stronger. She made straight for the lift, no staring out of the door now that she knew she could be seen. The lift was coming down from the third floor, probably to the laundry on the lower ground floor. She propped herself on the edge of the table and made it move somehow so that the flowers fell over. Horrified, feeling like a schoolgirl caught out in some stupidity, she shovelled the flowers back into the vase and scooped the water from the table with the sleeve of her cardigan.

'Level One,' said the disembodied voice from the lift, then 'Ground floor.' She went on using her sleeve to polish the table, waiting for the announcement for 'Lower ground floor.' The inner doors breathed their sigh as they opened then the fire door opened – rather shakily – and Arthur Wentworth practically toppled out.

She straightened as best she could, adjusted her sleeve and smiled. 'Good morning, Arthur. Are you going out for a walk?'

'Yes. Need some fresh air. The fish and chips yesterday . . . didn't sit well, you know.' He looked at her and obviously registered the slippers. 'Are you all right, dear lady?'

She forced her smile to widen. 'Yes. I heard Mrs Smithson wasn't very well and popped down with a card. She's quite all right now.'

'Was it the fish and chips, d'you suppose? Mrs Ballinger wasn't quite herself yesterday and I wonder whether she ordered them from the usual place.'

May frowned slightly. 'I'm not sure. I thought Mrs Smithson had slipped in the shower. She had a small glass of brandy and that certainly perked her up. Mr Smithson had one too. And so did I.'

He also perked up; just the thought of the brandy did wonders.

'Think I'll go along to the Hare and Hounds and do likewise.' He was already swinging towards the door, then he turned. 'Something I wanted to say . . . actually . . . apologize . . . was worried about you. Thought it was because those kids from the school had upset you. I made a fool of myself – went to see the head and told him he had no right to use us as guinea pigs. I might have lost my temper – can't quite recall . . . felt terrible before I did it, worse since.' He pressed his lips together and looked at her slippers again. 'That young Marsh thought I was an interfering old buffer – I could tell. He didn't say those words of course, but he didn't tell me I'd done the right thing either.' He took a breath and looked up at her. 'Best intentions, I do assure you. I'm fond of you, dear lady. Hoped that come the spring we might take short walks together. My arm would be at your disposal.'

She was holding the lift door open so that it could not go elsewhere. She made sounds indicating that she had to get in. If she let the lift go and continued this conversation she knew she would have to tell him that he might have hurt Daisy P'tek, and if Daisy P'tek could not visit Jenner House any more then he had certainly hurt May Thorpe. So she stepped inside, stabbed two on the key pad and just caught a glimpse of Arthur Wentworth, holding on to the outer door, head drooping. As if she had physically struck him. She wanted to call out that he could be seen from the kitchen window of the Smithsons' flat. But she didn't. He would go and drink his brandy and forget all about it.

She went into the safety of her flat, found her magnifying glass, opened the directory and thumbed her way to the list of Carters, then shortened the distance by concentrating the glass on the B's and miraculously finding what she wanted. He lived in Berkeley. Funny that this was the third time Berkeley had come up. Edward II had been murdered there, Jenner had lived there and now, it seemed, so did Barry Carter. She punched in the number and waited while the phone rang six times and then the answer machine clicked in.

She said very concisely, 'This is May Thorpe from Jenner House. I would like to apologize on behalf of Mr Arthur Wentworth who took it upon himself to complain about my recent visitors, Daisy Patek and Marcus Budd. This was absolutely uncalled for and unnecessary. I thoroughly enjoyed the visit, look forward to more of them and congratulate you on having the idea in the first place and the general demeanour of your pupils. Thank you very much.'

She replaced the receiver gently. A message was much better. He would have time to think about it, play it again and find himself praised instead of criticized. What had Daisy called him as she was descending in the lift? Was it Bum-Crack? If it was, then he would lap up those congratulations and reinstate the visits after half-term.

She smiled and went to microwave her lunch. And this afternoon she would put on her cashmere and perhaps the pearls, certainly her shoes, and go down to the lounge, where some of the men would be watching football. Norman had enjoyed football. She had liked Norman. He had wanted to marry her, especially when he was diagnosed with terminal cancer. He had pointed out that she could sell the business and retire immediately. But she had still said no, although there were tears not far away. Somehow she could not accept anything from Norman; he was much too nice. But she had taken the pearls. She was glad about that.

Ten

Daisy woke because the morning sun was framing her bedroom curtains. She looked at her clock; it was seven thirty and 1 March. She could hear Daddy making tea in the kitchen before he went to church and felt a little spurt of joy pop up from the lazy contentment of a good night's sleep. She was seeing Marcus tomorrow and she did not have to worry about school until Thursday. On an impulse she swung her legs out of bed and practically jumped into the clothes lying about everywhere from yesterday. She and Marcus had cautiously decided four years ago, after their Confirmation, that religion and superstition were one and the same but she still went to church with her parents now and then; just to please them, of course. Today she would go to the early service.

Daddy poured a mug of tea and she sipped obediently. 'Good to say thank you.' He nodded at her. 'I thought you might come with Mummy and me to Evensong. This is very special!' He grinned at her as he pulled on his shoes.

He went to get the car out and she poured the tea down the sink in case it made her need the bathroom. She had acted on impulse but he was right as usual; it would be a good thing to say thank you for Marcus and Alison. She did not know whether she was addressing her thanks in any particular direction; perhaps just to let gratitude float up through the church tower would be enough. She pushed her hair into an elastic band, grabbed her coat and went out of the back door and up the steps to the road.

The village church was on the other side of the valley, where the hills subsided and the road led on down to the M5. It had been built in the woods and only the tower was visible; a hidden sanctuary but with a view of the outside world from the crenellated top. It could have been a small castle or a fortress and had probably been fortified in its time. Now, the same colour as the grey woods, it seemed to have grown out of the earth. Daisy had always liked it; it was secret, mysterious, self-effacing.

They parked next to a big stone cube housing the family of a long-ago squire and surmounted by an enormous lichen-blotched angel. Daddy practically ran ahead; he had been churchwarden at one time and helped out at the eight o'clock services. Daisy lingered. It was a beautiful morning and the sun coming through the trees was spotlighting the smaller, slanting gravestones. There were moves afoot to remove some of the more decrepit stones in case they collapsed completely. She hoped they wouldn't. The lopsidedness of the small graveyard was part of its charm.

She wandered past the spotty angel to where a tiny clump of crocus waved their fragile orange flags. The stone above them was almost lying on its side. She read it with difficulty, leaning down and tracing some of the letters with her finger. 'Amy Jenner', she made out. She straightened, smiling. Jenner House. Jenner's vaccine. She knew that the name was not unusual and this was simply a coincidence, but she wandered into church feeling it was particularly meaningful that morning to find a connection with Miss Thorpe. She slid into their usual pew and knelt. She really must telephone when she got home.

Daddy finished lighting the candles and handing out the pew sheets and sat beside her. She glanced around; there were six other people in church, eight counting themselves. It bore out what she and Marcus had talked about in one of their discussions. They would be having another of those tomorrow . . . If only the weather held, it would be just marvellous on the tops. She must remember to tell him that church was definitely on the way out: eight people hardly added up to a congregation surely? How many had come when Dr Jenner's daughter was buried in the churchyard? She grinned suddenly; that would make Marcus sit up a bit. Could she possibly embroider the whole thing more and call Amy Jenner an illegitimate daughter? That would really get him going because he had done a study of illegitimacy in the early twentieth century and found the word not simply inappropriate but completely horrifying. Abhorrent. That was the word he had used. Abhorrent. She smiled and caught the rector's eye.

He said, 'The Lord be with you.'

And she was so surprised she forgot to join in the general response, 'And also with you.' Daddy looked sideways at her and she opened her eyes wide in apology and told herself to concentrate. And she did.

The short sermon was about Darwin, which Marcus would have enjoyed too. Far from seeing *On the Origin of the Species* as the death knell of Christianity, the rector considered it another reason for sheer awe at the wonder of God's creation. She liked the word 'awe', it was simple and direct. She wondered how the word 'awful' had degraded into fear and horror. And then they were standing for the Creed and she had lost her place again.

When they emerged into the sunshine, she tried to tell her father why she could not possibly be a Christian.

'Just because you do not like the taste of the wine?' He was genuinely surprised. 'Yes, all right, also because your knees hurt and you cannot concentrate on the service?' He sighed as he unlocked the car and held up his hand in salute to the other departing couples. 'None of that matters, Daisy. You know that. Let the words flow . . . that catchphrase "go with the flow" . . . it sums it up. You are caught in a current of thankfulness, bubba. A whole world of glory and thankfulness. To be part of that is to feel awe and wonder. Yesterday at the arboretum, you felt that. This morning you give thanks. The wine is one symbol – everlastingness – the knees are another – our human condition.' By this time he was waving his arms above the roof of the car. She could imagine him with bells on his wrists and ankles, dancing. 'You can be Hindu, Muslim, Buddhist, Christian, Humanist – it does not matter. You are part of the flow.'

She loved him so much she could have wept. Again. But the rector was emerging, locking the door, shrugging into his anorak.

She said quickly, 'I know what you mean, Daddy. But come and have a look at this.'

And she led him away from the path to the gravestone of Amy Jenner. He was instantly interested and bent over it, tracing the letters as she had done and discovering the age at death. Three years old. The rector waved. 'See you tonight, Nehru,' he called. Daddy nodded and went back to the grave.

'March the first,' he said and looked up at her. 'Today, Daisy. It's her birthday today!'

They talked about it on the way home. For some reason, the coincidence became a mini-miracle. Mummy was up and making toast. 'I nearly poached some eggs, but as it's Sunday – eggs for tea – and we also had them yesterday . . . bad for cholesterol.'

They both tried to tell her about Amy Jenner at the same time and she joined in with what she thought was a joke and produced three candles. They sobered.

'Only three years,' Daisy said.

'But how wonderful that we can still celebrate her birthday.' Daddy buttered his toast liberally. 'I could not see the year of her birth or death but whenever it was she is still remembered. By us.'

Mummy said, 'Happy birthday, Amy.' And then, 'And happy new month to all of us!' Daisy felt a current of energy run through her and knew how the Mad March Hare must have felt.

The next day was overcast but there was no valley mist and she was glad when Marcus phoned at ten thirty to say he would pick her up in half an hour. 'Might as well start from your level. We can make for the beacon and then walk along towards the woods.' His voice was different somehow. It was nearly a week since she had seen him.

'I'll bring a picnic.' She knew he was going to demur and went on quickly, 'Mummy made two Cornish pasties yesterday afternoon. Specially.'

'That was . . . kind.'

'She didn't want me raiding the fridge!'

'Ah.'

He put down his receiver and so did she. Why did she always say things that highlighted his own lack of any normal family life? She gritted her teeth and clenched her hands, frightened by her own insensitivity.

She was ready in ten minutes and he was late by ten minutes. She waited outside, rucksack on her back, dithering about whether to invite him in for a mug of coffee. She knew he would not want to; he loved the big calm basement kitchen with its enormous views but not now, not after what had happened. But he surprised her, as he so often did.

'Hi, Daisy!' He stopped by her, holding his side. 'That hill is steeper since I climbed it last; how do you do it every day?' He grinned and it looked genuine. 'Any chance of a coffee before we take to the hills?'

'Course!' She went ahead down the steps and opened the kitchen door. He followed. In the short time since last Tuesday she had forgotten how tall he was. None of the Pateks was tall; Mummy looked taller than she was because she had what Daddy called 'presence'.

Marcus fell on to a chair. 'God, Daisy, this is great. Seems yonks since we did a ramble. I forgot the map but it doesn't matter. It's all there.' He jabbed a finger at the view. 'Good light today, quiet, grey, no clouds coming over from Wales.'

She reached for the instant and spooned it into mugs. The kettle started to rumble. She said, absolutely without thinking, 'Good bombing weather.'

'What?'

She was surprised. 'Sorry. I'm certain that Miss Thorpe pops things into my mind now and then!' She poured boiling water on to the instant and stirred vigorously. 'The enemy aircraft had to have a clear night to find their way – they

133

followed the Severn up to Gloucester and Worcester, then turned right. Yes?'

He accepted one of the mugs. 'Yes. Probably.' He looked into the mug. 'Any milk?'

'Oh, yes. Sorry.' She went to the fridge.

He said, 'I'd almost forgotten Miss Thorpe. Like I said, it all seems yonks.' She poured milk into his outstretched mug and he thanked her and sipped. 'Have you been back?'

'Yes. I'll tell you about it when we get to the beacon.' She thought, relieved, that Miss Thorpe was a safe subject. Even Arthur Wentworth and Barry Carter might sound funny. And there was Zack too. She wondered if Zack was all right now.

Marcus said, 'We could drop down by the woods and come back through the village. Mum would love to see you if you've got time.'

'Oh!' She put her mug down, almost overcome. 'I didn't think she would. I mean, I'm sort of like a bit of an interloper really.'

He opened his eyes wide. 'What are you on today? Interloper, no-hoper, mini-moper . . . I don't think so!' He swigged his coffee, gathered up her mug and went to the sink to wash them up. 'So that's OK then? I wouldn't mind dropping in on the churchyard to look at some of those old gravestones before Health and Safety have them dragged away.'

It really was eye-popping time. She couldn't get over the way minds tuned in to other minds. She told him all about it as they hauled themselves up the muddy incline to the beacon. 'It's like me just now. This Coventry thing. Seeing the weather from that time rather than this time. Like one of those books where you make a time jump. Only I'm not really making it, just thinking it.'

Marcus did one stride to her three and paused to haul her over an outcrop of rock. 'Perhaps Miss Thorpe really makes the jumps though. When we got her talking I thought once or twice she actually *was* in that place and time.'

'That would account for Mr Wentworth being so angry with us.' She was panting badly and holding her side. 'And it could account for her passing out, of course. But we weren't even there then, so it wasn't our fault. Not really.'

He took another giant stride and almost lifted her off her feet as he pulled her up. He was grinning hugely; she was delighted, as he had been so quiet for the past week or two and now, when she had imagined he would be distraught or at least sombre, he was looking like a Cheshire Cat. They leaned on the big triangulation stone and she told him all about it and made it sound so ridiculous she started to laugh herself. She skimmed over the fact that she was forbidden to see Miss Thorpe and described her mother's total stillness before her subsequent explosion. He rolled his eyes.

'That's how she was in court that time . . . d'you remember? When we went to see her and she didn't know we were there because your father said if we told her she would be inhibited?'

'Yeah. Just like that. But I've remembered something not so good, Marc. Mummy said to ring Miss Thorpe and I tried to and couldn't get her – she must have been in bed. And then we went to the arboretum and I forgot till now. Oh blast! I'm such an idiot!'

'No, you're not an idiot, not even a fraction of an idiot, which is all you could be as you're such a tiddler. You can ring her now. On my mobile.'

'I've got my own. And I will. And then I'll do my judo hold on you.'

She scrolled down to Miss Thorpe's number and pressed the button. It rang just once and then Miss Thorpe said, 'Is that you, Daisy? Listen, I don't want you to worry about any of this any more. I know what has happened. Mr Wentworth is with me at this moment and he's going to see Mr Carter again and apologize for his groundless accusations of Thursday evening and then we will forget it.'

Marcus, who was sharing the phone, drew away to open his eyes at Daisy. It was so obvious that Miss Thorpe's rather loud and clear speech was for Mr Wentworth's ears as well as Daisy's.

Daisy giggled – hopefully for Miss Thorpe's ears only – then said in a low voice, 'I was ringing to apologize for not phoning earlier. Mummy was livid. She said you were a personal friend and BC had no right to put an end to it . . . oh, you know.' She paused while Miss Thorpe told her how pleased she was, then she said, 'Oh Miss Thorpe! It's so beautiful up here – we're by the beacon and the sun has just come through the cloud – oh, it's gone again but it was shining all down the valley.'

'How lovely. Is Marcus with you then?'

'Yes. Do you want to speak to him?'

'I won't now. Is he . . . all right?'

'You mean apart from being so tall?' She giggled again as Marcus put on Mrs Arbuthnot's expression when she found jam in a returned library book. 'Yes, actually he is fine. We're going to walk right along the tops, then down through the woods to look in the churchyard. There's a little girl buried there whose name is Amy Jenner. We want to find out more.'

Miss Thorpe made joyous sounds at the other end. 'Enjoy being alive, time detectives!' she almost crowed.

*   *   *

They got as far as Rook's Wood by one thirty and climbed a tump so they could eat their pasties and see over the trees and down to the flatlands around the Severn Estuary. The sense of exhilaration made them grin, first at the view and then at each other.

'It's being so high,' Marcus said as if discovering a scientific fact. 'That's why people talk of being "high" when they take drugs.' He laughed at her expression and said, 'I'm serious. When we're old and decrepit we'll come up here and feel young again.'

She held her breath for a moment then let it go in a laugh. 'You'll be a famous investigative historian by then. And I'll still be starving in a garret, painting stuff no one wants.'

He said judiciously, as if seeing her future in the land below them, 'You will be a set designer . . . I think for the RSC, or maybe the National Theatre. Our work will dovetail neatly. Rather like your parents'.'

She stopped breathing again. He seemed to have no idea that he had said anything earth-shaking. He gathered up the greaseproof paper and stuffed it into the plastic box which had contained the pasties, then stood and stretched.

'The only thing is, if we're too decrepit we might have difficulty getting up here!' He held out a hand. 'Come on, old girl. Into the woods we go. D'you remember playing Hansel and Gretel here when we were kids?'

She stood up without taking his hand and croaked, 'Yes.' Of course, it was just another game.

He said, 'While they were pumping out Mum's stomach I had a walk round Gloucester. There was a shop in Westgate. Cameras. Binoculars. I went in and looked at some field glasses. I'm going to get some with my carer's allowance.

Save up a bit of course because they were almost a hundred pounds. We can bring them up here.'

What was he saying? She said angrily, 'When we're old and decrepit, d'you mean? When we can't see very well? When we'll probably fall over and land in hospital?'

'Probably.' He grinned at her. 'Stop being coy, Daisy. We used to talk about being married when we were eight years old and since then we've taken it for granted. That's how it should be, surely?'

She couldn't see the big picture. She stammered, 'But – but – sod it, Marc – you've never even kissed me!'

'That's not true.' He was still grinning and it was infuriating; as if she was eight years old.

'OK. A peck. And usually on the cheek. Never – not once – a proper kiss!'

'D'you want one now?'

She was so breathless she could barely speak but she managed an explosive 'Not if it has to be squashed into a bloody timetable!' And then there was a long pause and her lungs and pulse calmed down and she said sadly, 'We're not Romeo and Juliet, Marc.'

He said, 'Thank God! We've got a future. And – before you can say it – we've got a now. We're very much in the present tense. We're at a place in our own histories, Dais. And it's just wonderful!'

'Did you work this out when you were looking at the field glasses?'

He was surprised. 'Yes. I did. I knew Mum was going to be all right. I could relax and see things – *see* them – properly! The old, tired city still full of the marching feet of the Roman legions and the smell of smallpox . . . being regenerated – I have to go and see the plans some time, Dais. And I remembered the stuff in your portfolio . . . regenerations again. And I thought of Miss Thorpe and the people there who have done things, made their voices heard, been happy and sad and – and – and – and everything!'

At first she thought it was just a mood; euphoria perhaps. And then – when he mentioned Miss Thorpe – something happened. She could not put a finger on it then or later but she knew in that instant that she and Miss Thorpe were together in a peculiar other-plane sort of way. Her own voice was still flat, not cynical but unenthusiastic, as if this was a special moment and she did not know whether she wanted it or not. But still she used Miss Thorpe's words.

'All will be well.'

Marcus grinned. 'Julian of Norwich? Not your thing, Daisy!'

'Actually, they come from Mabel Thorpe,' she said, already coming back to herself, beginning to smile.

And he said dramatically, 'Can anything good come from Mablethorpe?'

And they both laughed and he held out his hand and this time she took it and they went down towards Rook's Wood.

He became completely absorbed by Amy Jenner's headstone. The light was not good but he had the torch she had given him last Christmas and the intense blue beam picked out the information he wanted. He knelt in the mud and relayed it to her as she crouched above him.

'Born seventeen sixty-eight, died seventeen seventy-one.' He scraped away at the turf, then pushed the torch close and leaned after it, muttering letters, scraping, looking again. At last he looked up and said quietly, 'It says, "from the dreaded pox". My God, Daisy, she died from smallpox. And he went on to make a vaccine against it.'

He stood up and she straightened and moved away. 'You're saying this is his daughter then?'

'Of course not. He was only nineteen, there would have been a scandal.'

'They married young in those days. Or Amy could have been illegitimate. Hushed up.'

'In which case she would not have been called Jenner and she would certainly not have been buried in hallowed ground.' He scrubbed his hands on his jeans. 'More likely to have been the child of his brother or even a latecomer to his parents.'

'Doesn't it say "dearly loved child of" or something similar?'

'That's all that is there. Just her name, dates and cause of death.'

'It's a bit of a let-down.'

'Yes, it is.' He looked at her face. 'Cheer up.'

'I wanted something a bit more . . . whatever . . . for Miss Thorpe. The sort of thing she gave us.'

'Listen. Have a look in one of your reference books about the sort of clothing a three-year-old would be wearing in the mid-seventeen-hundreds. Hairdos. That sort of thing.'

'She'd have a cap or a tiny brimless linen bonnet with ties under her chin.'

'Her hair would still show.' He grinned, knowing he had got her interest. 'Get going with the charcoal. Make some sketches. Give her a face.'

'Stop patronizing me!'

'Have I ever patronized you? I'd have to get ahead of you somehow. And I'm always far behind you, Daisy Patek.'

'Oh . . . *Marcus!*'

'It's true. You're like a firefly darting everywhere, finding out things . . . I follow behind.' He gave her an upside-down smile. 'I *need* field glasses, Dais.'

She was frightened she was going to cry and wondered what on earth was the matter with her.

'Come on,' she said. 'I *need* a cup of tea.'

They went to her place first to drop off the rucksack, use the bathroom and make tea. Mummy was already there and although she smiled a welcome Daisy knew she was holding herself still inside.

'I took the afternoon off and went to see Alison.' She put a hand on Marcus's shoulder. 'You're doing a wonderful job. I'm glad that your aunt and uncle are helping out now.'

Just as she had known about Mummy's conscious self-control, so she knew that Marcus was . . . *glowing* . . . inside. She tried to tighten her facial muscles again.

He laughed. 'She can't stand Aunty Gert. And Ted's pretty hopeless in the kitchen.'

Mummy got on with making tea as if none of this mattered but her voice was very steady when she spoke. 'Nevertheless, you must let them do their bit, Marcus. Ted is your father's brother. It's a family thing.'

He went on smiling. 'Oh well. We'll see.'

Then Daisy knew, quite suddenly, why he was so settled, so normal, so happy. He had given up Leeds. He was going to stay at home and care for his mother full time. He had talked of the present and how important it was. He had decided to keep the present as it was and let the future take care of itself.

Mummy asked him to stay to supper. 'It's bangers and

mash because I'm cooking. Nerrie is going to be late. Do stay, Marcus. We could have ice cream for pudding.'

Daisy watched him, anticipating practically every word he was going to say.

'I'd love to, Aunty Etta' – how long since he had called Mummy that? – 'but I couldn't eat another thing after those enormous pasties. They were great. Thanks so much. Anyway, I'd better get back. Miss Thorpe's tomorrow, Daisy?'

She said they could meet at Jenner House, ten thirty, to give Miss Thorpe time to 'get sorted' after breakfast. 'I'll phone her and make sure it's OK.'

'No. Let me, Daisy. Then I can thank her for being concerned about Mum.'

He was going. She didn't see him off. He had forgotten that she intended to go with him to see his mother. When they heard the door close she said, 'He's giving up Leeds, isn't he? That's why you're so rigid.'

Mummy relaxed suddenly, put out her arms and they held each other.

'They're so close, darling. Marcus has taken Stan's place. And Stan would never have left her on her own or with Ted and Gertie.'

'But he did! That's what he did!' Daisy heard herself; she was wailing like a banshee.

'He had no choice,' Mummy said. She kissed the top of Daisy's head. 'It's hard for us to understand. We just have to accept it – all of it.'

Daisy thought of Marcus's anger last Tuesday when he had told her that she did not understand. And then his immediate joy when he had heard that he had a place at Leeds. How long had it been before he realized he could not accept the place? Had it been solely because his mother was so ill?

She sighed and said, 'I suppose all will be well. Somehow.' She drew away slightly and grinned. 'I'm OK, honestly.' She looked around the kitchen. 'I'll peel some potatoes, shall I? When will Daddy be in?'

'Not sure. He's gone to Gloucester. He's working with a family there. They're having a hard time . . . well, you know Daddy.'

'Yes. I'll do extra potatoes. He'll be hungry.'

'He wants to ask you to help him with this job, actually. There's a boy, must be about your age. Wondered whether you could talk to him.'

Daisy looked sideways at her mother. 'Just talk?'

'How do you mean? Oh . . . Daisy, we are in England, you are half English. The English don't have arranged marriages and your father thinks they are barbaric.'

'No, not really. He fixed up the aunties and that has worked out well. And he was looking at the dating columns in the paper the other day and said something about the custom following him from India to England.'

'And that means something?' Mummy jumped back as one of the sausages spat at her. 'For goodness' sake, Daisy! He was making a comment! And Vera and Mitzie *asked* him to get in touch with the Birmingham church!'

'Yes. Well.' She almost announced that she was going to marry Marcus. But stopped herself in time. She did not like the sound of the family in Gloucester. Not one bit.

Eleven

By Sunday the atmosphere in Jenner House had changed. Subtly at first then increasingly throughout Saturday afternoon it became obvious that the ship – if you could call a solid block of bricks and mortar a ship – was without its captain. Although Zoe was not officially in residence at the weekends she generally returned to her flat on Sunday afternoon, but this time she had let it be known that she would not be there until Monday morning. The residents could no longer pop down to the office to 'mention' that their hot water was not as hot today as it had been yesterday or that someone had left their laundry in the tumble dryer overnight. If anything really bad happened they had their emergency cords, of course, but that usually meant you ended up in hospital without so much as a comb.

Zoe often gave them mini-lectures on what she called 'community living', which – as one resident pointed out – was another way of offering a licence to be nosy. 'Keeping an eye on each other is certainly not being nosy,' she said firmly. 'It's being caring. We live together, though separately. There is never any need to feel isolated. Sit in the lounge for a moment reading a book and someone will join you.'

144

It was a safe bet of course, especially if it was a good book.

But for some reason May found herself, that Sunday afternoon, sitting in the lounge with the encyclopaedia on her knee and her notepad at the ready. She checked the clock by her wristwatch and decided that in ten minutes – four o'clock prompt – she would go into the communal kitchen and put the kettle on. That would definitely bring someone running.

She knew what it was; Daisy had not phoned. Of course she would be busy helping Marcus to settle his mother back into the cottage. That's what it would be. Unless Mr Barry Carter, MSc, had found a way of breaking that up too. May looked at her notepad: she had put a line through 'Barry Carter'; now, uncertainly, she added a question mark at the end. He might not be quite the bum-crack Daisy thought; he might be devious and clever and want to subdue someone as bright as Daisy Patek. She gripped her pen hard at the thought. She had been naive to imagine that a phone call from a woman of eighty could sway someone like that.

She stared at the notepad; there must be something else . . . There was. She wrote 'cleaning lady' next to the question mark. One of the team of cleaners was a relative of Daisy's. She remembered her trying to get past the dinner lady last Thursday to ask whether Daisy could call. She would ask Zoe for her name. Or perhaps she could lurk in the hallway tomorrow morning; Zoe had enough on her plate without worrying any more about May Thorpe. Yes, that was what she would do: she would pretend she was waiting for the post and when the cleaners arrived and she was saying good morning she would add ever so casually, 'Is Daisy all right?' Then she could say, 'Will you give her my very best wishes?'

Then perhaps Daisy would telephone. She put a tick next to 'cleaning lady' just to emphasize the point, stood up with some difficulty, grabbed her stick and made for the kitchen door to make some tea.

Four trolleys were lined up by the counter, all laid with milk jugs, sugar bowls and two cups and saucers; May leaned on her stick and opened the fridge to get out milk. As she waited for the kettle to boil she looked through the window at the alternative view, which was the back garden. She wondered where they would put the greenhouse. Not too far from the door, she hoped; she wouldn't mind planting a tray of something and later pricking out the seedlings. She could imagine herself leaning on one of the slatted shelves and very gently lifting a tiny, fresh green sprout into its pot. There was something really wonderful about growing a plant of any kind from a tiny dry seed . . . participating in a miracle. She had intended to grow parsley on the window sill and hadn't got round to it. Nothing quite like parsley sauce. Her mother's favourite dish had been a threepenny gammon hock smothered in parsley sauce. May had made it herself when her mother became ill and had presented it with new potatoes and carrots from the garden. Her mother had been grateful but had hardly touched it and said, 'Cooking is not your strong point, May, is it? But you enjoyed growing those potatoes and carrots. Like your father. A gardener, like your father.'

The kettle switched itself off and May used one of the smaller teapots and made tea. Mother wouldn't think much of teabags though she had tried one when they went up to London once. Earl Grey. She had pronounced it 'disgusting'. Mazawattee tea was her favourite. Enamelled plaques bearing the strange name were fixed in columns in most of the

THE PROMISE

stations. May smiled as she hooked her stick on to the side of
the trolley and leaned on it to trundle back into the lounge.
What a very basic form of advertising. Two words hammered
into millions of heads over and over again. When she had
worked for Norman they had got in on the first commercial
television advertisements. 'Gorridge for Porage for Breakfast' had become a national catchphrase. She had modelled
for the young housewife providing a substantial breakfast for
her two children. There hadn't been a husband in the small
film. Why was that? Norman had said casually, 'Well, you
haven't got one, have you?'

'And neither have I got two school-age children!' she had
snapped.

He had thought the exchange was simple badinage and
came back with, 'Have you got proof of that, May?'

She had turned away quickly, feeling the heat rise to her
face, and he had said no more. But it hadn't been long after
that when they had taken their product and advertising
campaign to Scotland to try to persuade them that porage
oats could come from places beyond their borders. That was
when, in the unfriendly atmosphere of a hotel in Glasgow,
he had confided his own story to her. She had already heard
most of it from the office messenger boy; it was the same one
she had heard from Walter Partridge, council chairman in
Warwick. The men working all hours to put food on the table,
the children growing up, leaving home, closely followed by
the wife. Walter had eased her into his situation by asking for
help with cooking, with cleaning, with shopping. When she
had protested he said she was so much more than a private
secretary, she was his personal assistant in everything. 'I
got over the kids, I got over Maggie. I'd just shrivel and die
without you,' he said. And he had started to cry.

She had stood out against his advances but she could not stand out against him when he cried. She held him to her shoulder and rocked him. She was twenty-five. It was ten years since her mother had made her promise never to tell a soul. She did not tell Walter but she felt better for sleeping with him. She thought they would marry and she would devote her life to making him happy and there would be a purpose to everything again. But he was twenty-five years older than she was and it would not have looked good. Three years later she applied for the job with Gorridge's and left for London and an entirely different life.

When Norman Gorridge had finished his sad little tale – almost identical to Walter Partridge's – she sighed and looked at him wryly. 'It happens, Norman. All the time.'

He thought she was talking from personal experience and nodded. 'I know that, my girl. I guessed right from the start you knew the score.'

'Did you?' She was genuinely surprised. She would have been a devoted wife to Walter Partridge but she hadn't loved him, not really.

'Of course. I recognize a broken heart when I see it.'

She stared at him, even more surprised.

He laughed. 'Well, we both know where we stand, May. How about it?'

'How about what?'

'Us. Together. Making something of Gorridge's, together. Making a life together. Dammit, May, making love together!'

She had laughed, pleased she had forced him into the open. She had been about to shake her head and then suddenly thought, why not? She liked him; he was honest; he wanted company out of bed as well as in it. And he hadn't once asked her to clean or cook.

Now, trundling a tea trolley over the lounge carpet at Jenner House, she wondered why she felt no regrets and certainly no guilt for sleeping with either Walter or Norman. She had left Walter because their relationship could never develop into anything more than it was; she felt no guilt about that. And Norman . . . she had not left Norman. Their relationship had developed into the sort of companionship she had dreamed of; they could work together, play together, laugh, even cry together. And now . . . blessedly . . . she could relive those exhilarating times without falling down in a stupid faint! Although she had no wish to share her memories – they were, after all, very personal – she had made no promises to anyone to keep them secret.

So, she sat down, poured her tea, fingered the pearls worn discreetly beneath her twinset, pushed aside the encyclopaedia and let herself think of Norman. Norman before cancer . . . not a big man physically but so full of energy and ambition he often appeared a titan among his peers. The Chicago business conference; was that in the early seventies? She had had a tape recorder in her bag and managed to capture what the main speakers were saying and when it was Norman's turn she had thought suddenly that he reminded her of James Cagney. Leaning on the table, head thrust forward, he managed to make Gorridge's porage sound practically inspirational. She smiled as she sipped her tea and remembered snatches of that speech . . . *I'm not selling just a good breakfast, my friends. I'm selling a warm blanket on a cold morning, a family ritual, care.*

It sounded so ridiculous as the words popped into her head that she laughed aloud. Since then, that kind of pitch had become so much more sophisticated and tough. But then . . . she had teased him about it after. 'You sound like the flower people – you're selling love, man!' But for once he had not smiled; in fact he had looked surprised. 'I meant it, May. And yes, in a way I am selling love. Or at any rate a sense of security in the world. That's what it means to me – a hot breakfast.' He had been forced to laugh at the expression on her face and somehow he had turned it round, calling her his 'hot breakfast'. She laughed again and sipped her tea. And then let herself remember the time after he had known his days were numbered. Ah.

He had wanted to stay in America; he loved it there and it seemed his natural home somehow, but he had come back to England. 'Can't expect people to come to a funeral in the States, May. The exes will want to be there.' He called his family the exes. His wife had remarried, both sons had married. There were grandchildren too. 'Listen, May. Marry me. Become my next of kin. Please. You are the only one who will really regret my departure and you'll be fixed up for life then.'

Of course she could not. That was when he gave her the pearls. He did not tell her that he had also arranged an annuity for her.

Her smile became wry but it did not disappear because after the funeral, when she had lurked inconspicuously at the back of the church, there had arrived a square parcel from the solicitors' office. It had been a packet of Gorridge's Porage and a note inside had simply said, 'Here's to a hot breakfast.' She had decided there and then that Norman's real bequest to her was laughter; she had done her best. And when it was hard, something usually came along . . . Daisy and Marcus, for instance. Her smile widened humorously again and she poured more tea and drank it quickly and then picked up her notebook and began to write out the entry listed under 'Jenner, Edward' in the encyclopaedia. The more she wrote, the more random it sounded. He was apprenticed to a surgeon in Gloucester. Had he wanted that? Or had he simply not wanted to follow in his father's steps? And he had gone to London to learn surgery. That had probably meant some kind of refined butchery in those days, so he was a man of his times, not squeamish at the sight of blood.

She stopped writing, suddenly feeling chilled. The lounge was overheated and she wore her cashmere twinset, so it could not possibly be that. She was chilled because she *was* squeamish; the sight of blood had always chilled her to the bone. Why was that, for goodness' sake? She had grown up at a time when rabbits and chickens arrived in the kitchen wearing fur and feathers and the Shambles in Worcester was still where meat was butchered. There had been plenty of blood in her childhood and she had turned a blind eye, trusting that death had come quickly and before the blood. Her mother reassured her. 'We have to drain them before we can cook them, May. That's all it is. They don't know a thing about it.'

But then there was Dad. Dad who had sheltered them with his own body, spreadeagling himself over the hole in the ground so that though the blast pinned them to the earth and sucked the breath from them, they stayed alive. Dad did not. He regained consciousness when the ambulance men got him on the stretcher; he screamed before he died.

When she and her mother were bundled down into the crypt, she told her mother that Dad would be all right because he bled first, not after. Her mother cuffed her so hard she fell at the feet of one of the ladies, who picked her up and said, 'You must be brave, both of you. Your dear one is with Jesus now.' And her mother said in her normal voice, 'Stop making a fuss, Mabel.'

So she had. It had been cold in the crypt, bitterly cold. Even the hot sugary tea had not warmed her. And now, looking at her careful script in the notebook, she could feel that same cold. Edward Jenner must have felt it, surely?

There was some tea left in her cup and she finished it, her thoughts jumping between the young man of over two hundred years ago and the girl in the crypt seventy years before who seemed to have so little to do with her yet sometimes dragged at her so persistently. The glorious VE day was still to come; she and her mother had over four years to get through before then and though Florrie came home as often as she could they had had to cope alone . . . *then*. At that moment. In the crypt. With one of the ladies crying behind the trestle tables because she had opened a tin of evaporated milk and cut her finger on the jagged edge . . . more blood but no screams.

She put down her cup, lifted her eyes and saw someone was standing in the doorway of the lounge. And in that instant she knew very well how she and her mother had coped . . . then. She had put down the thick white cup and lifted her tear-streaked face and registered her mother's fear and desperation and then her eyes had gone to the low doorway of the crypt and the man standing there, stretching his neck, looking for someone. The man was her brother. They thought he had been lost at Dunkirk. He was there. Standing there in his khaki uniform, wearing a tin hat, and she had leapt to her feet screaming, 'Jack! Jack!' And she had knocked her gas mask to the floor with the cup and there was another hullabaloo within the big hullabaloo and the three of them hugging and hugging, her mother saying over and over again, 'Jack . . . Jack.'

Toby Marsh got to her just before she fell out of her chair. This time she did not faint and he tucked her carefully back and said, 'I hope you're not going to make a habit of this, Miss Thorpe.'

Her heart was beating hard and she was cold and hot at the same time.

'It's just – I'm really sorry – I never let myself remember. At the hospital they told me I must move on – but recently it's been difficult. And I thought for a moment you were my brother.'

'Ah . . .' He drew up another chair and sat down. 'And what was his name?'

'I promised I would never . . . It was Jack.'

'Jack. A name that has become very fashionable again. Rather rakish then, I imagine. Jack-the-lad. Was he a Jack-the-lad, May?'

It was all too much, he was getting too close. Jack's name, her name . . .

She said, her voice stifled but clear, 'He was a deserter.'

'Ah.' He had a way of making that outgoing breath sound understanding. It didn't mean anything, not really. How could he possibly understand the awfulness? He said, 'Was that why the medics advised you to move on?'

She was surprised. 'I don't think so. Nobody knew about Jack. He would have been shot, you see.'

'But surely – he was older than you. Forgive me, May, but I rather thought – isn't he dead? Could you not speak of him now?'

'I promised . . .'

'Ah.' He stood and picked up the teapot. 'Listen, I'm going to make another pot of tea. There are two cups and saucers here and it seems rude not to use them both. Will you join me?'

He did not wait for a reply. She watched him go into the kitchen; this was her chance to get up and leave but she did not. If her stick did not hold her she might well go down and then there would be another kerfuffle worse than last week's. She could well end up in hospital without a comb. But . . . she had to find a way to stop him talking about the past. If she could turn the conversation somehow and get him to tell her about his childhood . . . Men enjoyed that. Even Norman had enjoyed that. Though mostly it had been because of the porage. His mother had kept bees, that was what had started it. Porage and honey, and he had found a way to combine the honey with the oats . . .

She smiled up at Toby Marsh. 'Yes, I will have another cup, just half. I'm making notes from this ancient encyclopaedia. Edward Jenner. Trying to make him into a real person.'

He went along with that. 'Fascinating. Of course if it hadn't been for him we might not be here having this conversation today.'

'Quite.' She watched him pour. 'And how did your daughter's birthday party go on Friday, Mr Marsh?'

'Oh, please call me Toby. I seem to have slipped into using your first name.' He smiled. He was familiar with her and familiar to her. It confused everything. He said, 'There were crackers and paper hats and jelly and ice cream and sausage rolls.' He laughed. 'I was required for the games. The little boys get rowdy. My wife thinks that scares the little girls but I'm afraid they rather enjoy it. So I'm looked on as a – provocateur!' He leaned down to the bottom tray of the trolley. 'There's a biscuit tin here. Oh, nice biscuits too. Do have one, it will help to soak up some of the tea.'

He made it sound clandestine and she took a custard cream, smiling as she recalled the little boys who had come to the bring-and-buy last Tuesday and waged a war over the biscuits. He told her about the party, the rather old-fashioned games, like pass the parcel and forfeits. She asked how old his daughter was and he said she was four and then added almost shyly, 'We have another on the way. It's a boy. We couldn't resist asking about the gender.' He looked at her and said, 'Strangely, our daughter is called May. She was christened Mary after Eve's mother, but we call her May to differentiate . . . you know how it is in families.'

She did. Her father was John and his first son was christened John. Tradition. But called Jack. She dropped the custard cream on to her lap and closed her eyes quickly. The past was like Pandora's box; once you let it out it would not go back. Her mother had been right to make her promise.

He said, 'Are you all right, May?'

She said, 'Yes. Perhaps I had better go back to my room.' She knew she could not stand up for a moment. 'I'll just finish my tea.' She forced a smile. 'When is your new baby due then – er – Toby?'

He smiled, reassured. 'This coming week actually.'

She had not expected that and was surprised and interested. 'How wonderful. Will you be taking paternity leave?'

'Yes. That's why I'm here now actually. I'm taking a number of files from the office. I can familiarize myself with them over the next three weeks. Nothing personal of course, that's Mrs Ballinger's area. We are looking at estimates for a new heating system. And garden maintenance too.'

They were on safe ground at last. She remembered the

pearls and slid them from beneath her jumper. 'I know I mustn't have them on show, of course, but just for today . . . They are rather precious. You are very generous and I hardly know how to thank you—'

'I wanted to put something into the funds, May. And I wanted to do it anonymously – as far as the residents went. Zoe and Arthur Wentworth know, but they are the only ones. So you can wear them as publicly as you like.' He smiled. 'It was my pleasure. I mean that.'

'Oh . . .' She was overcome again but quite differently. She smiled. 'I have to confess that when I opened them I felt immediately . . . well, better! As if there were still unusual and exciting things happening. First Daisy and Marcus and then the pearls.'

He smiled back, delighted. 'The two from school? Arthur mentioned them as you know. I like that idea. Possibilities . . . waiting round every corner.'

'And now your new baby.' They sat for a moment in complete accord, smiling at each other. And then she said, 'What will you call him – have you thought of a name?'

'Oh yes. Eve wants to call him Jack.'

Her face changed; she felt it tighten and stretch at the same time. It was as if he had planned this all the time, perhaps to trick her into some kind of reaction. She had to stop it. Now.

She got to her feet somehow and unhooked her stick from the arm of the chair.

'It's not a lucky name, Mr Marsh. My brother . . .' She swallowed hard. 'Jack. My brother Jack . . . he committed suicide.'

He leapt to his feet, astonished, apologetic, not really understanding – how could he understand? He gathered up her books, thrust them into her bag, took her arm, apologizing all the time. It was all a muddle and though she kept telling him she was perfectly all right, he still escorted her to the lift and stepped inside with her. She held the grab rail and kept her head down and tried not to listen to what he was babbling.

'It wasn't just a coincidence that I took this job – you must have guessed that right from the start – the connection. I started in Birmingham and then found that – years later – you had been in a sanatorium in Droitwich. It was my mother, you see. I was impatient – said it didn't matter – she wanted it. So much. And she died. And it became something else. Like a promise I had to keep. A promise to my mother . . .'

He seemed to be goading her in some way, goading her into telling him about *her* promise . . . Was it part of his psychology degree or whatever he had? Get them to talk it out and then they'll be suddenly well again?

The lift stopped and the doors sighed open and she was at her front door, key ready, and . . . he was gone. Once inside, she sat down and closed her eyes for a moment and gradually the room settled around her and she remembered to breathe deeply. What an idiot she was; he wanted to use her as a confidante, that was all it was. Perhaps, like Walter and Norman, his marriage was rocky. But it had been his mother; he had wanted to talk about his mother. He admitted he was a provocateur. He was stirring up his memories just as she stirred up hers. Maybe he wanted a confessor.

She frowned and shook her head gently. And the phone rang. Praying it was Daisy, she lifted the receiver.

Arthur Wentworth's voice came over uncertainly, without a trace of his usual bluffness.

'May – Miss Thorpe – I realize I have – um – offended

you as well as making a fool of myself – no fool like an old fool, eh? My intentions were – um – well-intentioned. I assure you of that. But if my – um – intervention – was – could be – seen as interference, then I apologize. Profusely. Humbly.' He stopped speaking and waited for her response.

She felt a peculiar lightness expand her lungs, as if a small breeze from the hills promised spring. This was happening now. This was nothing whatsoever to do with the past. This was where she had moved on to. A place. Her place. And she knew, in that instant, that if she liked she could make room for Arthur Wentworth.

She smiled into the receiver but of course he could not see that and he said quickly, 'Don't put the phone down, May. Let me come and see you. Have a cup of tea, talk about it.'

The thought of more tea was too much; the thought of Arthur being here in this room with her was too much. She wanted to treasure this lightness on her own.

She said, 'Not this evening, Arthur. I've been in the sitting room most of the afternoon and I am tired. Come and have coffee tomorrow morning.'

He made sounds of relief and pleasure. She said, 'Thank you for explaining things to me. It has been . . . difficult.'

The sounds stopped. She added, 'It's all right, Arthur.' And put the receiver down. Immediately it rang again.

Mary Smithson said, 'Are you all right, May? We saw you go to the lift supported by Mr Marsh and we were a little anxious.'

'I'm absolutely fine. No, honestly. So kind of you . . . no, I'm fine.'

And as she replaced the receiver she thought that this was what Zoe meant by communal living and in fact she really was fine. It was ridiculous that she kept linking Toby Marsh with her dead brother. Toby was a nice young man who was as keen as mustard to do a good job at Jenner House and had somehow latched on to her as being like-minded. And Jack Thorpe . . . was dead. The past was dead.

She gave a wry smile and murmured, 'It's all right, Mother. I haven't broken my promise.'

Twelve

By the time Daisy and Marcus arrived at Jenner House on Tuesday morning, it was snowing. Marcus would not admit it.

'I've counted six flakes since you first started screaming,' he said. 'The rest is definitely rain.'

Daisy jumped up and down on the pristine carpet and her hair shed two or three white flakes. She screamed triumphantly and Dot, who had let them in, made calming gestures. Marcus grinned. 'Dandruff,' he said. And Daisy attacked him with her scarf. The door to the visitors' toilet flew open and Vera emerged, yellow-gloved and clutching a bottle of bleach.

'I knew it was you. This is a house for retired people, Daisy Patek! We do not need screaming teenagers. We do not need wet carpets!' Her voice changed to a wail. 'I have just this very moment vacuumed all this area and now – look!'

Daisy apologized and hugged her aunt and was instantly forgiven. Marcus was hugged and told he was taller and thinner than ever. Dot herded them to the lift and stabbed the up-button, then held back Vera, who was in the middle of telling Daisy that Mrs Eve Marsh had gone into labour that very morning and Mrs Ballinger would be sending a congratulatory card round for signatures. The lift doors swished closed and her words were cut off.

Daisy said, 'Sorry, Marc. You know how it is.'

'Aunts.' He rolled his eyes. 'I'd prefer yours to mine. Aunty Gertie is only interested in bad news. Yours are at the ready to rejoice.'

'Not always. But we couldn't manage without them. They are kind of like a framework.'

'Supportive?' Marcus screwed up his face consideringly and she thought how beautiful he was. 'I suppose . . . Ted and Gertie are supportive. At the moment. But it's all so . . . disapproving. They never criticize exactly. They just emanate disapproval.'

The lift doors parted and he pushed open the fire door and let her walk beneath his arm. She knew that she was happy but as she left the shelter of the long sleeve of his jacket it was as if she caught a glimpse of the other side of everything and for an instant felt a pang of terror. And then, before they could ping-pong Miss Thorpe's doorbell, the door opened and she stood there grinning like a Cheshire Cat.

'I heard the yelling so I knew you'd arrived! The kettle is on, the biscuits aren't quite stale. And I just looked out of the window and saw the snow! I love snow, don't you?'

And Daisy forgot the other side of the coin and rushed forward to peck Miss Thorpe and hand over some more snowdrops and ask how she was.

They eventually sorted themselves out. Marcus made the tea and they took off their outdoor stuff and draped it on the radiator in the kitchen and Daisy pulled a packet of seeds from her pocket and wondered whether Miss Thorpe might like to plant them. 'They're only cress, but they grow fast and cress makes such a nice sandwich.'

'How strange! I was thinking just recently that I might start some parsley. Cress is much better. I've got one of those foil trays on the draining board and it can grow on some damp kitchen paper – we used to do it on blotting paper, you know. It works well.' She turned her wide smile on Daisy. 'That's a case of telepathy, surely? And please call me May.'

'OK, May.' Daisy laughed at herself. 'Listen, we'll get some parsley seeds and some soil.'

Marcus said, 'They're hard to germinate. Don't you have to do something?'

'I'll look it up.'

They were pleased with each other, smiling, exclaiming as the snow became thicker. May said, 'Is everything all right now, Marcus? Daisy was very anxious.'

'Mum? She got her pills mixed up but she's more relaxed now than I've seen her for ages,' Marcus said, nodding. 'My uncle and aunt are staying with us for a while so she's got company. And the social worker seems . . . nicer. Probably Aunty Gertie has had a bit of a go at her.'

They all laughed at that. May said, 'The social worker – her name isn't Longsmith, is it?' Marcus could not remember. 'I had a social worker who wanted me to go to an art class. I wish I'd had Aunty Gertie to deal with her.'

They drank tea and Daisy ate biscuits. May said, 'I think we've sorted out the business with BC, haven't we, Daisy?'

'He phoned late last night. Mummy picked up the phone and Daddy took it from her. Forcibly.' She blew crumbs as she giggled. 'Mummy would have gunned him down with words. Daddy listened. Apparently he got your message, Miss . . . May. And then another one from Mr Wentworth apologizing profusely.'

'Mr Wentworth was here yesterday. He told me.'

'We guessed he was when we phoned you from the tops.' She giggled again. 'Actually I feel quite sorry for Mr Wentworth. And for BC.'

'It's not weighing you down though, is it, Daisy?' Marcus said, taking the last biscuit before she could. He smiled at May. 'Yes, everything will be back to normal when school starts again.' He looked at Daisy more soberly. 'I'm glad poor old Steve is off sick actually. He'd have got the brunt of what you had to cope with, Daisy. And he's not as resilient as you.'

'Thanks,' she said. But she also nodded, knowing what he meant. She reminded May that Steve Coles was their personal tutor and had been off sick last week. Then Mrs Arbuthnot. 'Librarian and Disseminator of Information,' she intoned. 'Bit like this place, I suppose.' She remembered Aunty Vera's message. 'By the way, Aunty Vera says a congratulations card will be coming round later for you all to sign. Apparently someone is having a baby. Like *now*. Can't remember who it was.'

'Eve. Someone called Eve something,' Marcus supplied. 'My favourite name – next to Daisy of course.'

Daisy's predictable reaction was lost in May's exclamation. 'Already! It's Toby Marsh's wife – he's taking over the finances here apparently. He told me on Sunday afternoon that they were having another baby this week. No wonder he was in . . . a bit of a state.'

Marcus lifted his mug solemnly. 'Here's to the new baby!' They sipped decorously and May said, 'It's a boy.' She looked past them and through the window where the snow was outlining the skeletons of the horse-chestnut trees. She took a breath. 'Jack. They're calling him Jack.' She came back to them and smiled. 'I had a brother called Jack. He died in the war.'

There was a little silence then Daisy said uncertainly, 'It's a nice name.'

May nodded. Marcus said, 'Is that the reason Mr Wentworth was so angry with us for making you talk about those days?'

'I'm not sure. But I enjoyed it, so don't worry.' She shook her head. 'Though perhaps we could leave it for today.' She put down her mug and leaned forward. 'I'm very interested in that gravestone you found in the churchyard.'

Marcus picked up the change of topic. 'Nothing very exciting, as it happens. Amy Jenner, born March the first, seventeen sixty-eight, died April seventeen seventy-one aged three. We need to get hold of the parish records. We think she might have been a latecomer to Edward's parents. Or possibly the child of a brother . . . cousin. The name Jenner was probably not unusual and she may have been nothing to do with Edward at all. The interesting thing is she died of smallpox.'

'Interesting?' Daisy looked up from rummaging in her bag. 'Tragic. Poignant.'

'I meant interesting because Jenner may well have started to research a vaccine because of Amy's death. It's another tenuous link between them, that's all.'

May was busy scribbling on her notepad. She bit the end of her pen. 'So he was nineteen when Amy was born. It's possible.'

'What?' Daisy asked, pulling out her sketchbook.

'That she was Jenner's child.'

Marcus went into the reasons why this could not be and May looked as deflated as Daisy had felt when he had expounded them to her the day before.

Daisy opened her sketch pad. 'I've started a sort of graphic biography of Amy. This might have been the sort of cradle she had . . . It's wooden with a fixed hood. Those are rockers; they stick out like that so that whoever is in charge can rock the cradle with one foot while she peels potatoes or spins wool or something.' She laughed. 'I don't know how Amy would have been wrapped up – we might have something in the library at school – so I just did this fist waving at us.'

May was delighted. 'Daisy! What a brilliant idea! We'll probably never know for sure who Amy belonged to, of course – so many secrets within small communities – but we can give her a fairly accurate background. It's a lovely idea.'

'Not mine actually. Old clever-clogs here thought of it. I'll have a check in the history section. Make a few sketches of caps and those smocky things they wore.'

'Strangest thing . . .' May looked down at her notepad. 'I've been thinking of Jenner as a young man – same age as Marcus really. Blackberrying. Don't know why . . . late summer . . . wonderful time in the countryside. And there has always been someone with him. A girl. One cannot help wondering . . .'

Daisy said, 'A cousin perhaps. The same name. Jenner.'

Marcus looked embarrassed. 'This is the very thing you're not supposed to do when you are researching the past. Already you've fallen into your own trap. If you are suggesting that this baby was conceived in late summer – say, the end of August – then it would have been born three months prematurely. Such a premature baby would never have survived in the seventeen hundreds.'

'Miracles do happen.' Daisy flattened her sketchbook. 'And look – there's her fist waving to prove it!'

'Plus' – Marcus looked sternly at Daisy to silence her – 'plus the fact that first cousins could not marry, so Amy would have still been illegitimate and not eligible for burial in the churchyard!'

'Oh . . . bollocks!' said Daisy.

Marcus glanced at May, alarmed. But May had not noticed a thing. She said slowly, 'They believed in miracles then. And they loved Edward. They would send her away, of course, but when the child died they may well have let her come home.' She looked up and grinned at Marcus. 'Research does not allow for the unexpected reactions of people.' She turned to Daisy. 'And for someone as feminine and sensitive as you are, your epithets are definitely coarse!'

'Sorry, May. Shall I have a look in the library and see what I can find?'

'I expect you will. And Marcus will investigate the parish records and I will make some phone calls.' She beamed. 'Are all the biscuits gone? Then we can have the doughnuts. Arthur Wentworth offered to get my shopping this morning and I asked him to bring some doughnuts and a pot of jam in case there wasn't enough in them. Sometimes they can be so mean with the jam, I find.'

She produced the sugary buns and some plates while Marcus made more coffee and Daisy put the snowdrops in a glass. The feeling of accord in the crowded bed-sitting-room was tangible. Outside, the snow had stopped and was already melting slushily on the path. Below, the front doors opened and Aunty Vera emerged. Daisy opened the window to wave and Vera waved back and called upwards, 'Tell Miss Thorpe. It's a girl!'

Daisy closed the window and turned towards the kitchen. 'Did you hear that, May? Aunty Vera just called up to say that the baby is a girl. You thought it would be a boy, didn't you?'

May emerged holding a plate of doughnuts. She put them on the table, dusted her hands on a paper towel and nodded then chuckled.

'You see, Marcus? Even in this predictable age, the unpredictable happens! The scan showed a boy – Jack – and it turns out to be a girl!'

Marcus grinned good-naturedly. 'That's what makes it all so exciting, I suppose. And they can always call her Jacqueline – Jackie for short.'

They started throwing suggestions at each other as they resettled themselves around the table. Marcus said how unusual it was for this kind of mistake to be made. Daisy wondered whether they might sue, especially if they'd bought everything in blue.

May shook her head. 'They're not that kind of family,' she said. And then wondered why she had spoken so definitely. She had talked to Toby Marsh perhaps three times and hadn't known about his wife and daughter until Zoe mentioned the birthday party last Friday. And all that gibberish Toby Marsh had talked last Sunday afternoon had been just that. Gibberish.

Daisy washed up and tidied the kitchen before they left. They both felt that the visit had been really good, though Marcus said he wondered whether they would ever talk about Coventry again. 'I think your Colonel Blimp had a point, you know, Daisy. There's something there . . . she's frightened of it.'

'Of course she is, you goop! It was carpet bombing on a grand scale.'

'I think it was more . . . personal.'

'Well, her father was killed, it seems. That was personal.'

'It could have been later . . . I don't know. I've got a feeling. It's weird. I'm somehow connected to it.'

She looked at him then nodded. 'Actually I know what you mean. We are both, like, connected with her. And perhaps Amy is in there somewhere, too?'

'Shouldn't think so. But it's obviously a topic which has grabbed her. She should have been a history student.'

'According to you, everyone should be history students!'

'Well, you are for starters!'

'Don't be freaky. You know bloody well I'm into art big time.'

'You should do art history, Dais. Seriously. We're both part of a long line of people and we need to know what went before. Oh, and another thing, stop swearing. May doesn't like it!'

She was going to argue the point and then suddenly didn't. He probably meant his mother didn't like it. And that was where they were heading now.

Aunty Gertie had invited her to lunch. 'You can have a nice chat with Mrs Budd then,' she had said. 'She's very fond of you, apparently.' Daisy had felt the disapproval Marcus had mentioned; like a damp blanket tucked around her neck. She said to Marcus now, 'OK then. Sorry. But . . . bollocks!'

However, it was a lovely lunch and they sat around the dining-room table, Aunty Alison in a chair by the fire, and ate every scrap. Marcus waited on his mother as if she were a child and was obviously delighted at her eating so well and so appreciatively.

'See, Ma?' He hugged her shoulders into his arm. 'It's all for the best. A new start.'

She smiled up at him and Daisy felt a little blip in her chest. Everyone was different of course, she knew that. Her relationship with Mummy and Daddy had nothing to do with Marcus's relationship to his mother; he was taking the place of his dad. Of Stan, who had worshipped his beautiful, blonde Alison. This was what Marcus had meant when he told her she did not understand.

Her phone rang and she reached into her jeans pocket and raised her brows. 'It's May,' she said.

May's voice was amused. 'I had to share this with you two – sorry if it's an inconvenient moment.' Daisy made reassuring noises and then listened and laughed. She pressed a button and looked up at Marcus, who was just offering a bowl of bread-and-butter pudding to his mother.

'You'll never guess. The baby – the one who was supposed to be a boy and turned out to be a girl . . .' Marcus looked round quizzically. 'Well, they've chosen a name. They're not bothering with Jacqueline. She's going to be called Amy. They called the first one Mary after Mrs Marsh's mother. And this one is after Mr Marsh's mother! What you might call a bit of a coincidence.'

Marcus still hovered with his mother's pudding. Then he made a gesture of surrender with his spare hand and said, 'OK. We'll try and have a look at the parish records this afternoon and I'll get on the school computer asap.'

He told his mother about Amy Jenner and she nodded, interested. Aunty Gertie frowned. 'I don't get it. This new baby has no connection with the earlier one or any of the hundreds of other Amys who are being born right at this moment!'

Marcus said, 'How do you know that, Aunty? It's unlikely there's a connection, but nobody really knows.' He looked at Daisy. 'The more things are researched, the more unpredictable they become.'

Daisy smiled at him, and noted that at last he passed his mother her pudding and sat down for his own. She would have liked to say that the more she knew, the less she understood. But for once she said nothing. The bread-and-butter pudding was delicious. She knew that much and understood it only too well.

Thirteen

The rector was strangely reluctant to produce the parish records. Marcus said later that actually the poor man was reluctant to leave the comfort of his study and tramp across the slushy snow to the vestry, and if Daisy made up one more mystery about this very simple research he would drop the whole thing. But because Daisy felt as if they were intruding – or trying to intrude – into something that could have been a very private disgrace all those years ago, she insisted that his reluctance was part of the 'whole thing'.

'Perhaps all the rectors ever since seventeen sixty-eight have been sworn to secrecy.'

'For Pete's sake, Daisy!'

'OK, OK. But surely other students must investigate parish records? I mean, they're not bloody sacred or anything, are they?'

'No, they're not bloody sacred and they're not even just sacred. And other students would make a similar request. Yes. And probably meet with the same reluctance because, whatever people think, priests work more than one day a week and are usually very busy people.'

'Sorry, sorry, sorry. Anyway, did you manage to write it down?'

'Apology accepted. And when I produced my pen and
notebook and actually used them, then surely it was obvious
I was writing down the relevant entries. All right?'

'Oh, shut up being all disapproving. You must have quite a
large portion of Aunty Gertie's genes!'

He approached her twirling his long scarf like a ball and
mace. They both started to laugh. Then he huddled back over
the table where his school notebook was open and pressed
flat. They were in the big Patek kitchen and the enormous
brooding sky outside was darkening quickly; Daisy was
making tea and was now hunting for the biscuit tin which
her mother regularly tried to hide from her.

'Don't know what to do about supper. Do they want me to
start anything? They just abandoned me this morning and
there's no note . . . nothing. Perhaps they were kidnapped
. . . abducted . . .'

'They must have said something other than goodbye.'
He looked up and grinned. 'Your father would have had to
have a hug and your mother would have been incapable of
silence.'

'Little do you know.' But Daisy frowned then relaxed. 'I
was still in bed and I pretended to be asleep because I didn't
feel like getting an earful of instructions. But no note – it's
just incredible. I feel totally abandoned.'

'It's because you can't find the biscuit tin. I can see it from
here actually. Just out of your reach behind the top sauce-
pan.'

He went back to his notebook, so she had to drag the step-
stool over and climb on to it to reach the biscuit tin. He was
right, she instantly felt better.

He said, 'OK. I've coherenced my notes—'
'Co- what?'

'Coherenced. A verb from a noun. OK? May I go on?'

She munched happily, wishing she had thought of the noun–verb thing. She ran through a few experimentally and without success.

Marcus said, 'Amy's mother was also called Amy. Amy Mary Jenner.' He looked up at her. 'Her maiden name was Amy Mary Jenner. Got that?'

'Father?' Crumbs sprayed the notebook and Marcus shook it at arm's length, mouth stretched with disapproval. Daisy intoned, 'Aunty Gertie.'

'She's not even a blood relative. But I understand her fastidiousness.'

'Sorry. Again. Go on. Tell me that the father is unknown.'

'Actually, no. He was called John Smith and he's listed as a cowman.'

She was going to jeer at the name but then paused. 'Surely that should be cowherd?'

'Well, it's not. Perhaps it means he was an expert with cows.'

'And John Smith was an alias for Edward Jenner?'

'No. But I think it makes the name and occupation . . . genuine. I mean, it's before the days when John Smith was a sort of smutty cover-up identity. It sounds like a farm labourer's name. And cowman sounds like a superior farm labourer. I've got a feeling that in those days a cowman would have also been a self-taught vet.'

Daisy was instantly caught up in possibilities. 'Sooo . . . the daughter of the house – presumably Edward Jenner's sister – fell for the cowman. And baby Amy was born. And was sent away?'

'Well, perhaps not. Because she was christened in our church too. Two months later.' He pushed his original notes towards her and pointed. 'See? The end of April. Seven weeks. They liked to get them christened early.'

She nodded. 'What about the first Amy's parents?'

'Not entered. And I managed to flip backwards and forwards looking for a marriage. John Smith was married four years later. To Amelia Worthy, domestic servant at River Farm.'

Daisy was aghast. 'So Amy Jenner must have died at the same time as little Amy? Oh my God. How awful.'

'What makes you say that?'

'John Smith would not have married anyone while she was alive. He loved her. And she loved him.'

'Why didn't they marry?'

'Her parents. This really is a Romeo and Juliet situation. And with a baby too – oh Marcus.'

'You're getting carried away again. But . . . it must have been grim. What I don't actually get is why little Amy's stone – and the entry in the records – labels her a Jenner and therefore illegitimate, yet she still gets a place among the legitimate.'

Suddenly, Daisy bunched her sweatshirt to her chest and said, aghast, 'It's the day for aunties!'

'It could mean that the Jenner family had forgiven her, taken her back, insisted that the baby should have a Christian burial—'

'My God, Marcus! Mattie and Saul and the kids and the aunties are here for supper! Two tureens of curry and green tea and talk, talk, talk! And Daddy's not even here! He's in Gloucester fixing me up with a husband who is probably half my age!' She was already at the counter setting out chopping boards and an array of knives. 'You lay the table and I'll start on the vegetables. Mummy's probably got chicken marinating somewhere. Nine places. Oh my God!'

Marcus went into action automatically but still said, 'Pull yourself together, Dais. Your father does not believe in arranged marriages. He's on that Equal Opportunities thing anyway. And he never involves you or your mother so stop dramatizing every little thing.'

'Why didn't Vera *say* something this morning instead of just moaning about us dripping snow on the carpet!'

'Presumably because we were dripping snow on to the carpet. Oh – and she had to tell us about the woman – Eve – who was giving birth to *her* baby Amy. Daisy, slow down. You're going to chop your finger off at any moment.'

Daisy did indeed stop. She turned and stared at him and her chin wobbled, then her enormous dark eyes filled up. She whispered, 'It's the other side of the coin, Marc. So much unhappiness and fear and – and – awfulness.'

He held out a hand but she did not take it. He said, 'People survive, Daisy. That's what is so marvellous. They don't always die. They find a way to . . . *survive!*'

She stared at him then spoke again in a whisper. 'I know you're not going to Leeds, Marc. I know you're going to stay with your mother and help her to . . . survive. And I don't understand.'

He grabbed her hand and pulled her to him and she wept against his chest.

He said, 'It's not like that, Daisy, I promise you. They've deferred my place for a year. That's all. And I'm going to make it my gap year. I'm going to consolidate Mum's new outlook. Listen to you rabbiting on about your art foundation course and start making notes for my thesis.'

She stopped crying and pushed back her head to look at him properly.

'*Thesis?* You don't know yet what sort of area you might

175

want to—' He was smiling and she tried to punch his chest but he was holding her too closely.

'Listen, gabble-mouth. It came to me. In Rook's Wood, yesterday. If you're going to design costumes for the National Theatre, I'd better research the history of theatre in Europe.'

'But I don't know whether I'm going to . . .' She looked up at him and wept again. 'Oh Marcus . . . how do you put up with me?'

'It's a question of keeping up, actually. And of course making allowance for all the hormonal activity going on in such a small area—' She managed to find enough space between them to deliver a half-hearted punch. And then she laughed and so did he and then they kissed. Properly. Fearfully.

They drew apart when they heard the car pull up outside. Then the Pateks came down from the front hall with their usual flurry and made a fuss of Marcus. They asked about Alison and were delighted to hear that Aunty Gertie had cooked lunch for everyone.

'Stay and eat with us now, Marcus,' Daddy said. 'You know my sisters but Saul and Mattie are strangers to you. And the little boys will love you.'

'I'd better get home, Uncle Nerrie. But thank you.' Marcus looked at Daisy and she thought that he looked incandescent with happiness, then saw that her mother had switched on the light behind him and it aureoled his head. 'We've been . . . looking into parish records. Lots to think about.'

Daisy forced herself to look away from him. 'I thought you were in Gloucester, Daddy. I didn't know what was happening.'

'I wrote it all down in the note,' Mummy said, eyeing the

chopping boards and knives with a kind of resignation. 'And put the note on top of your duvet.'

Daisy realized she must have covered the note as she flung back the duvet to get out of bed. She started to laugh and then couldn't stop. Marcus left through the back door and she climbed the steps with him and they both admired the clarity of the sky. 'No more snow,' Marcus said when they reached street level. 'Look . . . stars.'

She said, 'It doesn't worry me any more. About not understanding.'

He was silent for ages. Then he said, 'We've got to wait, Daisy. You do understand that, don't you?'

'I suppose I do. I don't want to. But . . . yes, I understand that.'

He didn't kiss her again and she understood that too. And then she went downstairs to the pungency of curry smells and the array of stock pots on the cooker hob, all 'ready to go' as her mother put it.

Zoe Ballinger brought the card in during that afternoon. It had 'Congratulations' in silver across the front and inside a cartoon of a stork carrying a shawled baby to its destination.

'I know it's ghastly but I couldn't find anything interesting.' She listed the high street shops she had scoured. 'I should have had a look in Bristol at the weekend but he didn't tell me the baby was due quite so soon.' She pegged the card to her clipboard and produced a pen. 'He seems so frank and open but then you trip up on something he hasn't told you.'

May nodded. 'I spotted him last Tuesday going up to the top floor and thought he looked mysterious.' She took the pen. 'Just here?'

'Yes. Write "and" before your signature. I saved you till last as you are so special to him.' She met May's raised brows with a smile. 'Your necklace. When I showed it to him that Wednesday he immediately bought it and I knew he planned to return it.' She shook her head gently. 'Apart from Arthur, no one else knows, May. It's not only the necklace anyway. He carried you up here so . . . tenderly.'

'He is a natural carer, I'll give you that. But we are not friends. Not at the moment anyway.' May spoke very definitely and Zoe did not pursue the subject.

Instead she said, 'My sister and I had a proper shop-fuddle in Bristol on Saturday afternoon – not at the Mall, up and down Park Street. It was fun. A waste of time and money but . . . fun!'

May was delighted. 'That's how I feel about Daisy and Marcus. Especially Daisy. There's a lot to them besides, but somehow they bring that fun element into so much.' She changed her smile to a grin and added, 'Actually it's your haircut. It's like a passport to . . . somewhere else!'

Zoe turned faintly pink but said normally enough, 'They turned up then? I wondered – when I saw the snow . . .'

'I'm amazed you didn't hear them greeting Daisy's aunt in the hall.'

'Is that what it was? I kept my head down in the office. The cleaners do a lot of arguing.'

'Wise woman.' May handed the card back and watched as Zoe stuck down the envelope. She knew something else was coming.

Zoe said, 'On Saturday night Barbara and Dennis – sister and brother-in-law – took me to a very nice restaurant for dinner. Just off the old A38. A converted barn, I think.'

'How . . . nice.' May smiled encouragingly; she liked the sound of Dennis and Barbara.

'I was going to have duck and orange but then I had venison which I don't usually enjoy but this time I did.' She grinned. 'Have you noticed that when you're low and depressed and unsure of yourself, you don't enjoy things and then something nice happens and . . .' She laughed and shook her head. 'So silly! I am being so silly, May. The truth of the matter is that Philip was there and he came over and chatted away so naturally – even Dennis said what a decent bloke he was. For a hairdresser.'

May opened her eyes wide. 'The *hair*dresser! Zoe, how nice! How very, very nice!'

'I knew you'd say that. It was. He's a professional charmer of course but there's something underneath all the banter and chit-chat. He's kind. That's what it is, May. He's a kind man.' She sat back, waving the card as if it were a fan. 'Anyway, he persuaded me to try the venison. Probably that was why I enjoyed it this time.'

May nodded . . . Philip. Philip and Zoe. It sounded right. She said slowly, 'Let it happen.'

Zoe looked as if she might prevaricate, but then she said, 'It may be nothing.'

'But it may be something. A friendship. A friendship worth having, Zoe. Don't be defensive. You've got another hair appointment?'

'I made one last Friday. Four weeks.'

May waited, hoping Zoe would tell her that Philip wanted to see her before then. But Zoe was standing up, her beautifully sculpted hair leaning forward with her, highlighting her jawline. 'I'd better go. The social committee are meeting in the lounge. They want me to produce a newsletter once a month. As if there isn't enough to do.' She grinned and turned at the door. 'I nearly forgot – you'll enjoy this one, May. Mrs Smithson informed me this morning on the tannoy that she is all right now after almost falling but she might have a touch of post-natal shock!'

May was still chuckling as the door clicked shut. Then she closed her eyes, leaned back and thought about Zoe and the hairdresser, Philip. Zoe had always seemed so officious, so . . . uptight. That buttoned look must have been a direct result of her husband's desertion. And not helped by her job probably; the residents, including herself, made demands. All the time. She had heard one of them say once, 'That's what she's paid for!' And of course she did not mind when people genuinely needed her, but . . . Arthur wanting the newspapers ironed, Mrs Smithson having 'post-natal shock'. And of course, Mabel Thorpe collapsing all over the place! May opened her eyes; that was one thing she could do – not even think about Coventry . . . move on. And perhaps . . . maybe . . . could she offer to produce copy for a newsletter? It need not be long. Dates of coffee mornings, visiting choirs and conjurors, any local gossip she could dredge up. Her experience with Norman and Walter would be useful. But she would have to be a bit stronger than she felt now.

She switched her mind to Daisy and Marcus and closed her eyes again, smiling foolishly. She had sensed Daisy's tension and thought she knew what caused it. And Marcus . . . Marcus had reached a harbour of some sort. It had to do with Daisy. And it must have to do with his mother also. Was that what Daisy could not bear – was she jealous of the mother-and-son relationship? Surely not. And yet during that very first visit only a week ago, she had called Alison Budd a 'bitch'. Not a good word. But Daisy was not jealous.

She was warm and open and protective. Perhaps that was it, perhaps she was over-protective and resented Marcus taking on the role of his mother's carer?

And then, just before she fell into a dreamless sleep in her chair, May switched her thoughts to Arthur Wentworth. She was glad he had asked her to go for a walk with him. 'A step further each day, dear lady. By summertime we'll be able to walk down to the shops and back again.' Such a practical suggestion; one step a day. It was another of her mother's sayings.

He might seem fuddy-duddy but he was a kind man. Like Philip the hairdresser, underneath that top layer he was kind. That was why he could not bear to remember Coventry and the war and had lashed out so foolishly, so thoughtlessly. Poor Arthur Wentworth. There was nothing for it but to move on.

She slept.

Fourteen

Arthur turned up promptly at ten o'clock and helped her with her tweed coat. She had already adjusted the matching woollen hat and scarf and stuffed the gloves into her pocket. Norman's daughter had sent them for Christmas; she had not missed one Christmas or birthday since Norman's death.

Arthur said in his gallant voice, 'You look like a schoolgirl, dear lady!'

'Oh, I hope not, Arthur!' She emphasized his name in the hope that he would drop the 'dear lady'.

'Why not?'

'Well, if I look like a schoolgirl what does that make you?'

He looked at her uncertainly and then laughed. 'D'you know, May, I had no idea that under that demure exterior lurked someone so – so—'

'Cheeky?' she supplied quickly in case he said something really awful.

'That's not quite it, but it will do.' He opened the door and she went through and then had the usual fiddle to lock it. He said, 'I've tested the pavements. The slush has all gone and there's plenty of grip. How are you feeling? Could we go into the park?'

'That would be lovely. Are there any snowdrops left?'

The lift was waiting and they got in.

'I haven't walked in Folly Park for years. There used to be a little café somewhere. It might be open.'

'It won't be licensed,' she warned.

He shepherded her through the main door and she glanced at the Smithsons' kitchen window; the venetian blind was angled against onlookers but she smiled and held up her hand just in case they were there.

He took her gloved hand and threaded it through his arm. 'I feel you see me as a drinker, May. A whisky pensioner! It's not true, you know.'

She burst out laughing. 'Oh Arthur! I like that – a whisky pensioner! Even better than a whisky priest!' They crossed the road gingerly; nothing was about but May had to concentrate on the gutters and kerbs. She realized with a little jolt that she had not been outside Jenner House since the Christmas shopping trips. She held on to Arthur tightly.

She said, 'I apologize if I have misjudged the reason for your daily walks. But it would not worry me unduly if they ended up at the Coaching Inn.' She laughed again. 'Whisky pensioner indeed!'

He opened the side gate of the park and they went through a little avenue of rowan to the wide lawn. She stopped in amazement. The borders and central flower bed were covered in bedding plants, many of them blooming in spite of the snow. The lawn itself was starred by snowdrops and crocus, drooping but still showing mauve, orange and white.

Arthur said, 'I saw the council lorry last week. They must have done the planting then. This was worth coming to see, May – what?'

'Oh Arthur, yes.' She was so pleased that he was as delighted as she was.

They walked slowly around the circular lawn, still exclaiming at the sheer tenacity of the frail blossoms, some of them apparently weeping the remains of the snow. But it was when they entered the little copse dividing the park into two that their combined wonder made them stop suddenly and stare at a blob of pure gold among the leafless trees.

'They're wild,' Arthur said.

May nodded. 'Isn't that just amazing!'

'Of course the trees are protecting them.'

'Yes, but even so . . . in this weather.' They both stared down at the clump of daffodils in full bloom. By now May was clutching Arthur's arms with two gloved hands and he had covered both of hers.

'The way we're staring at them, anyone would think they're going to be whisked away in two seconds!' She laughed again and tried to drop her arm to her side, found it difficult and left it where it was.

The café, built as a Gothic folly three hundred years ago, was at the far end of this second lawn and by the time they reached it May was praying silently that it would be open for business. She had not brought her stick and knew she was hanging heavily on Arthur's arm. He was rambling on about using the laundry room as a workshop to build some shelving for the proposed new greenhouse and she realized that he was covering for her sudden silence. She was surprised by his sentience; he knew she had to concentrate all her energy on putting one foot in front of the other.

He said, 'It really gets me that Mrs Ballinger has decreed that all carpentry must be done in the rubbish room. When I reminded her that the bins weren't exactly fresh, she said I could leave the door open! I ask you!'

She eyed the four steps leading to the portico of the café.

There were pillars on either side, so if she angled Arthur that way she could manage by using them as an occasional support.

'It's not as if sawdust is unhygienic. I understand that if I was suggesting using paint or wood preserver in the laundry room it could be a problem. But I simply want somewhere . . . Of course it's the Smithsons. They object to everything on principle.'

Two more steps to go. Arthur slid one hand beneath her elbow and used the other to grip her wrist firmly. They stood for a moment before the arched windows of the wide door. Lights were on, tables were laid, a fire was in the grate. May said, 'Thank you, Arthur.'

'Nothing to do with me, May. Just good fortune.' His smile went from ear to ear. He did not let her go as he opened the door and ushered her inside.

They were the only ones there so they got a personal welcome from the local ladies who ran it as what they called 'a community café'. They had a table by the fire, and conversation from the one while the other went into the kitchen to make the instant coffee and pop the scones in the microwave.

'The Village Vixens suggested to the council that before this place went to rack and ruin we could bring it up to scratch and provide cheap snacks for visitors. Proceeds to charity of course. Last summer we did so well we kept going through the winter. We work on a rota system and Jeannie and I do one week in six. You should tell them at Jenner House. It's a nice walk across the lawns and the flowers are such a treat.'

The coffee and scones appeared and the two women returned smilingly to the kitchen to cut sandwiches. 'Just give us a shout when you need more coffee!'

May sipped thankfully and whispered, 'You know what they're saying, don't you? The two old dears. That's what we've become, Arthur.'

'Little do they know. No call for them to be condescending.'

'But affectionate as well as condescending. And they do know . . . well, they *guess* . . . that you probably saved their grandparents and therefore made it possible for them to be born!'

'Steady on, May. Imagination running amok.'

'Well, imagination has to run amok at times, especially where imaginative identification is concerned.'

'Sorry?' He looked confused.

'What else have we got? The bare facts are not enough, Arthur. We need to clothe them.'

'You're going too fast for me, May.'

She looked at his face, noted the broken veins, the blue eyes watering from the cold. 'Sorry, Arthur. It's just that I didn't sleep all that well and I started to think about Edward Jenner.'

'Edward Jenner? Oh, you mean Dr Jenner – the one who gave our house its name.'

'Well, yes. But the smallpox vaccine too.'

He nodded. 'Sorry.' He glanced upwards. 'Sorry, doctor! And thanks for the vaccine and the house!'

She was heartened again by his humour and smiled as she said, 'That's the sort of thing I meant. Imagining him. Talking to him. Asking him things.'

He guffawed. 'You can do all that, May, but I've a feeling he won't give you any answers.'

'How do you know that what comes into your head isn't an answer?'

She was smiling and he did too; this was still a joke after all.

'It rather depends on what comes into your head.'

'Well . . .' She cut her scone into bite-sized pieces. 'How about Dr Jenner when he was just Edward Jenner. Maybe Ted Jenner. Or just Ed . . . Eddie.' She experimented while she nibbled one of the bits of scone. 'It was autumn. And he was picking blackberries along one of those lanes that meander down to the Severn Sea . . .'

She waited, munching appreciatively; the scones were good. Arthur was nodding judiciously. 'Yes. Yes. It's not my usual cup of tea – but I can see it's the sort of thing he might have done as a teenager.'

'Can you see what he is wearing?'

'Of course not. But I might make an educated guess. Rough woollen breeches, perhaps. And a very loose – baggy – shirt. Fine cotton because they weren't poor. But not lawn. After all, he might mess it up.' He frowned, really concentrating, entering into this game of hers very seriously. 'What about footwear? Boots?'

'Don't know.' She swallowed the last of her scone and dusted her fingers on the paper napkin. 'I'll ask Daisy to look that up – she seems to spend a lot of time in the school library!'

He sat back, deflated. 'Those schoolkids again! They're the ones who have got you imagining all this stuff. Truth or fiction, it doesn't seem to matter to them!'

'Well, the footwear must be truthful of course. But perhaps there are other things that might have happened and would explain just why he turned to that particular research.' She made a face. 'They need not be factual but there could be a certain truth – fidelity – about them.'

'So if they are half a truth, they are also half a lie. Yes?'

She laughed. 'Too true.' She leaned forward. 'When you were up there in your plane, did you never imagine you were a bird? Didn't your Spitfire become part of you and you of it? No, don't brush it aside like that, Arthur. Think about it.'

'Let's talk about something else, May. Shall we have another cup of coffee?'

She sat back slowly, her eyes on his face. Neither of them spoke for all of two seconds, then she said, 'I'd love one, Arthur. She asked us to give her a shout.'

He reached across and touched her hand then sat well back from her, lifted his head and yelled, 'Jeannie!'

Murmured conversation in the kitchen stopped and a woman appeared wearing a flimsy polythene apron and a huge smile. 'We're both Jeannie. Can I get you anything?' Arthur asked for two more coffees and made a joke about genies of Aladdin's lamp and she laughed and said, 'You're not the first one with that, sir. Our favourite though is that we are both Jeaniuses.' She made a face. 'A smile makes the world go round and costs nothing.'

'That is most definitely correct!' Arthur spoke heartily and when the coffee arrived he lifted his cup and toasted the geniuses of Folly Park, then flinched as the scalding coffee burned his lip. But after Jeannie had flown back with a glass of cold water and he was cooling his lip, conversation lapsed again. May mentioned the clump of daffodils in the copse and he nodded vigorously. May said, 'Wasn't it nice that Toby Marsh and his wife have had another little girl?' And he nodded again. She said, 'We ought not to be much longer. The meals on wheels sometimes arrive at midday.'

He lowered the glass, put some cold milk into his cup and sampled the coffee. He nodded, satisfied. 'That's better. A really nice cup of coffee, May. And we've got plenty of time, it's not eleven o'clock yet and it took us only fifteen minutes to get here.' He looked at her ruefully. 'Habit of a lifetime, checking the time.'

She seized this new topic gladly. 'I suppose so. Even a second could make all the difference between life and death.'

She realized she had said the wrong thing and held her breath while he made a point of drinking his coffee down. She thought he would stand up then and she reached for her gloves and hat. But he did not move. He sat there staring into his empty cup as if it were a crystal ball. Then he sighed.

'You're right, May. I did imagine things . . . when we were flying. I couldn't do much of that on the way out, concentration was everything. But coming home . . . then I thought.' He looked up at her, then quickly down again. 'I didn't ever say I was in Fighter Command, May. But when the rumour started I did not discourage it. To fly a Spitfire in defence of my country . . . wonderful to be one of the First of the Few.' He sighed. 'I was actually in Bomber Command. I try not to think about it, of course, but sometimes . . .'

She said quickly, 'You don't have to talk about it, Arthur. We have to move on. Sometimes there are things best not remembered—'

He said, 'I had a name for myself. It was Death Dealer. Because that is what I did. I took that enormous buzzard out to hunt. And I became the buzzard. Dealing cards that were always black. I used to hand over to Ginger McIntyre when we reached the Channel. So that I could be sick. I was always sick.'

She had no control over her tear ducts and they filled and overspilled immediately. She made a small sound of distress and reached for the hands cradling his empty cup. But he was already standing, pushing on the table so that the crockery rattled alarmingly. He seemed to have forgotten her and the coffee they had just had and not paid for. As he stumbled towards the door, May reached into her pocket and found two pound coins and put them on the table and scrabbled her hat on to her head. He was through the door and at the top of the steps by the time she had thanked the two Jeannies, who stared rather blankly at the coins which were supposed to pay for four coffees and two fruit scones. Somehow without her stick she got to the door and closed it behind her and reached for the first of the pillars.

'Arthur! Please wait!'

He stopped, obviously in a daze, and looked round at her.

'Dear lady! Just stay where you are – no – stay—' He was moving as fast as he could but she could not stop herself and knew she was going to fall before it happened. But she also knew that Arthur would save her and she left the pillar and reached for him and the next thing was they were clinging together like shipwrecked sailors and he was staggering backwards on to the grass and still holding her tightly and then, as his heel caught on the small notice that told him to keep off the grass, they tumbled backwards on to the slushy snow that still lay like flimsy lace on top of the lawn.

Neither was hurt; they fell like children, rolling uncontrollably, still clutching, and then laughing.

She said, 'Oh Arthur! Are you all right? What about your poorly back?'

'Very therapeutic to roll like this. I never do it because of getting back up again. So let's keep it up for a minute or two. Left . . . now right . . . how are you doing?'

'I'm fine,' she spluttered. 'But how on earth are we going to get up? I'm no good at it either!'

'I'm going to roll away from you and then think about it!'

He rolled and she stayed and lay there, concentrating on her breathing. There was some panting and grunting going on behind her head and then Arthur was standing above her, holding out his hands. He pulled her up as if she were a feather, then he dusted her down, adjusted her hat, tugged at the hem of her coat and told her she would 'do nicely'.

She said, 'I'm really sorry. I knew it was going to happen but I couldn't stop it.'

'It was my fault, May. I was caught up in my worst nightmare. Are you all right? Can you manage to get home? I promise that won't happen again.'

'I feel grand actually. Rolling around like that . . . couple of children again! I'm really thankful the Jeannies didn't hear us – nobody heard us, it seems.'

'And the grass was spongy. Almost springy.'

'Let me have a look at the back of your coat – oh, it's such a mess!'

'Yours is too. I'll take them both to the dry cleaners this afternoon. You'd better have a nap after your lunch.'

'I will. I will.'

They walked into the copse and admired the daffodils again, then across the first lawn and through the side gate. Jenner House loomed above them, somehow comforting.

He said, 'What were you going to say about Dr Jenner – you know, when he was a boy and went blackberrying?' They both stood, leaning against the park wall opposite their home.

'When he was just Edward, or Ted? I was only going to say that he could have had someone with him. A girl. A companion.'

'I suppose he could. Does it matter?'

'Only that it helps to make him real. A human being. Who might have . . . I don't know . . . had a child. Had a child who died young of the smallpox. And that was when he decided to find a vaccine.'

'Well . . . yes.'

'I can tell you think it's wrong. But what if he had stood here and looked across at the empty fields and said to himself, one day there will be a communal home built here and it will be named in memory of me.'

'He is allowed to have his own dreams, May. That's his business. But for you to suppose an affair and a child and whatever else you've got up your sleeve – don't you see, he's not here to refute any of that. He's not here to tell you to mind your own business. It's not . . . it's not *fair*, May!'

She looked at him, wide-eyed. Then she hugged his arm. 'Arthur, you're right. Of course you are! That's why I've kept my promise. Of course. I was keeping it for them, to protect them. And my mother made me promise for my own sake, not theirs at all! And they're gone. So I am not bound to keep it any longer! Oh, thank you, my dear. Thank you so much.'

He stared back, then smiled, understanding. 'You mean . . . you have a choice. To keep a secret or to share it.' He hugged her closer to his side. 'I feel the same, May. I've kept my secret – lied about it actually – because of shame. You know half of it already, my dear girl. Here's the other half. I was in the squadron that bombed Dresden. I took part in the revenge of Coventry. And you were there, May. You were there.'

She looked up at him. She could barely see him; her eyes were full of tears. So much she had shared with this man already. She blinked hard and nodded, still unable to speak.

And then they crossed the road and Arthur used his key to open the glass front doors. As they waited for the lift, Mrs Smithson opened the door of her flat and said, 'My goodness, you two are in a mess. Whatever have you been up to?'

May felt Arthur stiffen beside her and she had to say something; she had to protect Arthur. She turned and smiled blindingly at Mary Smithson.

'So many things have happened – I don't know where to start! Best not start at all. I know you can keep a secret, my dear. Not a word. All right?'

Mary Smithson was startled into silence. The lift sighed as it arrived and Arthur pulled at the fire door and they went inside. As it began to climb up to the second floor, they clutched each other again and laughed helplessly.

And then, without a word of warning, he kissed her.

Fifteen

After her mother left for work early on Wednesday morning, Daisy knew she was in for a depressing day. Marcus had made no mention of them getting together for their last bit of half-term and she wondered now whether their conversation at the top of the steps had meant they were going to cool things for a while. And after two strange but wonderful days together, and . . . that kiss . . . she surely had to give him some space now. Just in case he needed it. He knew where she was anyway. He could telephone or just turn up. But as she shoved her cereal bowl into the dishwasher, she knew he would do neither.

She stared out at the mess of muddy snow and past the garden, far out to where the sea must still be. The horizon was blurred. A pinprick in the mist meant that the lighthouse at Flat Holm was getting through. She watched it, screwing up her eyes then forcibly relaxing her whole face. Then she counted her breathing in time to the flashes. Neither technique worked. The jumble inside her head refused to recognize the enormity of the space outside and it certainly did not respond to the mundanity of clearing up the kitchen. Mummy had recommended both methods for sorting out a racing brain; Daisy thought wryly that she could have done with some help when confronted by that blessed gene pot.

However, it seemed she was stuck with what she'd got, so she grabbed her sketch pad and, after a few seconds hovering over a clean page with an HB, she started to draw.

She did it without thought but with infinite care. Caps, frilly ones and plain skullcaps; aprons, knitted stockings and wooden pattens. Then Red Riding Hood cloaks; a muff, goatskin leggings with twenty tiny buttons on each and – suddenly and unexpectedly, a button hook.

She was totally absorbed. The post plopped on to the floor of the upstairs hall, a police siren screamed, the dog next door barked furiously: she heard none of it. It was eleven thirty when she surfaced and she was drained of everything except an urgent desire for coffee and biscuits. And her mother had not bothered to hide the biscuit tin.

Half an hour later, sated physically, the turmoil began again and she opened her sketchbook and grabbed the pencil. This time nothing happened and, what was worse, her bonnets, aprons and cloaks looked meaningless. Just for a moment she considered ripping out the two pages and tearing them into stamp-sized pieces. It was the sort of thing you saw in films and read in books. She couldn't do it. With a little scream of self-disgust she closed the book and flung it across the table, which was better than just leaving it where it was to taunt her.

She walked around the house, right upstairs to her bedroom, which was a tip, across the landing to the spare room where their 'lodger' would be sleeping, down into the sitting room and the galley kitchen. It all looked slightly unkempt and just for a second she thought about fetching the duster and spray and polish. And then flung that idea across the table too.

She couldn't really believe that Daddy could have done this to her . . . been so underhand, so secretive. Kept it all to himself until after the aunties and their husbands and the two little ones had left and then just announced it. As if it was nothing at all.

The telephone began to ring in the lower hall and she nearly fell down the stairs in her anxiety to pick it up. It was bound to be Marcus.

It was Shirley Gray of the tulip-shaped skirt.

'Daisy. We're the same size so I made you a skirt. Don't worry if you don't like it. Just that I didn't have much to do over the weekend and I thought I was going mad so . . . Anyway, I'll bring it tomorrow so wear some tights.'

'But, omigod, that's so great of you. How absolutely bloody marvellous. What colour?'

'Red. I know your aunty will say it makes you look like a street woman – I can just hear her, can't you? – but it was the only spare fabric I'd got. Left over from those hot pants I did – d'you remember?'

'Yeah.' Daisy had no idea which hot pants. Shirley had lived in hot pants for a whole term.

'It's pretty sexy. Are . . . your people . . . funny like that?'

'Probably. But no. Not like you mean.'

'Good. Only, my dad says I might as well wear a large arrow inside my leg saying this way for you-know-what.'

'Your dad doesn't sound the most sensitive man in the world.'

'He's cool though.'

'OK.'

'Got to go. Things to do and so on. See you tomorrow, thank God.'

'Likewise.'

Daisy put the phone back and it fell on the floor. She actually lifted her foot to kick it and it rang again.

'Marc?'

'It's me. Mummy. I'm going to be late. Daddy just phoned. He's bringing the student home with him. Can you rustle up some kind of meal, darling? Fry those chicken breasts with vegetables and use the sauce at the back of the fridge—'

'I know, I know.' This was definitely the last straw. 'What time?'

'Not sure. Rush hour and so forth. But if you do rice . . . well, Daddy can take over. Are you all right with this?'

'What do you think?'

'Yes. I know. Didn't think it would be so soon. But of course, school tomorrow . . .'

She sounded awful, worse than Daisy felt.

'Listen, it'll be fine. Stop worrying. I'm just fetching the polish to go round the lounge and his room. Shirley rang. She's made me one of those tulip skirts and her dad reckons they're the sexiest thing on earth.'

'Lovely.' Mummy sounded resigned.

Daisy deliberately misheard. 'Me too,' she said and put the phone properly on to its rest. She stared at it and it still stayed put. She said loudly, 'Bollocks!' then went for the fridge.

The trouble was, Mummy had been brought up by foster parents who boasted about her in public, then, in private, told her she was a naughty, precocious little girl. 'They called me Marietta because it was the name of a heroine in a magazine story – you know, golden hair and gentle as a lamb – so they felt cheated there. And of course I was born argumentative, which was so antisocial in their circle. Useful for a lawyer though!' She had grinned about it but when Daisy flung her arms around that long elegant neck, she said, 'Darling, don't be upset – I met Daddy, remember. I could have married some awful men – nearly did – and then . . . I didn't.'

But that had simply made Daisy cry more.

Now she wished she had more of the strong, tough Marietta genes and fewer of the Nerrie ones. Daddy was so . . . soft! He could be talked into anything – Daisy knew because she had talked him into so many things. And out of so many things too. And if he'd come home and talked over all this lodger business first, she could probably have talked him out of it. But he'd kept them at arm's length for a whole week! How could he have *done* that?

She remembered last night with a sudden touch of guilt. It had been late of course, nine thirty when the people carrier had driven away, but normally that wouldn't have made a bit of difference. Last night was different. She was angry and refused to listen. 'I'm tired. I've had a busy day. Sorry.' And she'd gone upstairs as if she expected – perhaps hoped – that he would chase after her. And he had not done so. How *dared* he simply tell her that they would be having a nice young Indian boy for a few days and that she could make a real difference.

She went through to the utility room and fetched vegetables and began slicing viciously. Then frying. Oil. Chicken pieces. Veg. She couldn't find the sauce for ages and when she did it hissed in the pan and made smoke signals right up to the ceiling. 'Bollocks three times,' Daisy hissed back. She shovelled the lot into an iron pot and stuck it in the oven. Swilled hands perfunctorily and fetched cleaning materials.

'I'm nothing but a drudge,' she muttered as she set the timer. 'And when Daddy sees all this he's going to realize he can't arrange a marriage for me and make me a drudge for the rest of my life.' Then she remembered Marcus, who had been his mother's carer for so long. And she was at last ashamed.

The lodger's room looked good. She stood by the door and surveyed it with something like satisfaction. It gleamed. And it smelled good too. She glanced at the can of spray polish in her hand. Primrose Valley. Nice one. And yes, it did smell of primroses. On an impulse she turned to go outside and see if there were any early primroses she could pick; that would be a nice touch and perhaps offset the sheer pretentiousness of the Kafka book on the bedside table. She caught her toe in the cable of the vacuum cleaner and nearly went headlong and Aunty Mitzie's voice echoed eerily in her head – 'Too quick, Daisy Patek – too quick.'

She said aloud, 'OK. So no primroses. Water glass? And the Rupert Bear annual from 1940? Yeah. Definitely yeah.' She stepped delicately over the cable and across to her own room. 'All will be well,' she intoned to the empty house.

She went downstairs, opened the oven door and sniffed. Nice. It was two thirty and she really should eat something. Three hours since the biscuit binge. Amazingly, she wasn't hungry. She could go back upstairs and do the lounge. And perhaps tidy her own room. She went into the hall, seized the phone and picked out Miss Thorpe's number.

Miss Thorpe sounded a bit hyper herself.

'Of course it's not inconvenient, Daisy! It's . . . delightful! The icing on the cake, really. You don't have to have a reason for telephoning. If you simply said hello it would be a treat.' A pause and then she said in a different voice, 'But . . . is there something? Marcus's mother?'

'She's fine. It was great having lunch there yesterday.

And great of you to phone with news of the baby's name. I mean, it cannot be coincidental all the time, can it? The way that name keeps cropping up. Amy. I've been doodling away, hardly conscious of what I was doing – and discovered I'd drawn a whole page of caps and bonnets and cloaks . . . They're rubbish but they happened.'

'When was this?'

'I don't know . . . just before biscuits and coffee . . . ten thirty-ish.'

'That was when I fell over. Actually, that was just after my coffee and scone. How strange.'

'You fell over? Oh, May! Are you all right? Why didn't Aunty Vera phone me? I asked her to keep in touch—'

'Stop!' There was silence, then May's chuckle came over the airwaves. 'I fell on top of Arthur Wentworth. Not a scratch but plenty of snowy mud! We took a walk in the park. I kept thinking of Edward Jenner. And you were drawing his daughter's caps and cloaks. I know I must not assume that Amy Jenner was anything whatsoever to do with Edward Jenner – yet there we were, both assuming just that and at the same time. That is . . . *interesting*.'

Daisy felt her eyes popping. 'You fell on top of Arthur Wentworth? The chap who yelled at BC? In the park?'

'Exactly. It sounds bizarre, I know. But it's quite a good way of finding things out . . . We're friends now.'

'But, May – you can't be all right! You fell over, for Pete's sake!'

'I am fine – better than . . . before. Honestly. Now, tell me about yesterday first. Did you see the parish records?'

Daisy squeezed her eyes shut then opened them. She swallowed. Then, in quite a small voice, she told May about yesterday.

May was silent, digesting it. Then she said, 'I don't think we're going to find out anything more about Amy Jenner, Daisy. You see, if someone back then made a promise that they would keep her secret, and if they kept that promise, then we have to respect their secret and trust that no one was hurt by it.'

'Oh dear.' Daisy felt her body begin to relax into some kind of normality. 'I hear what you are saying. But . . . perhaps you and I could be allowed to think of her? Not to resurrect her or anything. Just . . . think of her.'

'Yes.'

But May sounded hesitant and Daisy knew that Arthur bloody Wentworth had got to her somehow. She could not bear to leave her like that so she blurted, 'Guess what? When we got back here after the vicarage and everything – oh, and he made loads of notes too – anyway . . . Marcus kissed me. Properly. He's never done it before.'

There was another silence, startled this time. Daisy wished to goodness she'd kept her big mouth shut. Somehow, in some way, she had shocked May Thorpe. She had thought May was unshockable. And she was not.

But then, a thread of a whisper said into her ear, 'That is the strangest thing of all, Daisy. I cannot tell you why, dear girl, but believe me. That is strange. And wonderful too. You and Marcus. You are meant to be. You are like brother and sister, friends, and now lovers.'

Daisy said hastily, 'May, it was just a kiss. Mummy came in then and anyway we wouldn't – Marcus wouldn't – he's sort of tied to his mother—'

'I know. It's difficult. But it's as it should be. You have to acknowledge your love. And you have to share it too, Daisy. You can do that. I promise you – you can do that.'

'Oh Miss Thorpe . . .' Daisy started to cry.

'Call me May. Please. And don't cry, Daisy. This is how it should be.'

Daisy wailed, 'I'm not sure – not sure,' but May had already replaced her receiver and Daisy knew it was because she too was crying.

She sat on the chair in the lower hall, dropped her head into her hands and howled like a wolf. Then deliberately recalled the words Steve Coles had used when he told them first about Miss Thorpe who lived in Jenner House and might welcome a visit from two people who were interested in her past.

'This woman went through the Coventry bombing as a child. When she had a spell in hospital before coming to Jenner House she was delirious. It was obvious that that time still haunted her. The hospital psychiatrist was satisfied that she had reached a stage where she could move on. Mrs Ballinger wonders whether that advice has made her . . . close up . . . even more. So . . . let her do the talking. If she doesn't want to speak of it, leave the whole thing.'

Daisy straightened her back and said into the empty hall, 'Well, it worked, Steve. For her as well as for us. Heaven alone knows what sort of probs you're coping with, but this one is going to be OK. This one is . . . your big success!'

She laughed and stood up and went upstairs again. The vacuum was still plugged in and she tore around the lounge with it and then used the rest of the spray polish on every-thing above floor level. The smell of primroses nearly knocked her out. She put the stuff away and began to lay the table for four. This was how it was going to be for a while. They could do it. The Pateks could do it.

*   *   *

She knew a moment of panic when Mummy rang again to check that everything was all right. 'Daddy phoned. They're on their way. Are you all right?'

'Sure am. The visitor's room looks great. Likewise the lounge. My room is fainting with surprise at being tidied. The chicken hotty-potty thing smells like heaven and—'

'Yes. But are *you* all right, honey pie? Can you face this?'

The panic began. 'What's to face?' She spoke jokingly but Mummy knew and started to placate her. She interrupted. 'God! They're here. The car . . . gotta go, Ma. Don't be long. Need you.'

She threw the phone on to the hook and it actually stayed in place. Good omen. She ran up to the top hall and flung open the door. Daddy was getting out of the car. He held up one hand in greeting and then threw her a kiss as he walked round to the passenger door and opened it. Someone got out. It was foggy but not dark and she could see him clearly. His duffle coat was ripped across the back and when he turned and looked at her she could see the bruises on his face. It was Zack. He had been beaten up. She couldn't believe her eyes. She stood, frozen, her face wide open.

Then she went to meet him.

'Oh Zack . . .' Tears poured down her face. 'What have they done to you?'

He was crying too. He went into her arms as naturally as her toddler cousins and she wrapped herself around him like the aunties always did with her when they came to supper. Daddy followed and wrapped himself around them both.

He said, 'Let it out, Zack.' And to Daisy he said, 'This is

the first time he has wept since he was found in the alley behind the fruit market.'

They both bent their heads over the black, henna-streaked hair. And then they went inside to the smells of chicken hotty-potty and primroses.

Sixteen

May spent Wednesday afternoon in her armchair, eyes closed, head back. Arthur had called for her coat after lunch. She had not expected to see him; he had quite suddenly stopped laughing as they came up in the lift, stared at her with bulging blue eyes as if he had never seen her before, then practically bolted when they reached Level 2. She had managed to hold the fire door and get through on to her landing and when she peered towards the staircase she saw just the back of his muddy coat disappearing into the end flat. She opened her door and went into the narrow hallway, closed the door with her back and leaned against it, put one hand over her mouth and spluttered with helpless laughter.

Her meal arrived half an hour later. It was cottage pie and pineapple upside-down pudding with a tiny carton of cream. Balanced precariously on the layers of tinfoil cartons was a single daffodil.

'Mr Wentworth sent this.' The dinner lady did not approve. 'He said to tell you he'll collect the dry cleaning about two o'clock if that's all right.'

'Absolutely fine.' May placed the cartons carefully on her tray, which already held cutlery and condiments.

'I told him I was not supposed to convey messages. I cannot

take responsibility, you see.' She paused and when May did not offer reassurance or apology she said, 'I'd be careful of that one if I was you. He's a regular ladies' man. Offered me a pound.'

May twinkled. 'Did you say thank you?'

'I did not take it, Miss Thorpe! I was brought up never to take presents from men. They never give freely, there's always something behind it.'

'Oh dear.' May was still twinkling. 'I wonder what he was after?'

'I don't know, I'm sure. It's usually a roll in the hay.'

'Ah. And a shortage of hay at the moment. You would have got frightfully muddy just rolling on the grass. The snow has turned to slush.'

The dinner lady followed May's gaze to the duffle coat spread over the radiator. Pink with embarrassment, she made her farewells. May put the daffodil into her glass of water and looked at it thoughtfully, no longer smiling. She had been enjoying the sense of 'moving on' but if Arthur was going to get hurt in some way, it wouldn't do.

She ate her lunch with relish; her particular roll in the mud had given her an appetite; so had the kiss. Afterwards she cleared away the cartons and her cutlery and put the offending duffle coat into a plastic bag and settled into her chair.

The phone rang.

Daisy said, 'I'm sorry if this is inconvenient, May. Is it inconvenient?'

'Of course it's not inconvenient.' Something wasn't quite right, Daisy sounded much too bright. She talked about Amy Jenner, then her sketches, then thanked May for phoning about Toby Marsh's choice of a name for his new baby. 'It's all so . . . I don't know . . . unpredictably predictable.'

'Do you mean coincidental?'

'More than that. The fact that it was a girl instead of a boy . . . unpredictable. Then that they chose Amy. Unpredictable. Yet, because we know what we know, very predictable.'

May laughed. But then she mentioned her fall and Daisy went flying over the top with anxiety. And then calmed down. And then May told her about the daffodils and the Village Vixens and Daisy remembered that Aunty Alison had been one of the original 'Vixens'. Other things were said and then May replaced the receiver and put her head back. She let herself flow. Perhaps this was the end; perhaps he was waiting for her and had been waiting all week. She would not prolong that wait longer. She let herself go. And then the bell rang and the blue lights flashed and it was Arthur for her coat. He looked all right.

She said, 'Oh Arthur . . .' Immediately he turned deep brick-red; she was aghast. She said, 'Please don't feel . . . awkward. Or . . . committed. Surely friends can exchange a kiss without—'

He cleared his throat so loudly she was afraid people would come to see what was wrong. She pulled him in and closed the door. Somehow she became jammed between him and the door; the hallway was ridiculously narrow.

She said, 'I do understand, Arthur. It's the others, isn't it? You don't want the Smithsons gossiping and after my stupid remark—'

He said strongly, 'Couldn't care less about the bloody Smithsons, May! It's you I care about. It wasn't a kiss between friends. It was me showing my real feelings towards you. Have I offended you, my dear?'

She looked at him, his face so close to hers, battered by ... so many things. Why on earth had she giggled foolishly? Now she wanted to cry. Tears were in her throat and nose. She swallowed fiercely, put her veined hands to his face and touched his lips with hers. Gently. But tenderly too.

He stood very still, hands by his side. She drew back and smiled at him, feeling her mouth tremble.

'You have not offended me, Arthur. How could I be offended by a loving, living kiss? We are connected. Because of the past which neither of us dares look at too closely, we are connected. Can we – shall we – take it from there? I do not know you very well and you do not know me ...'

'I know enough, May. I know you are special. Full of surprises. Please – please – come for a walk with me now and then.'

It was such a reasonable request and she smiled and nodded. 'Of course. That's what I meant.'

'It was rather good today, wasn't it? You felt it too?'

'I did. But perhaps we had better not roll in the mud next time. I'm afraid the dinner lady spotted my coat and I let her think the worst. I'm sorry, Arthur. It seemed ... funny. At the time.'

He grinned from ear to ear. 'That's what I meant about your unexpectedness. And that business with Mrs Smithson when we got into the lift. As if you wanted to shock the whole of Jenner House!'

'Actually, I think I did. And then it occurred to me that it might hurt you and I regretted it.'

'It might have done at one time. But ... if we're in it together, May, then ... I think it could be fun!'

'That's a word I didn't think you knew, Arthur Wentworth.'

'I didn't until now.' He looked at her in the dim light of the tiny hall and whispered, 'Oh May.'

She stared back into the faded blue eyes and for an instant saw Pilot Officer Wentworth, tall and slim, taut facial muscles holding back the terror of imminent death; not much hope so no future. And now, at this moment, he had hope and he had a future, however short it might be.

She cleared her throat. 'Will you take my coat now, Arthur? It's in that bag by the kitchen door.'

'Of course.' He moved away and she almost collapsed on to the floor. 'Will you come for another walk tomorrow? If we're going to set the place talking, we'll have to keep it up, you know.'

This was how he must have talked to the girls he danced with, the girls he might well have slept with, but who were now memories like Norman and Walter.

She said, 'You're right, my dear. After all, we have to move on.' She came to him and put her arms round him and the unwieldy plastic bag. She smiled so that her dimples were deep. 'It's going to be fun, my dear boy. It's bound to be short, so let us make it sweet.'

And they kissed again, the bag between them keeping them apart yet making them closer than ever.

Daisy thought she would never stop crying. Zack was almost as bad but then he had something rather personal to cry about. In the end, Daddy had to bundle them into the house all anyhow before someone sold tickets. He took them straight into the lounge, put them in separate armchairs and knelt down to light the fire. Zack's deep, shaking sobs began to subside but Daisy, bereft of two sets of arms, put her own hands to her face and let the tears slide through her fingers.

Daddy said, 'I'm going downstairs in a few moments to make some tea. I'll bring it to you and then leave you again so I can cook our meal. Does that sound good to you both?'

Zack made a sound that could have been a slurred 'Yessir'.

Daisy wailed through her hands, 'I've done chicken in sauce with lots of veg and it's in the oven – oh, how can we bear this? How can we *bear* this?'

Daddy, still on his knees, put a hand on her knee. 'If Zack can bear it, bubba, then so can we.' He squeezed gently. 'Thank you for making a meal. Would you like me to do some rice?'

'Ye-e-e-s, p-p-please.'

'And shall we have it in front of the fire? And you can watch the flames and they will become the Dancing Dervishes of Byzantium!'

Zack made another sound that could have been 'Yessir'.

Daisy again said, 'Ye-e-e-s, p-p-please.'

The flames licked from kindling to the small logs. 'See them? Can you see the Dancing Dervishes?'

Zack leaned forward and said clearly, 'Yes, sir! I can see them!'

Daddy put his spare hand on to Zack's head. 'I thought you agreed that you would call me Uncle Nerrie. Marcus calls me Uncle Nerrie.'

'Sorry.' Zack looked across to Daisy as if for permission. She moaned and covered her face again. One of his beautiful Kashmiri eyes was swollen half shut. He dropped his voice, 'If Daisy does not mind I would like to call you Uncle Nerrie at all times.'

Daisy tried to tell him she did not mind but it was difficult to say so many words in proper sequence and she ended on another wail. Daddy stood up, took her head in both hands and said quietly, 'Daisy, it was no one we know. Some hooligans who were drunk. They have been caught and most unfortunately bailed. That is why Zachariah will be staying for a while.' He bent down and kissed the top of her head. 'It is so good that you have made supper and tidied in here.'

She looked up. 'I thought – thought it was the Gorms . . . all my fault.' And then, reverting to a ten-year-old, she muttered something almost unintelligible about Zack's room.

'Then why don't you show Zack where it is? While I do the rice?' He turned to Zack and said, 'Is that all right with you?' Receiving a nod he reached to the top of the television set and handed Daisy a box of tissues. 'Zack could do with some of these. And possibly the bathroom. Can you manage?'

She took a handful of tissues and dragged them down her face. 'Yes,' she said without a single stammer.

The tour of the top part of the house was marked by staccato phrases like bullets fired into the air.

'Bathroom.' 'My room.' 'Your room.'

He looked at the bed. 'Oh Daisy! It's a Rupert annual! My amah had a Rupert Bear book – brilliant!' He ventured a look at her; she met it and pushed the sodden ball of tissues against her mouth. He said, 'It doesn't hurt now. Honestly. And the Gorms will be impressed.'

She removed the tissues and asked in anguish, 'How?'

'I'll tell them they ought to see the other chap!'

'Oh . . . *God*!'

'Daisy, please stop crying. I'm not crying now and I want to talk to you properly. I don't want to stay if it makes you cry all the time. Or if you feel uncomfortable about it. It's not your fault and—'

'Oh shut *up*! You crazy kid! Androgynous, for crying out loud! No wonder everyone picks on you – I told you what to do and the next thing I know . . . oh *God*!'

'Daisy, I did what you told me and it worked all right. And then . . . well, you know what happened then. And you know I'm in love with you and it was worth getting beaten up to come and live with you.'

She threw the damp paper ball across the pristine room and it fell with a wet plop on to the bed. Suddenly she felt unbearably weary. This stupid, stupid kid had no idea what was happening. If the 'hooligans' went to prison they would come out one day.

She said, 'Oh well. That makes everything all right, doesn't it?'

'It does for me. If it wasn't for being in love with you I would probably feel homesick and horrible. But I don't. We can go to school together tomorrow, can't we? Marcus won't mind?'

'Probably not. Is that your bag in the hall? D'you want to unpack and do the bathroom bit? I should help my father.'

'All right.' He accepted the bag she passed to him and put it on the bed. 'Will you be long?'

'Course not. Look. Come down with me and see the kitchen. It's where we are most of the time. Does it hurt to go up and down stairs?'

'No. It's all sore. And it feels funny. Specially my eye. And nose. And the ear. They can do a graft if I want it to look right but I thought it made me a proper Dennis the Menace. What do you think?'

She went ahead of him down the stairs so that he could not see she was crying again. She managed to articulate 'Yes.' Then she let him babble on about finding Dennis in a second-hand bookshop . . . That was when she wondered whether she could ever stop crying. Ever.

Of course, she did. She had her precious ten minutes with Daddy when he just held her and rocked her and said the words from two continents, mixing and matching them into layers of comfort. The tears subsided exhaustedly and she managed a little snigger as she told him that she had actually suspected him of trying to arrange a marriage for her.

'Crazy bubba! I could arrange a thousand marriages and Daisy Patek would still marry Marcus Budd.'

She was shocked, holding herself away to stare at him incredulously.

'What made you say that?'

He gave Daisy the enormous grin that nearly split his face in half and reminded her of a watermelon.

'Your mother prophesied it when you were at playschool.'

'Oh Daddy . . .' She wanted to drown in that grin; or even eat the watermelon. She said, 'He – he – sort of – like – asked me. On Monday. Near Rook's Wood.'

The grin settled into a smile. 'Darling, that is so . . . good.' He shook her shoulders gently. 'And this young Zack. I have wanted to tell you about him for some time. A very special boy. I have wanted him to come here and be with us occasionally. But then he seemed to be settling. How could I have guessed that by my shilly-shallying it would come to this . . . When I saw your face, bubba . . . I am sorry. It was a bad thing for me to do without warning.'

'No. No, it was not. I would have . . . I did . . . resent the whole idea.' Her eyes filled again. 'It's real life, Daddy. It is what you deal with. And I must deal with it too.' She forced a smile. 'Alison. And now Zack.'

He nodded, then turned her and tapped the seat of her jeans. 'Go back to him and let him talk. He likes to talk. I will bring supper upstairs in fifteen minutes precisely – check your watch.'

She did so. It was six thirty and only just light. She said, 'Will it be dark when Mummy drives home?'

'She said eight o'clock. We must see. Now go.'

He turned to the cooker and she went through into the hall and climbed the stairs slowly. They seemed steeper, so that she had to pull herself up by the handrail. She was thankful there was a lift in Jenner House. Perhaps this weekend she could take Zack to see Miss Thorpe . . . May. And she could tell him about Jenner House and Dr Edward Jenner. And, perhaps, Amy.

Seventeen

The very next day, which was 5 March, Mary Smithson managed to find an opportunity to cut May Thorpe stone dead. She must have seen Arthur Wentworth arming May out of the front door for their walk across the park, and made sure that on their return she was in the foyer reading the noticeboard. She turned, met May's gaze and immediately swept into her flat. May still thought it was funny; Arthur less so.

The next day, Friday, was fish-and-chip day in the lounge. Zoe joined Arthur and May at their table and handed two snaps to May. Little Amy Marsh featured in both, one in the arms of a very fair, attractive girl who was Eve Marsh and the other held rather gingerly by the now familiar figure of Toby. Somehow, probably because Toby had been misled about the sex of his new baby, May had forgotten her defensive anger with him last Sunday. She found her glasses in her bag and put them on.

'I can't usually see that babies resemble anyone, but Amy . . . my goodness, she is like her father.'

She leaned back in her chair. 'Shall I pass them round, Zoe? Mary dear, just look at these. Don't you think the baby looks very much like Toby Marsh?'

Mary Smithson did not know what to do with herself; she was desperate to see the photographs, but equally desperate to continue to ignore Miss Thorpe. Arthur Wentworth too, of course, but especially Miss Thorpe, who had duped the Smithsons into thinking she was a kindred spirit. She dithered for a vital second, long enough for May to say, 'Never mind then, pass them on round the table.'

Then, as she was practically forced to accept them, Mary swallowed visibly and said, 'Well, of course I'd love to see them!' She turned to her neighbour and presented a very cold shoulder to May as she said, 'What do you think, dear? This is Mr Marsh's new baby. I didn't know he already had a daughter, did you?' Zoe opened her eyes wide at May, who smiled and shook her head slightly. Arthur, who had been ready to wade in if May showed any sign of distress, remembered that this was all part of the peculiar game they were playing and went to find the tomato sauce.

The meal proceeded. Most people enjoyed fish and chips so practically everyone came to the Friday lunch. It gave them the opportunity to enquire informally about arrangements they might have missed over the tannoy or on the noticeboard and Zoe stood up twice, first to tell everyone that Roland Knight was still in the cottage hospital getting used to his new hip and would welcome visitors; secondly to remind them of the outing to the garden centre when they hoped to look at greenhouses. Small greenhouses.

People began to drift away; it was time for a nap. Others had coffee and went on chatting. The Smithsons invited one of the other couples for a cup of tea later; they dropped their voices on a last few words and the other two glanced nervously in the direction of May and Arthur.

Zoe said, 'What's going on?'

May pretended to misunderstand. 'Well, I've got Daisy popping in after school to introduce me to a little boy who is staying with her for a few days.'

Arthur said, 'I thought I'd have a game of snooker with the Reverend – he's booked the table.' There was an annexe off the lounge optimistically called the billiard room.

Zoe registered May's smile and Arthur's heightened complexion. She said, 'And Mary and Cyril are giving a little tea party in their flat so that they can spread the word further.' She turned to May. 'It's marvellous that you have come out of your shell but we cannot have a house divided against itself. Tell me your side of it.'

'You've heard the other side already?' May was amazed. 'We fell over on Wednesday and did not hurt ourselves, yet on Friday morning you know about it?'

'A possible accident was reported to me on Wednesday afternoon and since then I have waited – courteously – for you to tell me about it, May. Now I find it has become the subject of gossip. No, I can see you are not hurt, either of you, but you may well be if the residents take sides. Come on. What happened?'

Arthur said quickly, 'It was a joke. We fell over in the park, it was slushy and muddy, no harm done. But when Mary Smithson popped out of her door like a jack-in-the-box, we gave her the impression . . . we'd been . . . up to something.'

'They keep an eye on arrivals and departures,' May expanded. 'And it was me who started the rumour – non-rumour actually – not Arthur at all. All I said was that we could rely on her to keep our secret.'

Zoe looked from one to the other and then her shoulders dropped and she smiled. 'Actually, as far as I'm concerned, she did. It was the meals-on-wheels driver who reported that your outdoor things were covered in mud.' Her eyes settled on Arthur. 'She was annoyed with you for asking her to take a message to May; also a daffodil.' She sat back. 'Yes. I can see it's tickling the two of you to bits. But now that the Smithsons have decided to spread the word – it could be tricky. And I'm responsible for keeping a good atmosphere in Jenner House.'

'Dear lady, I do apologize if we have made your task more difficult—'

'It's all right, Arthur.' May wanted to kick him sharply under the table but she wasn't sure about his varicose veins. She smiled ruefully at Zoe. 'I will deal with it. I promise. I'm sorry Mary took it so personally – I've upset her and I didn't mean to do that. I'll apologize.'

Zoe stood up. 'Thanks, May.' She turned to Arthur. 'And thank you for getting May out and about again. Short walks are just what the doctor ordered – but keep her upright if possible!' She made for the kitchen.

May said, 'Funny how things turn sour on you. Don't worry, my dear, I can see you are hating it now. I won't do it again.'

He said, 'Whatever you do is all right with me. We could always elope.'

She said, 'Go and find the Reverend. And let him win.'

'That's a form of cheating, May.'

'Actually, it's called diplomacy.'

She made her way to the lift and then peeled off to flat number one and rang the bell.

She was strangely tired by the time Daisy arrived with Marcus and the visitor. He was the same size as Daisy and was probably beautiful like her but his face was disfigured by an enormous bruise that was half closing one eye. His mouth and nose did not seem in alignment either.

She held out her hand and he took it and shook it vigorously. May noticed the warmth of his. He looked like someone from a Mediterranean country.

She said formally, 'I'm pleased to meet you . . . ?'

'Zachariah. I'm usually called Zack.' He smiled and his mouth became a proper shape. 'Daisy calls me Dennis. Like Dennis the Menace in an old-fashioned comic book.'

Daisy said, 'You sit here and let Miss Thorpe get used to you. I'll make some tea – d'you mind, May? We've brought some biscuits. And some parsley seeds.' She settled both boys in chairs; May had put cushions on the footstool and was glad that Daisy assumed it was for her; Marcus would have had to fold himself painfully to sit so low.

She kept smiling as she thanked them and then enquired about Marcus's mother. Marcus still looked as he had on Tuesday: utterly content. As if he could see his future and had already settled into it. Daisy was doing the worrying for him; May could see it in the movement of her slight body as she came and went with plates. And there was extra tension now because of this battered boy. He had been beaten; or perhaps had an accident. May guessed the former, otherwise Daisy would have mentioned an accident when she telephoned. May noted the way she tucked a piece of kitchen paper under his chin; the way the boy looked up at her. He loved her. May closed her eyes for a moment. To receive love like that was . . . a responsibility.

Marcus said, 'We're getting on surprisingly well, actually. Uncle Ted is less bossy because Aunty Gert does it for him! And we've never taken much notice of Gert, so somehow

. . . it works!' He laughed. 'I've got a feeling about it. A good feeling. We're in a happy place, May. Zack knows what I mean, don't you?'

Zack nodded and the paper bib fell on to his lap; he stuffed it back quickly into the neck of his T-shirt.

Probably because of the hurly-burly of the fish-and-chip lunch and the business of the 'joke' – which had seemed to her no worse than laying a false trail in a paperchase – and then the feeling of ignominy when her apology to the Smithsons had been so graciously accepted, she was extra-tired. And because she was extra-tired she saw these three young people as fragile and unbearably vulnerable. She wanted to protect them, to keep them as they were here and now, to stop time.

Daisy said, 'May, are you all right? Have a sip of tea. I'll hold the mug . . . there you go. Now another.' She put the mug on the table and crouched, her arm around May's shoulder. 'Are there too many of us? Shall we go away and come back on Monday?'

The boy stood up. 'Is it because of me, Miss Thorpe? I'm all right now, honestly. I'm not frightened any more.'

May smiled and shook her head. 'I'm tired, that's all. And . . .' Her smile widened. 'For a moment I wanted to stop time. To hold it and look at it before it went on . . . and became something else.'

The boys were silent. Zack sat down hesitantly. Daisy exclaimed, 'I want to do that too! How amazing, May – honestly, I'm not making it up – lately, just since talking about Coventry and Dr Jenner and his beautiful girlfriend and then Amy Jenner . . . I've wanted to hold on to everything and really see what is happening!'

They looked into each other's eyes, so close, yet over

sixty years apart. Then May suddenly relaxed against Daisy's arm and shook her head as if surrendering to fate.

'We can't do anything about it, Daisy. Only savour each moment as best we can. The boys will think we've gone crazy.' She switched her gaze to them and decided that their blank faces masked anxiety. She said, 'I can hardly remember my dad but he had a great sense of fun. Always teasing Jack and Florrie and me. It drove Mum mad. He used to sing a hymn just to . . . what do you call it – wind her up? Yes. It did wind her up too. Would you like to hear it?' Daisy said yes, and the boys continued to look carefully blank.

May took a breath and sang in a reedy but steady soprano,

'Days and moments quickly flying
Blend the living with the dead;
Soon our bodies will be lying
Each within its narrow bed.'

She could barely hold the last note before bursting into a joyous laugh. 'Have you ever heard such a dirge? Mum used to yell at him to shut up and he would come behind her and swing her round and say things – they were naughty then, nothing now of course. And she would scream and say, "Not in front of the children!"' The laughter died. 'It must have been so bad for her without him. I didn't really understand. And then, of course, losing Jack. Losing him over and over again.' She looked again at Daisy. 'People die and we hold them in our hearts, peacefully. When things go wrong we talk of "losing" them, and we lose them constantly. We have to learn to let them stay quietly with us.'

Daisy's eyes were full of tears. She said, 'So much to learn and no proper study time.'

There was a silence and Marcus said gently, 'Drink your tea, May. You too, Daisy. Let's all drink our tea. I know, let's drink a toast. Come on – hold your mugs up like this. And now . . .' his voice changed sonorously, 'to my dad and Mr Thorpe. May they rest in peace.'

They drank. May said, 'My dad would love that!'

And Marc blinked and said, 'So would mine.'

And Daisy said, 'So would mine.'

Zack looked apprehensive. 'But he's not dead, Daisy!'

'He would still love it. I love it and I'm not dead or a dad!' She laughed and sat on the footstool. Her head was within an inch of May's hand. The small space was filled with a feeling of celebration. Marcus produced the parsley seeds.

'I don't know how true this is but I was reading an old magazine in the waiting room of the hospital and there were some gardening hints. It said that parsley seeds were notoriously difficult to germinate and one of the ways was to put them in the freezer for a day or two and then plant them in a pot and put the pot over a radiator so that the frozen outer case of the seed would expand quickly and break – a bit like a frozen water pipe. Shall we give it a try?'

May directed them to an eggcup and they shook some seeds into it and placed the cup in the fridge. 'The cress is through – have a look, Zack. On the tallboy over there.' They crowded round.

Daisy said, 'Didn't it amaze you finding something so – so – *relevant* in an out-of-date magazine in a strange hospital at a time like that?'

'Of course.'

'You didn't mention it before.'

'There were so many synchronicities, tiny things relating to other tiny things. The Amy Jenner thing, for instance.

That's taken up all our time.' He made a face at her. 'Actually the parsley thing was quite a comfort. Commonsensical.'

She hugged his arm and teased him about such a long word as synchrowhatever and how he must remember not to use it when he was wearing false teeth. May, watching and listening, felt that contact as if it were her arm. She remembered Jack saying, 'I can't go back. You're only a kid but you understand that better than Mum, don't you?' And she had nodded and hugged his arm to her side.

'So next Friday can we come and plant it?' Zack was loving it too; it was making him feel safe.

May nodded. 'Come whenever you like, Zack. I remember Dennis the Menace very well and with that poor face of yours at the moment, you look just like him! Make the most of it because it won't last!'

They laughed and Daisy poured more tea and opened some biscuits and eased out a handful.

May, looking at Zack's bruises, remembered that Jack had been beaten up several times and had decided to leave Coventry before his so-called friends and neighbours reported him to the Military Police. One of the barns out towards Stratford had received a direct hit and he had gone there, making a shelter in the middle of the rubble, living like an animal with a sheet of corrugated iron as a roof and a dustbin for a fire. Every night he used the ashes to douse the flames and put a lid on the bin so that not a glow could be seen by marauding planes. Every morning he rekindled the hot ash with papers Mum sent him and stuffed potatoes through the air holes he made with his bayonet. But the wardens had still seen the light of the flames on a foggy day. May had been with him as she so often was and he had crawled into the mass of broken, charred beams and piled bricks just in time and she had run towards the two men in their navy-blue uniform and babbled, 'It's only a bit of fun, sir! I found the ashbin and there were some mangolds lying about so I made a fire and cooked 'em. I was hungry, sir.'

And the air raid wardens had been so taken with her Shirley Temple curls and her red-raw hands, they had found a packet of chewing gum and given her a lovely minty piece of it. 'Better come along with us, my girl. And don't do it again. That fire might burst into flames tonight. It would be as good as a landing flare to a Messerschmitt! Come on now, don't dawdle. We got to get back. Folks seem to think that if they can't see each other through a fog, the Jerries can't see them! They'll not be bothering to put up their blackout – just you see!'

She came back to the present when she heard Daisy speaking two inches from her right ear.

'May, you haven't eaten a crumb! Would you prefer one of these?' She held aloft an unopened packet of plain biscuits.

May forced herself to concentrate. She smiled tightly and her dimples appeared. 'You want to get me on to yet another research project, don't you?'

'What do you mean?' Daisy was uncertain; May's eyes had been looking at another world. Was that why poor old Mr Wentworth worried about her?

But she was laughing now. 'Those were the biscuits we always had when I was young and lived in Coventry. They had a girl's name and Jack said they were named for Marie Antoinette.' May's laugh turned into a chuckle. 'I never knew whether he was teasing or serious. He said that the quote they always use was wrong. When the peasants told Marie Antoinette that the poor had no bread, she is supposed to have said, "Then let them eat cake." But Jack said the real quote was, "Then let them eat biscuits!" And that was why those biscuits were given her name!'

Marcus said, 'He was teasing of course.'

'I was never sure. Any more than we are sure that Amy Jenner is not connected to Edward Jenner.' She sobered and shook her head. 'Of course he was teasing.' She took a biscuit and stared at it. 'But true or not, these are the self-same biscuits we ate.' She took a small bite. 'And they taste the same too!'

Zack said, 'We have them sometimes at home. And we dip them into our tea.'

'Yes. We did that when the grown-ups couldn't see us.'

Daisy hoisted herself off the footstool and began to clear away the empty mugs. She glanced at Marcus and said, 'School started yesterday. And Steve is back. He didn't have swine flu after all.'

'Steve?' May frowned. She was still thinking of biscuits. She'd made a cocoa paste and sandwiched two of them together to make a chocolate biscuit and Mum had gone mad and accused her of wasting the butter and sugar. Dad had said, 'She's only nine, sweetie. And if war is declared there won't be much butter or sugar around to play with – let alone chocolate biscuits. I'll get some more on the way home from work tonight.'

'Steve Coles.' Daisy's voice was loud again. Anxious. 'He's our personal tutor and arranged the visits here.'

'Oh. Of course. And Mrs Arbuthnot is the librarian who is worried about his eating habits.'

Daisy smiled and looked relieved. 'She still says he looks thin. He was born thin.' She found a tin and put the biscuits into it. 'Don't forget these are here if you want something this evening.'

'No, I won't. Thank you all so much. Have a good weekend. Yes, I'm going for another walk tomorrow. Enjoyable. Most enjoyable. Of course you can ring me, Daisy. And give my regards to your parents. And to your mother, Marcus. And I hope you will enjoy living in the hills, Zack. You must go and see Amy Jenner's stone. See if there's anything the others might have missed. It's like being a detective and looking for clues.'

They saw themselves out and she put her head back again and thought she might take a nap before Arthur knocked to tell her how the snooker had gone. She was very tired. And Jack wanted to tell her something. It was something about looking after herself after he had gone. And she had wanted to tell him something too but instead she asked him where he was going and he said he had to find Dad. She was fourteen then and she remembered her bewilderment, her sheer naivety as she reminded him that Dad had died four years ago when he put his body between the shelter and the bombs. She started to cry and he held her close as he so often did and said he couldn't make it better, only worse.

She turned her head and tried to make her hand move to her face and mop up the present tears. She could not.

She called out, 'Jack! Jack! Don't do it – don't leave – Mum is ill – don't go—'

She must have reached him because the door clicked closed on someone and he was there bending over her chair, slipping his arm under her neck, lifting her slightly so that the tears ran down her cheeks and she could see him.

She whispered, 'Oh Jack . . . it's been a lifetime. I'm thankful it's over.'

And a voice, not Jack's, said grimly, 'It's not over yet. Not if I have anything to do with it. It's Toby Marsh here. And whether you like it or not, I'm your grandson. Apparently the image of your brother. I've spent a lot of time finding you, May. I'm not letting you go now.' His free hand was reaching round to pull the emergency cord and almost immediately the room was filled with static and he was telling Zoe to call an ambulance.

The last word she heard was 'pronto!'

It rhymed with bucking bronco. She had loved Western films. The physicality of them. No thoughts. Just actions.

Eighteen

On the way out of the building the three of them bumped into Aunty Vera, who was putting in extra hours to clean the cooker in the main kitchen. She had met Zack the evening before at the family supper and now embraced him fondly.

'I am Vera and not Mitzie,' she said, holding him from her and looking at his face searchingly. 'Mitzie is not as hard as you might think. Last night she said to me that she would like to get your persecutors in a dark alley when only she had a crowbar. But she seems hard. And I seem soft. Though I am not and I am very useful with a crowbar.'

Zack took the sting out of that garbled reminder of who was who by laughing delightedly. Daisy said sternly, 'That is the way to continue such behaviour, Aunty. Tit for tat. It is no good.'

Vera still addressed Zack. 'She is right. She is often right. And already you are looking very much better.'

Marcus chipped in. 'It's when he laughs. Everything becomes normal when he laughs. Daisy has done some sketches which show—'

'A pity that Daisy Patek does not use some of her spare time to help with the cleaning!' Aunty Vera announced but immediately put out one of her hands and took Daisy into the Zack-embrace. Then she leaned over the two dark heads to include Marcus. 'Have you heard that Mrs Ballinger has a boyfriend?' she whispered.

Daisy freed herself from the donkey jacket to say, 'No! Really?'

'He is a hair-cutter. He has a salon. Not a shop. A salon. And it was he who cut her hair.'

'I haven't seen it. We never see Mrs Ballinger. May calls her Zoe now.'

'Everyone calls her Zoe. Even the new boss.' Aunty Vera looked disapproving. 'It is better to say Mrs Ballinger. You should call Miss Thorpe "Miss Thorpe".'

Zack started giggling again and Vera obviously remembered he was almost inside her donkey jacket and gave a start.

'I have to get on. I cannot be talking to you children all day long. Tell my brother it is a good thing he is doing. His sisters are proud of him. And do not spend so long with Miss Thorpe, she is very frail.'

She was gone through the front door like a bulldozer and Daisy, laughing and waving, noticed that the venetian blind in the kitchen of flat number one was angled so that two pairs of glasses could be seen watching what was happening in the porch. On an impulse she blew a kiss towards the glasses and the slats of the blind were snapped shut. The three of them were laughing so much they almost bumped into another visitor who was just arriving and had his own front door key.

They had not met Toby Marsh, yet Daisy felt she knew him from somewhere.

*　　*　　*

Zoe held the door of her office and ushered Philip inside.

'Right. Now, you've seen my "workplace" – as you put it! And this is where I battle with the admin . . . though not so much now that they have appointed Mr Marsh. What do you think?'

'*Eccellente, signora!*' He swept in and sat at her desk, immediately twirling the chair round. He stopped it just before it dropped ignominiously almost to ground level. 'But it is not the building that makes a community, my lovely girl.' He slid from a so-called Italian accent into a Welsh one. 'It's the staff.' He rolled his eyes. 'I understand the manageress is having a torrid affair with the local barber! Is that quite the thing, d'you think?'

It was all a bit much for Zoe but she tried rolling her eyes too, even as her face, already hot, went into technicolour.

'I think your informant is exaggerating, m'sieur.' She looked at him seriously and even though there was the usual melting sensation in her chest, she said in her normal voice, 'This manageress would never have a torrid affair with anyone.'

He put his hands flat on her desk and looked at her. 'I was joking, Zoe. Sorry. I'm not very good at this.'

She had gone this far, she must go further. 'Actually, you sounded fairly practised just then.'

'And fairly sickening?'

She tightened her mouth and looked over her glasses humorously. 'Perhaps it was the mixture of Italian and Welsh. This manageress happens to know a hair stylist who is totally English and sports an excellent Gloucestershire accent.'

'Oh Zoe, I'm sorry. It was just . . . you know . . . going the rounds of the building . . . all so respectable and middle-class. And . . . I suppose I was scared it put you out of my league, so I tried to storm the citadel!'

She took off her glasses and smiled, then drew the visitor's chair forward and sat on it. Beneath the kneehole of the desk, their knees touched. She put her hands on the table so that their middle fingers also touched. The contacts were electrical and she moved away sharply.

He said quickly, 'Don't go . . . not any further.' She stayed very still; so did he. He said, 'How old are you, Zoe?'

'Forty-three.'

'I'm thirty-seven. Does that bother you?'

'Of course not. I thought you were younger, actually.'

He puffed a laugh. 'Was I going to be your toy boy?'

'Of course not!' she said again, though had she said something like that to May Thorpe? She could not remember.

'Then why not go in for the torrid affair? You told me your husband has remarried. I seemed to get on all right with your sister and her husband.'

'When my husband left me he took my confidence with him. That's why I've worked so hard with this place. It means everything to me.'

'Doesn't make sense. He took your confidence away? Yet you have made this place one of the most popular blocks of sheltered housing in the county. You had to have a bit of confidence to do that.'

She felt his right knee against her left one and her face flamed. She blurted, 'I couldn't have children. He said I was no good in bed.'

The knee was withdrawn but the hands reached over hers and held them warmly and he said, 'A-a-ah.'

She went on helplessly, 'You have obviously had relationships, Philip. I have not. He was my first and last love.'

She heard people outside the office. Had she locked the door? Sometimes Mary Smithson would burst in without knocking. She tried to withdraw her hands and could not.

He whispered, 'Give me a chance, Zoe. I think I love you. And I think you could love me. Sleeping together is like a crash course. We would know then if it might work – the whole love thing.'

She did not know what to think, do or say. He was outrageous. They had met two weeks ago and here he was proposing they went to bed together as a – a *crash* course? A crash course for the *love thing*?

The sounds outside gathered themselves together in an enormous laugh. She realized the voices were coming from the porch and she relaxed slightly. Construing this as encouragement, Philip's knee made contact again. She pulled back violently and almost tipped her chair into the filing cabinet behind her.

He said, 'Zoe – Zo – I'm sorry – don't go. Please! I should have told you that I have had four relationships, yes. And for a while one of them was very successful. But I could not afford then to offer marriage and someone else could. And we're now great friends! All of us. She jokes about her husband making her wear a chastity belt when I go to dinner—'

'For goodness' sake, Philip! *Shut up!*' She stood up. 'Every time you open your mouth you put your foot right into it! How could any of this endear me to you? A philanderer who wants no commitments, especially financial ones, meets independent older woman, earning good money, who also wants no commitments!' She shook her head. 'I'd be laughing if I didn't like you so much. As it is, I need you to go this very minute so that I can have a good cry then make myself a cup of tea and go to visit May Thorpe!'

232

Outside, the laughter was dying away. It had been Daisy Patek and her boyfriend. Oh God . . . they were so in love. May had told her about them. They were prepared to wait and work through enormous difficulties to be together. And they were seventeen. And she was forty-three and too old for all that.

He wasn't going to leave. He was standing too, holding out his hands and pleading with her to see him again, tomorrow, the next day, any time. There was something between them, something worth working at, surely she could see that?

She made for the door and he grabbed her and turned her into his chest and kissed her. And she let him. She tried to be unresponsive, to stand there like a zombie and let him see that her husband had been right and she really was a cold fish. She almost got there. And then he made a little sound against her mouth; it sounded like a sob; she stopped being unresponsive.

Heaven knew where it would have ended. She was literally saved by the bell from depths of passion she had not known could exist inside her middle-aged body. And the voice on the tannoy belonged to Toby Marsh. Toby Marsh of all people; the stereotypical successful young man, wife and two children. But strange. Definitely strange.

The speaker clicked in and his voice became very loud, filling the whole office, forcing them apart.

'Zoe, don't bother to pick up. It's Toby calling from May's flat. Ring for an ambulance double-quick. I know you're there, I saw you through the window. Hurry up – I think May's had a heart attack.'

Even as Zoe picked up the telephone, she wondered, horror-struck, how much Toby Marsh had seen through the window.

*   *   *

May woke up in a strange bed. She seemed to be propped almost into a sitting position and was wearing a Viyella nightdress with bits of lace at the cuffs. Probably at the neck too but she could not be bothered to investigate anything that required her to move her limbs or head. She felt relaxed, her body fluid, almost liquid, seeping into the pillows and mattress. She would have quite liked to open her eyes wide and see what was around her but she had a feeling her lids would not move, and anyway she was quite happy as she was.

Voices came close. Someone said, 'Will you have a drop of tea now, dearie? Nice and hot. Just like you make it at home.' A straw was pushed between her lips then clicked on her teeth; so . . . not a straw. A spout. One of those cups with a spout. The voice said, 'No? Not yet? You're almost there, dearie. Your eyes are moving behind your lids. You'll soon be back with us.' The spout was removed. May slept.

She became conscious of the soft Viyella again later. And then the same voice but not talking to her this time. The words ran together. They must have been comprehensible to someone because there was an answer, a protest, and suddenly, clearly, the words, 'If I leave it till tomorrow it might be too late,' followed by a regretful mumble and then another burst of proper speech. 'I'm her *grandson*, for God's sake!'

May slept again, but against her will this time. This was the second time someone had claimed to be her grandson. The first time, it had been Jack! What on earth was going on? Sleep pillowed her; it did not matter. Nothing really mattered now that Jack was near. Five minutes ago – perhaps ten – anyway, after the children had left her, she had rested her head against the back of her chair and waited to be taken to Jack; and it had happened. He was so close she could touch him if she wanted to. She would in a minute. She would lift her eyelids first and look at his dear face, and then she would put out a hand . . .

Just the thought of it brought a reaction. Through her sleep, she felt her face lift, making the tiniest of pops in both cheeks, and she had a bet with herself that the dimples were still there. She sank deeper into the mass of down that was nothing like normal bedding. It folded over her, under her, it was weightless and wonderful. There was not a pain in her body and in just a minute or two, perhaps three, she would wake and stand up and walk straight as an arrow to the bathroom. But then one of the voices became very loud. Strident.

'My God, she's smiling! Look – she's coming out of it!'

There was a bustle of movement, small puffs of air skimmed May's face and she felt her dimples shrink away. There was the rattle of curtains and then the voice said, 'Thank you. I won't stay long. I simply want to sit with her for a while. Be with her.'

Nothing more. She settled again like a bird in a nest. She thought of Zoe's haircut, beautifully layered, birds' feathers with the two points like wings on her cheeks . . . She must remember to tell her that a man who could give her a new face could possibly give her a new life. She thought of Daisy flapping like a fledgling, desperate to use the wings she had suddenly discovered. And Marcus, enclosing his mother in his wings, trying to stand in for his father, knowing instinctively that he could solve everything, do everything, with a steady flow of love.

And, as was usual lately, she came back to Jack. The

adored older brother – eight years older than she was – who had made her so proud by volunteering the moment Neville Chamberlain declared war . . . 'a state of war now exists' . . . and had come home from Catterick on embarkation leave in a uniform that was hairy and scratchy and much too big for him, and boots that were too small.

He had not turned up after Dunkirk. Dunkirk was a miracle, all those small boats going across to bring our beleaguered men home. But not all of them. Some of them were shot as they swam out to their rescuers, others were buried in the sand on the beach by bombs. She was told he had given his life for others. And he had; surely he had? Not then, not on those beaches. But later, when he had tracked down and killed her attacker, surely he had done that for her – for his sister?

Her father had died for her and Florrie and Mum; there was no doubt at all about that. He had heard the bomb as he came down the garden with a thermos of tea and he had thrown the tea ahead of him and simply spreadeagled himself across the mouth of the dugout. He could have jumped in behind the tea. But he understood about blast. About how it sucked the life out of people and animals. And he put his body between the blast and their bodies. And they lived and he did not.

He was a hero, there had never been any doubt about that. And Jack – yes, Jack her brother – he had been a hero too, she was certain of it. That time in the Home for Unmarried Mothers, she had worked it out that he was a hero because . . . because he had died. Did Mum think it was her fault that he had died? Was that why she made her promise . . . ? Did Mum think it was their fault that Dad had died? Were heroes and heroines acclaimed to assuage some kind of guilt?

How terrible it had been in the crypt of the church, with the urns and the shaking women . . . how Mum had shouted and she had cried . . . and then . . . and then . . . and then . . . the hero had arrived to rescue them. Jack. Alive. Almost well.

As if in response to that memory, she heard his voice. Not in her head; not from the past. She heard his voice almost next to her left ear.

'May. May, please come back to me. Please don't die.'

It did not make sense because, even through the wonderful relaxation, she had known she had to die to see Jack.

'May, you've been sleeping like this for three days. Where are you?'

She was confused: all she had to do was lift her eyelids, then she would know. She tried to concentrate. They moved a fraction and she could see the face two inches from her own. Very carefully, very slowly, she opened her mouth to make that first and last syllable.

'Jack.'

It emerged as a whisper but he heard and repeated the name and then added, 'Your brother.'

And she said something else, pursing her lips, pushing them forward.

'You.'

He could not understand. He thought she wanted tea and he struggled with the feeding cup and got nowhere. Her need for sleep was now overwhelming and he kept saying things. She repeated 'Jack' because he had seemed to understand the single syllable.

He was next to her ear again, speaking urgently.

'May, I want you to know. Just to acknowledge me. My mother wanted it so much . . . so much. Not for her sake –

she was happy – her adoptive parents were wonderful. She knew she was born in the Birmingham home. She knew you handed her over as soon as she was born and she grieved for you – she grieved terribly, May. She guessed what had happened – and that it had been hushed up. She wanted you to know that she was all right. And she wanted to know herself that you were all right. She could find no evidence that you were dead. And I could find no death certificate in the records. And then I did some work for the NHS. Pure coincidence. Statistics in a psychiatric hospital in the Midlands. Cases of post-war shock resulting in suppression and physical collapse. And there you were.'

May heard. The words came at her like pistol shots. They were entangled with the sounds of the pistol shots that had killed two people: 'the man' – the name popped up with the rebound of the pistol – 'George Hutchinson' – and . . . Jack. And she knew without a doubt that Jack no longer needed her to believe in his heroism. She wondered, almost idly, if that meant that her promise to her mother was null and void. Her secret was a secret no longer. And, after all, she had lived beyond the shame of it. She smiled into the face so close to her own and whispered the name he wanted to hear. 'Toby.' And then, in a wondering sort of way she added, 'Amy's son. May's grandson.'

She slept.

Toby stayed where he was for some time. He was exhausted; what with the new baby and May, he had had virtually no sleep since last Thursday. And now that dreadful wall of denial was down between May and himself, he could so easily have put his head next to hers on the pillow and gone to sleep.

He stood up slowly at last, stared down at her, noted the grey curls and the bone structure, small like a bird's, so like his mother's face. To his amazement, the skin over her cheekbones was already a mother-of-pearl pink; her whole body seemed more relaxed yet more present than on any of his visits. He leaned over her and ran his fingers through the curls so that they haloed her head.

He straightened again and with the same slow movements he took his chair back to the long corridor that linked the single wards. Daisy stood up and came towards him.

'Shouldn't you be at school?' he asked tritely.

'I am at school. No one knows I'm here. Not even Marc or Zack.' She had been crying again. 'Did she wake up? The sister thought she might be going to and then she didn't.'

'Well . . .' He was going to tell her, then did not. May must be the one to explain about this relationship. He smiled and began to feel better. 'She did and she didn't. She kept repeating her brother's name and he committed suicide back in forty-five. She wanted to go to him, Daisy. And then, quite suddenly, she seemed to focus on me. And she said my name. That's it. But I think she's turned a corner. I think she's going to be all right.'

She said, 'Oh God.' She swallowed hard. 'I'm going to go and look at her. Don't try to stop me.'

'I won't. I'll wait for you.'

'Don't. I have to go back to school before anyone notices . . . anything.'

She flew through the door of the ward, thrashed through the curtains and then stopped and stared. May was on her back, propped high; her hands were folded neatly on top of the sheet, her hair was a riot of curls and the beginning of a dimple was just visible. Daisy said, 'My God. You look good enough to eat.'

And May opened her eyes and deepened her smile and said, 'I've been asleep for ages apparently. Nobody told me to move on. So I didn't.'

Daisy was blubbering all over the place. She took the folded hands and unfolded them and put them to her face.

'They wouldn't let me see you. Only Mrs Ballinger and Mr Marsh were allowed in. May . . . did you love Jack like I love Marcus? You said something . . . I can't get it out of my head.'

May murmured, 'You are like brother and sister, friends, and now lovers.'

'That was it. You knew about it. You understood. Is that because . . . because . . . of your brother? Of Jack?'

'Darling Daisy. Jack is dead and I am alive. Just about.' She smiled. 'But yes, I understood. I understand that Marcus loves his mother in many ways. But he loves you in all ways. And I think Jack took my father's place and looked after me just as my dad would have done.'

'Oh May . . . bugger these damned tears. I don't want to upset you and here I am bawling all over the bloody place!'

'I understand that too. But you must go, dearest girl. I want to sleep again and I might snore and that would spoil everything for you.'

Daisy laughed but stood up, taking the hands with her, kissing them and then putting them back on the sheet. Then she turned and barged out as she had barged in, much too quickly. The ubiquitous Mr Marsh had gone and she was glad. She needed to let May's words settle into her head. May was telling her something; something about love. Something to do with the love Marcus had for his mother. And there was another need. She had to hurry. She had to use all her powers. She needed complete focus for this one.

She ran down the long village street and turned off into the row of cottages around the old lime kiln where Marcus lived.

Aunty Gert opened the door and blocked it unwelcomingly.

'Ted's back at work. Alison's gone for a nap. I'd just this minute put my feet up.'

Daisy was breathing heavily. 'Don't worry, everything is fine, Marcus is actually taking a history period with the first-years. I've been visiting May Thorpe in the cottage hospital and I've got a message for Alison.' She started off sounding heavily sarcastic, then suddenly changed, knowing what she had to do.

'Well . . . she's—' Aunty Gert, less aggressive, moved back slightly and Daisy was through and taking the stairs two at a time. Aunty Gert protested but not quickly enough. She closed the door resignedly and went to put the kettle on.

For some reason Daisy did not knock so she saw exactly what was happening the second she was in the room. She did not speak, she did not pause. The impetus of her small body carried her to the bed, knocked the water and the pills on to the floor, registered the ravaged, tear-streaked face and gathered it into her shoulder all in one movement.

Alison gave a cry, tried for an instant to fight off the intruder, then as Daisy's young arms proved unexpectedly strong, she surrendered to them.

Daisy held the thin shuddering shoulders of Marcus's mother, put her cheek against the faded blonde hair, remembered her when she had been Aunty Alison, the blonde bombshell who took her home with Marcus and said, 'You two are going to be friends all your lives, aren't you?' And when she stopped the awful moaning sound, Daisy was still weeping into the hair, quite unable to stop.

Alison put a hand up and drew down Daisy's head so that she was the comforter.

'Daisy . . . dear Daisy . . . I'm so sorry. But surely you understand? You of all people? Marcus must have his chance, darling. And just as your friend in Jenner House wants to go to her brother, Jack, so I want to go to my Stan.'

Daisy tore herself away and tried to speak coherently.

'May has lived for over sixty years without Jack – a good life – lots of laughs. And you have to live for Marcus – you wouldn't free him if – if you died . . . Not one bit. He would not be able to do anything much because of thinking of you . . . You have to go on till you're as old as Methuselah and you have to be happy! You *have* to be! Marcus loves you . . . he's trying to stand in for his dad . . . If you muck that up I – I – I'll *kill* you!'

She had used all her breath. She sucked in more, and then saw that Alison was . . . smiling. She was actually smiling.

She said gently, 'Oh Daisy. I love you.'

Nineteen

After Daisy had cleared up the mess, she went downstairs and offered to take Alison a cup of tea.

Aunty Gert actually smiled. 'That would be nice. Those stairs seem to get steeper every time I climb them!' She went into the kitchen and brought in a ready-laid tray. 'Will you have one with her?'

'No. But thank you.' There was a single daffodil in a glass on the tray and a cosy on the teapot. Aunty Gert was doing a good job.

'I could hear you two chattering away up there. She said to me the other day that you were like a daughter to her.'

Daisy took the tray, smiling but wondering how on earth the weeping and wailing could have been construed as chattering. She said, 'I'll see myself out – you try to have your nap. I'm sorry I practically broke into the house. It's just that May Thorpe has come out of her coma and I knew Aunty Alison would want to know.'

'That's good news. That will do her good.' She followed Daisy to the foot of the stairs. 'You youngsters, always dashing about . . .' She watched her go up as if she expected a fall at any minute and Daisy realized that aunties were the same the world over.

*   *   *

She put the tray on the bedside table but did not sit down again. Alison nodded and thanked her, then said, 'Daisy, I shouldn't have made you promise to keep this secret. If you need to tell Marcus . . . it's up to you.'

'OK. But I'll only do so under very special circumstances.' Daisy went to the window. 'You know those pills are meant to put you off alcohol?'

'Of course.'

'So you save them in case you need to do this sort of thing?' Daisy waved her hand vaguely.

'I suppose . . . yes. Listen – Daisy – I know I'm totally un-reliable but I also made a promise just now and I want more than anything to keep it. And if what you said about ruining Marcus's life . . . that was the reason, you see.'

'I know.' Daisy made a gesture through the window. Then she went on, 'It would be so easy if you took the pills properly. Presumably you would not then be able to look a bottle of vodka in the face. And then – also presumably – you would not want to commit suicide.'

She said the last words very deliberately and Alison winced.

'Yes. That's the general idea. The theory.'

Daisy swallowed but went on relentlessly. 'It's up to you to put the theory into practice, Alison. You can do it. Uncle Stan called you the blonde bombshell. You can do anything.'

Alison made a sound behind her. Daisy could hear her ragged breathing; she put a hand on the old-fashioned sash fastening and gripped it hard but still did not turn. At last Alison said, 'Yes. That was what he said. I didn't think any-one else remembered.' More breathing. Then, 'I was only . . . like I was . . . because of him, you see.'

Daisy squeezed her eyes shut and forced her voice to be steady. 'And now – and now – because of Marcus.' She tried to push her words physically across the room; to lay them across the bed for Alison to hear and see and touch. The sheer weight of love must surely make a mark in the duvet just as it had in her chest and her head these last days when she had recognized it, welcomed it, been terrified by it.

Alison did not speak. When Daisy turned at last, Alison was looking at the duvet as if she had never seen it before.

Daisy went to the door, praying her words had been true yet not cruel. She said, 'I have to go. I'm supposed to be at school.'

Alison looked up; her eyes were huge and very blue. She whispered, 'I don't know what to say, Daisy. I don't know if I can do it. But, thank you. Will you pop in? Just now and then?'

Daisy remembered her mother's outcry about their small, secure little trio. She felt unusually humble.

'Yes. I'd like that.' She met those wide blue eyes and remembered them full of laughter. She said, 'Thank you, Aunty Alison. For everything.'

And she was gone, leaping down the stairs and through the door and along the village street to the pub and past the pub to the school gates. She did not stop once. She took the short cut through the staff car park to the science block, where the glass doors were always unlocked in case of fire or explosion; Zack would be there, tidying the pipettes after a session of mixing chemicals, and for some reason she needed Zack. She rounded the last car – an elderly Triumph Stag owned by Steve Coles – saw that the doors were open already and crashed into the headmaster, who was standing just outside the block with a group of VIPs. Daisy recalled with horror that some people from the Min of Ed were coming to talk about extra funding for science. 'It will give us the status of a specialist school,' BC had announced proudly at the morning assembly. And here they were, having the specialist tour, undisturbed by the usual nuisance of eight hundred students. Until now.

She tried to spring back and then faint in front of them all. The only difficulty was, BC was supporting her with his arms, holding her up, then turning her towards a man in a suit with a waistcoat. A waistcoat. She thought she really was going to faint, especially as BC was now chuckling. She had never heard the headmaster laugh in the whole seven years she had been at this school.

He spoke humorously above her head. 'Now – as usual completely unexpectedly – here is one of our art students, Daisy Patek. She will soon be sitting her A-levels: art, of course, with history and sociology. She is one of the group we were speaking of at lunch.' He addressed the waistcoat. 'I believe you called it living history.' Then he looked down at Daisy almost fondly and said, 'This young lady has done sterling work with some of the older community members – what is the name of the sheltered housing block, Daisy?'

Block? She said very clearly, 'The house is called Jenner House. After Dr Edward Jenner who lived in Berkeley and refined a vaccine from cow pox in the seventeen hundreds and might have had a daughter called Amy who is buried—'

'Absolutely. Thank you, Daisy.' He kept smiling. 'I expect you are looking for your young protégé. We spoke of him too. The labs are closed just for this afternoon and Mrs Arbuthnot is showing his group the intricacies of the school library. Off you go. And no more running, if you please.'

'No. Sir.' She slid sideways and then round the Triumph

Stag and walked sedately along the drive to the main entrance and into the reception area. She glanced at her watch; three thirty. The school day was coming to an end and usually at this time the office staff were packing up and dealing with the younger children who had lost their PE kit, bus passes, bicycles and sanity. Teachers would be making their way to the staff room, loaded with books and hung about with children who had lost their timetables and did not know what was happening. Today was different. The school hummed with life; it was still full, but there were no sounds of running feet or raised voices; the office staff were still working, undisturbed; the armchairs grouped around a coffee table were in their right places; nobody was making an early exit; in fact the large light area was empty except for someone at the double doors which led to the teaching areas – Shirley Gray stood there speaking to Aunty Mitzie. Daisy paused and took it in; it was surreal. And all because of some men wearing waistcoats.

Shirley saw her and came over. 'Listen, I've got to go. Piano lesson. I've finished your skirt – was going to give it to your aunty but here it is. Try it on. Bring it back for alterations if necessary. How was your old girl?'

'Better, I think. Not sure. Oh God, Shirley, thank you for this.' She took the bag being thrust at her and held it against her like a lifebelt. 'I need this – I really do.'

Shirley looked surprised. 'Going somewhere nice?'

Daisy thought of home, Mum and Dad, and now Zack too. She nodded vigorously. Shirley said she had to fly and she flew. Daisy made her way slowly to the library and got there just as the buzzer sounded for the end of the school day. The library doors opened and children filed out in an orderly line, not talking. At the end of the line was Mr Coles

247

walking alongside Zack. They both hung back when they saw Daisy.

She grinned. 'My aunty Mitzie would like school to be like this every day.' She felt the world beginning to settle around her again. She hugged the plastic bag containing her new skirt and said, 'Come on, Jack. Time to go home.'

Zack grinned back. 'Is that my new name? Do I get a different one every week?'

Only then did she realize her mistake and file it away to tell Marcus. She wished she could tell him everything about this afternoon.

'Perhaps you do. Not a bad idea. Let's make tracks.' She looked at Steve Coles, smiling in the background. 'You OK now, sir?'

He raised his eyebrows incredulously; he had been 'Steve' to the sixth form ever since his arrival. He nodded and turned to go back into the library. 'See you and Marcus tomorrow, Daisy. I need a report on your visits to Jenner House. Typed, please. Your handwriting is confusing at times.'

'I know.' She should have felt gloomy; there went her evening. But she wanted to write it all down, before she forgot. And she did not want to think about Alison and grief; not all the time. She wanted to try on the tulip skirt and prance around the kitchen so that Mummy and Daddy laughed and Zack said she was beautiful. Of course, she did not believe him but it was nice to hear.

They waited by the school gates for Marcus to appear, then she told them both about May's sudden revival.

'It could have been just a – a – thing. You know, like bobbing up out of the water and then going under. I don't mean that, either. I just mean it might not last. It was after Toby Marsh went in to see her – he's the new accountant chap at Jenner

House. She wasn't allowed visitors and he got in by telling the sister he was her grandson! So I just barged in when no one was around except him . . . She was sitting up and she just smiled like she does. And she talked . . .' Daisy knew she would cry if she went on so she shut up abruptly.

Marcus said comfortably, 'That's good then. She might be better still tomorrow. I'll go in this time.'

'Oh, would you? I have to see Steve. He wants something in writing about the project generally. I want to do it properly. To show it stopped being a project . . . you know.'

Zack said, 'Can I do a bit too? I liked going there.'

They wandered down the long village street, talking randomly, irrelevantly, sometimes nonsensically. Daisy mentioned that she had dropped in to see Alison and rather liked Aunty Gertie and Zack wondered why Gertrude was shortened to Gertie and not Rude. And they giggled helplessly.

May slept and woke several times that evening. She knew that time was passing even when she slept. It was different from before, when Jack had been there but just out of reach. Then there had been no time; she had been shocked when she learned that two days had simply disappeared. Now, she could close her eyes when she wanted to, fall into sleep – or, as Arthur would say, into the arms of Morpheus – and wake up to sip tea from the spout of a feeding cup and smile at the nurse.

A grey light was filtering through the window when she opened her eyes next, and there were sounds of activity outside her door. She would have reached for her watch and her glasses except it would have meant moving her arm. She waited and while she waited she closed her eyes and – strangely – thought of Norman. How strong Norman had been as he slid awkwardly, painfully, towards death. A paradox: he got stronger as he got weaker. She had been fortunate, so very fortunate, to have known Norman. And then, in real old age, to have met Arthur, who was an old buffer, sometimes a bore, but who had seen something in the decrepit old woman on Level 2 and had got through her isolation somehow and made himself known. Friendship, then the unexpected tenderness of compassion and then the warmth of love. The warmth, the safety, the wonder of love. She felt her eyelids flutter as she came up from sleep and recognized that she loved Arthur Wentworth.

A voice said, 'Could you manage a cup of tea, Miss Thorpe?' And she smiled and nodded before she even opened her eyes. She wanted a cup of tea more than she had wanted one for years. And, for some peculiar reason, she appreciated being called Miss Thorpe instead of May. Just now and then . . . now and then.

She slept; woke for the bedpan and gentle wash, slept again. Woke for chicken soup sipped from another feeding cup and knew it was afternoon. There was a rhythm to sleep, she had noticed it before; rather like the old-fashioned swing boats at the fair but in slow motion. Up, up and up towards the sun, then the graceful glide down, the profundity of momentum as the boat continued into sleep then rose again towards the moon.

The voice said, 'Are you awake, May? He's come back.'

May's eyes opened of their own accord yet as if she was in charge of them again. Another paradox. 'Who?' she queried.

'That grandson of yours. Makes such a point of it. He's very proud of being your grandson, isn't he?'

She smiled and nodded. Grandson. It was a wonderful word. 'Grand'. And then 'son'. She waited.

Toby Marsh came in uncertainly. Almost apprehensively. His usual confidence had disappeared completely and she could see now why she had mistaken him for Jack. His sandy hair, blue eyes and round face were similar, but then lots of men had similar features. It was just that occasionally she had caught a glimpse of that uncertainty. And now it had deepened. And Jack had lived with fear the whole four years she had really known him. When she had run – every day – into the fields and woods around the wounded city with Mum's old hessian bag full of scraps, she had taken on some of that fear. She had held him tightly to her and told him it would be all right once the war was over. They could go to Scotland . . . Florrie would look after Mum . . . They could build a house and live there all their lives. But he had still been frightened. Consumed by fear.

Toby Marsh said, 'May. You look good. How do you feel?'

'Better.'

He had messages from everyone: Zoe and Arthur, the Smithsons, Aunty Vera.

She said, 'Aunty Vera?'

'The cleaner. She just said Aunty Vera.'

'I know. Daisy's aunty. Toby, I must see Arthur. I have to tell him how strong he is. He doesn't know, you see.'

Toby looked surprised; then nodded.

She said, 'I have to tell you something too, my dear.' She paused, taking shallow breaths, closing her eyes for a moment. He started forward and her eyes opened. He stopped. She said, 'I made a promise to my mother to keep . . . certain things . . . secret. I have honoured that promise until now.' She smiled at him; a brilliant smile that made

him blink. 'You released me from that promise. In fact you –
sort of – like – cancelled it.' She heard her own words, Daisy
words, and giggled, then visibly sobered and said, 'I want to
thank you, Toby. I want you to know I am . . . so proud of
you. Your love for your mother is – is – a wonderful thing.
And you are sharing it.' She firmed her mouth against tears
and nodded fiercely. 'I had no right to love her. I had no
expectation – ever – that she might love me. But you said
she grieved for me. And now I can grieve for her. That too
is a wonderful thing. I can grieve for Jack too.' She moved
her hand towards his and he picked it up and held it. She
nodded again. 'Thank you, Toby Marsh.'

Her eyes were already closing. He leaned forward as if
to say something. But then thought better of it. Instead he
did what Daisy had done; he put her hand to his cheek and
waited for her to sleep.

Twenty

Later, at Daddy's suggestion, Daisy phoned Stephen Coles at his home and asked for an extension for her report.

'The thing is, Steve, so much has happened and I am probably, like, going into irrelevant details so far as the Coventry bombing is concerned. But everything seems to hang on everything else.'

His voice was very slightly slurred and she wondered for a dreadful moment whether his illness was something akin to Alison's. Then he cleared his throat and was all right.

He said, 'I had a talk with Marcus this afternoon. After you had disappeared and before I took the youngsters out of the science block.' He gave her a moment to take this in and then went on, 'He filled me in with a few details. I think you should take tomorrow off, Daisy. Stay in bed and sleep for as long as you can and then, if you feel up to it, get your laptop on to the duvet and let fly. If you like, I will have a go at editing it before Mr Carter sees it.' He sighed. 'He is suddenly very interested in the Jenner House contact.'

'Yes. I picked that up while he was hanging on to me this afternoon.'

'Hanging on to you?'

'I nearly knocked him over when I was running. I ran.

Aunty Mitzie says I am always rushing about and she must
be right because I crashed into him and I tried to bounce off
and then faint but he held me up.'

He said slowly, 'Daisy, you sound hyper. I really do
recommend a day in bed. If you are sickening for the sort of
virus I've had, you'll need it.' He paused then added, 'May I
speak to your father?'

She was relieved. It was hard work to talk. He spoke to
Daddy and Daddy spoke to Mummy and the next thing she
knew she was being undressed as if she were seven instead
of seventeen. She hardly noticed being tucked up under
her duvet because she was already sinking into the most
marvellous sleep. She was very much reminded of the old
Barton Fair in Gloucester when she had sat on Daddy's lap
opposite Mummy in one of the red-and-blue painted swing
boats and soared up towards the early stars. She was conscious of Zack leaning over her and saying, 'Are you going to
be all right?' She smiled and he went away.

The next day she woke to an intensely blue sky filling the sky-
light above her bed. She felt luxuriously relaxed. The house
was silent and smelled empty. She closed her eyes again and
waited for sleep to return but it did not. Her toes started to
twitch; she rolled over and looked at the clock. Big hand
on twelve, little hand on nine and a sheet of paper propped
against a glass of water and covered in Mummy's spidery
handwriting. She struggled into a reclining position, picked
it up and began to decipher it.

'Darling D., Taken Z to school, back shortly. Working from
home. Out of biscuits so coming home via shops. Plan on
lots of orange juice with above-mentioned biscuits. You are
allowed trip to bathroom if necessary but not downstairs. If

you are hungry eat this note. Then go back to sleep. Your very loving but totally inadequate . . . Mummy.'

Daisy slid back down into the shape she had made over-night, put the note to her cheek and fell asleep.

Marcus arrived not long after Mummy but he wasn't staying. Aunty Gert was going to the dentist and he was taking over until the afternoon.

'Steve Coles told me what was happening with you and suggested we do our reports separately – more interesting that way.' He was sitting on the end of her bed, leaning forward, elbows on long legs, hands dangling between.

He said, 'You failed to mention that you had dropped in to see Ma on your way back from the cottage hospital.'

She stopped munching her way through the custard creams.

'There was so much to catch up on . . . the business with BC was, like, hilarious, really, and then Zack's theory that Mrs Arbuthnot was in love with Steve Coles – we didn't stop laughing really. Did we?'

'Don't be embarrassed – not you, Daisy!' He grinned. 'You didn't forget – you thought I might resent you dropping in unannounced! For goodness' sake, woman, it's two thousand and nine! You've been in and out of my house since you were three! And now you're shy?' He put on a strange face which Daisy knew was a ghastly parody of how he perceived her. She resumed pillaging the biscuit tin and grinned.

He said, 'Daisy – thanks. She was pretty low again. Aunty Gert said she hadn't eaten any lunch. Didn't want to get up. And then you roared in and she came downstairs – dressed – and the three of us had tea and toast and I told them about you barging into the VIP brigade and she couldn't stop laughing . . . Thanks, kiddo.'

'Kiddo?'

'One of the names Dad had for Mum. Kiddo. They were good friends, Daisy.'

She said, 'She's still got a good friend. You should call her Kiddo, now and then.'

He looked at her and she looked back. She started to speak and then stopped and bit her bottom lip.

He said, 'She told me, Dais. We talked and I cried and she didn't. It hasn't been that way round for a long time. Thank you again, Kiddo.' Then he nodded and was gone.

Her mother removed the biscuit tin and replaced it with the laptop.

At one o'clock they both stopped work. Daisy showered and dressed while her mother 'fiddled in the kitchen'. They shared a large tin of tomato soup with toast and cheese. Then they went to the upstairs sitting room, lit the fire and Daisy resumed work while her mother went back to the study. It was amazingly peaceful. As she typed, there were times when she became May Thorpe and could describe her gymslip with its big flat pleats falling from a braided yoke and the woven strip that was the belt and had to be fastened like a necktie.

At four o'clock Steve Coles parked outside the front door and Zack got out. Daisy opened the door before the car moved off.

'Can you wait, Steve? I just need to print out my stuff and you can take it with you.'

Zack said, 'You're better!' His face lifted. 'Good,' he added contentedly.

'I wasn't ill, Zack-Jack, just tired.'

Steve got out of the car grumbling ferociously. 'Can't have a few days off with a deadly virus without everything going pear-shaped. Make it snappy, I've got a home to go to.' He came into the front hall and his face changed. 'Oh, sorry, Mrs Patek. Didn't realize . . .'

'Come on downstairs, Steve. And the name is Etta. Have some tea while I thank you for putting up with my daughter and she prints out her work.' She was already on her way and Steve followed willy-nilly.

Daisy turned to Zack. 'That's how she does it. Sweeps all before her. I seem to be missing that particular gene.'

She explained about the gene pot while she fitted paper into the printer and set it going. He nodded sagely. 'My sisters have that gene too. And I expect that's why I'm androgynous.'

'You are *not* androgynous, Zack! You are outrageous. That's your strong gene.' She considered him across the room. 'It's what makes you special. But watch it carefully. I've got a feeling it might have been why those idiots beat you up. We'll work on it. OK?'

He looked soppy. 'OK, Daisy.'

She shuffled her papers into a tidy sheaf and found a paper clip and a big envelope. They went downstairs.

Later, after supper, when the two of them were washing up while Mummy sipped coffee and told them where they were going wrong, Zack referred to what he called the 'book love affair' between Steve Coles and Mrs Arbuthnot.

'I watched them yesterday when the VIPs were dumbing everything right down and I reckon it only happens in the library. It's not that they're soppy about each other,' he said, frowning prodigiously and drying the same plate twice. 'It's that they are soppy about books.'

'Are we talking about Mrs Arbuthnot's maternal concern for Steve Coles?' Daisy tried to sound austere.

'I suppose so. She wasn't very nice about his wife.'

'No. But it has to be a maternal feeling. She's about twenty years older than Steve.'

'Twenty years?' He stopped drying completely.

Mummy said, 'Actually, she is fifty-one and he is forty-six. I make that five years.'

'Too many years.' Daisy gave her mother a meaningful look.

'No, it's not.' Zack started drying again. 'There's five years between you and me.'

'Mummy, for goodness' sake, how do you know their ages? You're guessing!'

'You're right as usual, Crazy Daisy!' Mummy was spluttering into her tea, then snapped out of it. 'That's my phone. It'll be Daddy.' She fished in her briefcase. 'Hello, Nerrie . . . yes, missing you madly too. How's it going?' She got up and wandered to the back door and stood looking out across the dark garden to the intermittent flash of the lighthouse on Flat Holm Island.

Out of the blue Zack said, 'When my dad got the job in Gloucester, he was so happy. And he wrote to the Commission for Equalities to ask about schools and housing and he was happier still when he met your father. The school . . . and the school bus. And places for my sisters at Robin's Wood. And now . . . I am worried that he will wish to move again, Daisy.'

'It was just rotten luck, Zack.' Daisy dried her hands and took the tea towel from him to hang on the rail. 'The wrong place at the wrong time. It won't happen again.'

'But my mother . . . she does not believe that. And my parents are like yours – they are peas in one pod.'

'Ah.' Daisy glanced over at her mother's back. It was slightly bent as if protecting a very precious privacy. 'When you go home, you should call a meeting. A proper meeting. All five of you. And each one should produce an argument. For or against the motion.'

'My sisters are very young. They love living where we live but that's all they could say.'

'It wouldn't matter. But are you sure they couldn't give reasons? Robin's Wood is a very old hill – the only hill in the city – and very beautiful.'

'It has a dry ski run,' he offered.

'I wasn't actually thinking . . . but yes, that's a very good reason.'

'There are blackberries in the summer.'

'You've got the idea, Zack. What about your reasons?'

'You. And the school. Marcus. Mr Coles. Larry the Lamb.'

'What was that last one?'

'Don't you remember? The boy who sits at my table for lunch? You told him his nickname was Larry the Lamb. He loves it.'

She opened her eyes wide with incredulity and then clicked her fingers. 'That's the answer, Zack! Larry the Lamb will be your bodyguard! In fact, as from tomorrow, he will be your best friend.'

'But he likes boxing and hanging upside down on the bars.'

'And he didn't get any of yesterday's library talks, did he? And you already knew your way around the shelves. He needs you, Zack.'

'Does he?' Zack sounded very doubtful. 'When I learned the "Brave new world" speech for English, he called me a bloody queer.'

'That's because he knows he needs you. He might fight it for a while. I'll have a word with him. Explain how these things work.'

Zack frowned, then said, 'OK. But . . .'

'Don't worry about it. I'll wear my new tulip skirt tomorrow and he'll be eating out of your hand on Thursday morning.' She grinned at him and after a moment he grinned back.

Mummy pocketed her phone. 'Those two boys have been re-arrested and refused bail, Zack. You could go home, if you like.' She saw his expression and said, 'Not if you'd rather stay of course.'

'May I?' He looked at Daisy. 'I might be able to see Miss Thorpe later on in the week. Perhaps?'

'If she's up to it.'

Mummy pulled the blind over the door and stood with her back to the radiator, warming herself. 'That's settled then. Finish this week and see how you feel. Now, an hour's television while I do some work? Then bed.'

She went upstairs and built up the fire in the sitting room; Daisy gave the biscuit tin to Zack and took the fruit bowl herself. When Mummy left them to it, the biscuit tin went with her. Daisy looked at the fruit bowl with disgust but managed two bananas and an orange.

The next day, at two o'clock promptly, Arthur Wentworth was allowed into the single ward off the long corridor in the cottage hospital. May was propped up again but had slipped a little and was trying to push herself upright. He rushed to her, helped her expertly, reached over her head to plump the top pillow then settled her into it carefully. His eyes, four inches from hers, were full of tears.

He said, 'Oh May. Thank God. Thank *God*.'

She blinked and said without preamble, 'Arthur Went-worth, I love you.'

His tears ran down her cheeks. He said, 'Oh May. Oh May.'

'You know what I know, Arthur, you have survived. You are strong. And I must be too because I am still here.'

He whispered hoarsely, 'I have been looking for you all my life. And now . . . now . . . thank God, May.'

She moved her head into his shoulder so that she could look at him. It came to her that they were going to have a future together. It might not be a long one but it would last until one of them died. They would be married. And weren't there certain promises made in the marriage service that superseded all other promises?

She whispered, 'Lie on the bed, Arthur. I have to tell you some . . . things.'

It took time to settle themselves. She moved over to the edge of the mattress and he tried to keep his brogues off the sheet as he gathered her to him and she wrapped her arms around him. At last they were comfortable. They rested for a while and then she began.

She spoke of Dunkirk, when Jack was reported missing. She described the Anderson shelter in the garden; her father's heroic leap to cover the entry. Then the crypt of the church, full of shocked people drinking tea, her mother's outburst, Jack's appearance. The return of the hero. The wonder of it. Except that it had to be kept very quiet because Jack was not going back. He could not face it. And he became – 'sort of, like' – a fugitive.

She fell asleep then, in the middle of a sentence, woke after ten minutes and picked up exactly where she had left off. He shifted the arm that was beneath her head, kissed her curls, wept and whispered again and again, 'Oh my God . . .'

She told him about Florrie and her plans for moving them all down to the house in Devon. She whispered, 'Florrie and Bert and the baby . . . they were in that train crash – do you remember it, Arthur? The fourteenth of June, nineteen forty-six. I remember it because of Mum. They came for Mum's funeral and caught the midday train from Birmingham to Exeter. It was derailed at Cheltenham. Six people were killed and others injured. After the casualty lists coming back from the Far East, it wasn't made much of, really. It was so long ago. I would probably have lived with them. Florrie and I got on well. She was a good person and she needed me at that time. There was a place for me.' She sighed deeply. 'Anyway, her inheritance from Great-aunt Florence came to me and I sold the house and went on working for Walter Partridge. And then I left and worked for Norman Gorridge . . . I began to feel happy. It was easy to keep my promise to Mum. In fact I never thought of it. I never realized I was suppressing anything at all! Until Norman died and I went into hospital for the first time.'

Arthur whispered, hardly daring to interrupt her, 'What was the promise, May? Was it so awful?'

'Not in this day and age – not then, really. Lots of girls had babies and no husbands. But not when they were fifteen. And those that did were . . . sort of, like . . . marked. Different. They became sisters instead of mothers. The grandparents became parents . . . Mum was right. Nobody ever knew. I went to the home for unmarried girls in Birmingham, had a daughter, never even held her . . . The adoptive parents were waiting in the nursery. I came home, finished the commercial course, got the job at the Town Hall. That was that.'

'Oh May . . . my poor May. Did you say fifteen?'

'Fifteen when it happened. Just sixteen, I think, when Amy was born.'

'Amy? You named her?'

'No. Her parents did that. The parents who loved her and brought her up. Toby said they were marvellous. She was happy. But she did a bit of investigation and discovered . . . the facts. Toby said she grieved for me.' She moved her head so that she could see him. She repeated, wonderingly, 'She did what Daisy and Marcus are doing: she clothed me and imagined me . . . and she grieved for me. Isn't that wonderful, Arthur?'

'Toby?'

'Toby Marsh is her son. And when she died he went on looking for me. And it was one of those coincidences – surely not a random one – that he found my name in a hospital in the Midlands. I think I was diagnosed with suppressed post-traumatic stress. I was a statistic but Toby already had my name.' A trace of a dimple appeared. 'He's very conventional in a lot of ways but . . . open to possibilities. I think we're going to get on quite well.'

Arthur quivered a smile and she returned it. Her voice dropped unexpectedly to a whisper and he bent low again to listen.

'I didn't want to tell you, Arthur. You said that memories were sacred. But I was just frightened you would be shocked. Repelled.' He waited, hearing her breathing quicken. She said, 'Jack took me down to the town on VE night. Bonfires, dancing, burning effigies of Hitler . . . people kissing people. And there was a man on his own. His name was George

Hutchinson. I haven't remembered that name before, but I know that was it. He was our old neighbour, before our house was bombed. Not friendly . . . watchful . . . secretive . . . Dad said to take no notice of him. It was him.'

Arthur could not control a sob. He held her against him as if he might pick her up at any moment and run with her. Somewhere. Somewhere safe.

She put her free hand up to the back of his head, comforting him. 'I'll be quick,' she whispered. 'It did not worry me. Not then. What worried me was that Jack was being arrested at the same time. Manhandled towards some kind of armoured truck. And I couldn't do anything. He got to me – he was dragging the military police with him – nothing could stop him. He ripped the man away from me. He was screaming at him. The man ran – George Hutchinson – he ran. And he was squealing. Like a pig. And Jack was screaming that he would find him and kill him. And he did. He had a pistol – they were issued to the police after the bombing – in case we would all rise up and rebel against the war. They never had to be used and they were called in. But not all of them came back. Jack had got hold of one somehow and he carried it with him everywhere. And he used it on the man. And then . . . oh Arthur, then . . . he turned his pistol on himself. He killed himself, Arthur. Jack killed himself. We lost him as well as Dad. And Mum couldn't take it. She thought he was a coward. She started to die from then on – it took a year. Just a year.'

She was holding on to Arthur as if she might drown without him and for some time he simply held her close and gently rocked her.

When she began to relax, he put his cheek against hers.

They were both wet with tears. He made soothing sounds for a while and then they became words.

'May, if you hadn't promised your mother never to speak of this, never to think of it, you would probably have worked things out so differently. Don't you see, May, in those last few hours your brother was no longer a fugitive. He was a soldier again. And he was defending you. That man Hutchinson, he could have haunted you – and Jack would have been imprisoned, unable to do anything about it. This was his chance to set you free. The man became the enemy. And Jack was defending you just as your father defended you. Your brother was no coward, May. He was a hero.' He cleared his throat and said strongly, 'He gave his life for you. Oh yes, he was a hero.'

She clung to him. She heard his words and understood exactly what he meant. One thing stood out for her; there were many kinds of heroes. Her father had been one kind, Jack another, and, she thought very clearly, Arthur Wentworth had been a third. She had known he would understand. Heroes always recognized each other. It was a fact of life. She began to relax. Again, she slept.

The door opened, curtains swishing. The sister stood there, eyes popping as she saw Arthur lying on the bed, still wearing his shoes, well polished though they were.

'Mr *Went*worth!' she exploded.

He smiled and for a moment she saw the good-looking flying officer. She blinked.

He whispered, 'Let me stay till she wakes next. She naps for about ten minutes, that's all.'

She said nothing but went to the trolley, picked up the big roll of paper and tore off a generous length, then tucked it between his shoes and the top blanket on the bed. 'Basic hygiene,' she hissed. And left the room.

May was roused and managed a small laugh as the door closed.

'Do you always get your way, Arthur?'

'Not often. But it could be that things are changing. Since knowing you, May Thorpe, I feel very different. Almost . . . as if I'm in charge again.'

'But not quite?'

He put his face against hers, kissed beneath her ear, then her cheek, then nose and then, very gently, her mouth.

'Not quite,' he agreed.

Twenty-one

It was amazing how well the residents of Jenner House took the news of the wedding. The Smithsons seemed to think it was all their doing and even Zoe said, 'I just knew! He was so devoted.'

May came back to her room a week later and the social worker produced a walking aid that doubled as a tea trolley, had a hook for her handbag and could fold into a stool in case she met someone in the hall and wanted to stop for a chat. May demonstrated it to Daisy, Marcus and Zack in the lounge after she had explained about Toby Marsh being her grandson.

'Bloody hell,' Daisy said wonderingly. 'Technology and genealogy. This puts the Amy Jenner connection in the shade! What the hell went on in those dark Coventry days?'

May nodded and replied prosaically. 'Yes, the blackout had a lot to answer for. I think it can be filed away as a wartime incident.' She left it at that and knew that Daisy would too.

'How is BC?' she asked, just to prove that her memory banks were almost intact.

Daisy made a face. 'For some reason, I'm flavour of the month. He had to sort of sell me as a product of the school and I think he must have believed his own spiel. I'm taking the assembly on Friday. It's supposed to be a huge honour. I think I'll start off with a Pam Ayres poem.'

'Have you looked through Philip Larkin's stuff?' May glanced at Marcus, who opened his eyes wide and shook his head. She smiled. 'I gather from Marcus's sign language that you have not.'

Daisy looked from one to the other with suspicion. 'No. But I will.'

'You've done it now, May,' Marcus said. 'Just remember, Daisy, there will be eleven-year-olds present.'

Zack looked surprised. 'I know I'm almost thirteen but I've read Philip Larkin's stuff. My dad collects all the modern poets. He says the best way to learn a language is to read the poetry.'

May and Daisy were entranced and spoke in unison. 'How lovely!'

May said, 'I read him because he and Barbara Pym were good friends. And I do like Barbara Pym's novels.'

Daisy had pulled out her notebook from a bulging bag and was busy scribbling names. Aunty Vera looked in, smiled at May in a proprietary manner, straightened her face convulsively when she realized Daisy was wearing the tulip skirt yet again, and departed. Mary Smithson opened the door and waved but came no further when Marcus politely stood up. She said later to May, 'I know he's a lovely boy – you have told me that often, May dear – but he is so *tall*, one wonders whether he can be in control of such arms and legs.'

Then came Zoe wheeling the trolley laden with tea things and sporting an unopened packet of chocolate Bourbons. Zack looked delighted.

'This is a party now! Daisy's favourite biscuits too! Shall we wait for Mr Wentworth?'

Zoe glanced at May and then at the door. May smiled and said, 'Arthur has taken Philip for a walk, Zack. Who knows how long they will be? I think we had better get started.'

Daisy looked at Zoe and then at May. 'Everything all right?' she asked.

May purposely misunderstood. 'Everything is fine but I do have to rest now and then. And I would love some tea and biscuits before going back upstairs.'

Daisy was not satisfied. 'Is . . . Philip . . . another relative?'

Zoe glanced at May.

(Daisy said later, 'She was wild-eyed.' Marcus said, 'You have to make a drama of everything lately.' And Zack said, 'I thought she was wild-eyed too.')

May said comfortably, 'Not yet, Daisy. Would you open the biscuits, dear, and put them on this plate? Marcus, will you pour, you do it so well.'

May thought they probably looked a strangely formal little group sitting around a very conventional tea trolley, she in her grey pleated skirt and black top which showed off her cultured pearls to perfection; Zoe in her semi-official green dress and sensible brogues, her two tongues of hair outlining her jaw; the two boys, Zack and Marcus, both in school uniform; Daisy in her version of it, with black tights emerging from that peculiar puffball skirt and her white shirt tucked rigorously into the waistband.

May knew she had never been happy in quite this way before. She had made happiness, manufactured it like a knitted blanket, and laid it over what had happened in an effort not to think of Mum and Jack and her baby girl. It had worked. She had thought she could discard it with Walter; then – tougher and more experienced – she had discovered about fun with Norman. Her sense of humour had grown quickly, like a hollyhock. And . . . afterwards . . . when she thought she could lead an independent, interesting life in the London flat, she had been inveigled into what Norman called 'the voluntary sector'. It had started with administrative work for an orphanage. The word 'orphanage' had become debased in some way and the enormous building in Kilburn was being sold to make way for smaller 'village communities' around the country. She visited all of them with her clipboard and files, reporting back to the trustees. Facts and figures. No more than that. The blanket insulated her from loss and heartbreak. And there was time for other things; she loved the theatre and art exhibitions and reading.

There was no fixed retirement in the voluntary sector. The village communities spread north from London and she found it convenient to move to Warwickshire. She even visited Coventry again and wandered around the cathedral in a kind of dream, feeling nothing. The fields that had surrounded their old home were gone, covered in a shopping precinct and town houses; memories had gone with them. She went into Birmingham but could not find the home. She could have made enquiries through her own organization; she did not.

Age was a long time chasing her. She noticed it when her memory let her down. She did not simply forget; it didn't work like that. She would forget an appointment or an address, yes. But in its place she would remember something else. It was as if the blanket she had so carefully tucked in over her childhood was wearing thin. The things she wanted to forget came back to her; the things she wanted to remember were elusive.

She was visiting a community in Manchester during the

millennium celebrations; fireworks, a big party in a hall somewhere, paper hats and crackers and chocolate biscuits and children everywhere. She wasn't very good with children so why had she let herself work with them? For them. She worked *for* them. As if she had a debt to repay.

One of the house mothers said, 'Settle down, children. Let us listen to Miss Thorpe. She wants to tell you about the holiday plans for this summer.'

May had the facts and figures before her. She was a good administrator. She did not care for computers – she could use them but she always checked their immediate results with her own painstaking calculations – and had reason to be very satisfied with her own conclusions.

She stood up. She looked at a sea of faces. Eager faces. Faces looking forward to a new century. And then one little girl stood up and waved her chocolate biscuit in greeting.

That first hasty hospitalization had been one of several during the next ten years. Then, four years ago, a friend and colleague had visited and had offered a practical solution. She lived in Gloucestershire and had recently cut the blue opening ribbon for a new purpose-built block of flats. It was in the centre of a village tucked into the tail of the Cotswold range with an interesting history linked to Berkeley . . . Edward II . . . sheep farming. It was called Jenner House after the famous Dr Jenner. She could be a recluse there or she could mingle . . . or be a mixture of both.

May had heard of her friend's death the day she moved in and without any visitors she drifted inexorably into the recluse option.

And now, here she was, three years later, with friends of all ages, laughing like the girl with the chocolate biscuit. Because she was happy. Content, excited, living two or three lives all at the same time and accepting that was how it was. No more imagining that memories had to be smothered before she could 'move on'. They were the baggage, but they were also treasures beyond price. She needed them; and now she could share them. She shared Coventry with Arthur and he shared Dresden with her.

Philip came through the door first and held it for Arthur. He looked at the little group and grinned from ear to ear. Zoe let her breath go. She had not been able to stop Arthur from 'vetting' Philip and in a strange way she had not wanted to. If he couldn't take Arthur then he wouldn't be able to take the Smithsons, or indeed May, Zack, Marcus and the hummingbird that was Daisy Patek. She stared at him as he put a friendly hand beneath Arthur's leather-patched sports jacket and, grinning right at her, piloted him across the lounge. She felt herself getting warm; couldn't he take anything seriously? After his little speech in the office nearly two weeks ago she had suspected he was minus an important cog in his emotional make-up. Especially as he had followed it up with a marriage proposal just before May's ambulance had wailed itself to a halt outside. 'If a wedding is what it takes, then let's do it,' he had said just before she had walked out.

Since then she had been too anxious about May to listen to any other flippancies he chose to utter and when May had said to her, 'Look, I can see that the whole thing is worrying you to death. Why not let Arthur have a word with him? He will know instantly if he means what he says or says what he means.'

'But . . .' How could Zoe agree to the plodding Arthur Wentworth interrogating a man who lived entirely in the moment and therefore appeared . . . well, superficial?

May had said, 'Arthur understands so much, Zoe.'

But Zoe had still shaken her head. Philip was capable of saying something really shocking to Arthur. She could almost hear him. 'Sex is excellent therapy, Mr Wentworth. It's exactly what Mrs Ballinger needs.' Zoe closed her eyes momentarily before looking at Arthur as he walked towards them. Oh God, if Philip had shocked one of her dear residents with his ridiculous theories she would kill him.

But Arthur was looking . . . like Arthur. Solid. Dependable. Very dull. Zoe hoped very much that May knew what she was doing. After all, however shocking Philip was, he was never dull. He simply could not help saying the wrong thing and sometimes it wasn't the wrong thing really; it was the truth. And honestly, the way Arthur Wentworth had greeted him in the hall when Zoe introduced him – hadn't that been visibly manufactured? And by May too, who knew full well that Zoe had not wanted this to happen. Arthur had said oh-so-heartily, 'Very pleased to meet you, Mr Deakin. Just arrived for the tea party? The others won't be here till after school and I'm taking a short walk through the park. Will you join me? Get to know each other. Similar situations in a way.' He had held the door for Philip and armed him outside before the poor dear had known what was going on. Zoe had tried to stop them but May had started on about her walking aid as if no one else in the house had one, and Mrs Smithson had opened her door, smiled knowingly and closed it again. Almost as if she had been in on the whole thing.

And now, things were reversed. Philip held the door for Arthur and armed him across the room; Philip was grinning like a Cheshire Cat and Arthur was . . . Zoe looked straight at Arthur with her stern, matronly expression firmly in place. He was grinning too. Zoe felt herself crumbling, as if all the protective walls she had put up were coming down with a rush. She looked round at Marcus, so tall and smiling, already knowing what was right and what was wrong, accepting it, enjoying it. She switched to little Zack, who seemed to her like a chick breaking out of its egg, bright-eyed, full of knowledge and curiosity. And then to Daisy Patek, who was linked to May, perhaps standing in for the daughter May never knew, bridging the generation gap twice over. She said proudly, 'This is my fiancé, Philip . . . Philip, meet Daisy, Zack and Marcus. Good friends.'

She did not care what Arthur had said to Philip and what Philip said to Arthur. Philip had asked her to marry him and this was her way of saying yes.

He gave a whoop and dropped Arthur like a hot cake, gathered her up as if she was as light as Daisy Patek and held her to him while he looked at the others.

'Pleased to meet you all. I am Zoe Ballinger's fiancé! You heard that – all of you heard that! We are engaged to be married.' He whirled her round so that he was facing Arthur. 'We can have a double wedding! How about it, old chap? How about a double-bloody-wedding?'

'No need for the language – but if the ladies agree, why not?' Arthur somehow managed to look approving and dis-approving at the same time.

May clasped her hands delightedly and Zoe said sharply, 'Put me down this minute, Philip!'

Marcus reached for Daisy's left hand, Zack the right. Every-one was suddenly laughing. The door opened again and the flowered hood of a very modern three-wheeled baby's buggy appeared and was manoeuvred carefully into the lounge. It was pushed by a young woman almost as tall as Marcus, blonde hair in a topknot with lots of strands escaping around her fine-boned face. Behind her came Toby Marsh carrying a small girl.

May said delightedly, 'You are Evie! And you've brought May and Amy to see us! How marvellous!' She turned to Daisy. 'This is Toby, my grandson. And his family. Aren't they absolutely beautiful?'

It was as if they had all met before. Toby put little May down carefully and Zack immediately sat on his haunches to greet her. Toby reached over their heads to take Daisy's hand.

'The last time – first time too – I saw you was in the waiting area at the cottage hospital. You had been stuck there for ages, determined to see May.'

She nodded. 'It seems so long ago. Amy had just been born. I must see her.' She left him rather abruptly; she was not certain whether she approved of him. From what May had told them, he had almost played games with her, trying to trick her into admitting that she was his grandmother.

Daisy went to the pram. She looked up at the tall willowy girl holding the handle and gently rocking. Beautiful. Probably too good for Toby Marsh. She looked under the hood. Lots of blanket and a bald head. She hardly knew what to say. 'Another Amy. An anagram of May.' Then the head moved convulsively as if recognizing the name and a tiny fist struggled out of the blankets and shook at the interloper. Daisy took a breath. 'Oh . . . she's so like May.' She moved in. 'Hello, Amy. Hello.' She could have been talking to a dog or cat. Little Amy opened an angry eye and surveyed the interloper. The eye was encased in loose skin; there was a lot of loose skin around mouth as well as eyes. But Daisy was suddenly still, staring. At last she looked up at the tall, Nordic girl and whispered, 'She *is* like May. This is how May must have looked. Ready to take on the world!' She emerged from the hood and straightened. 'My God,' she said. 'This is why you wanted to find out . . . everything.'

The tall girl nodded. 'May – our May – is such a character. That's when we started to wonder. And then when we knew we were having another we thought we'd better do something about it. Toby's mother had just died and she had wanted so much to know that her mother was happy. So . . . Toby went back to the hospital where he had first identified Miss Thorpe. We worked out that she had been ten or eleven during the bombing and quite suddenly she became real and we desperately wanted to know her. We want our May and little Amy to know about her. It's not just nosiness – can you understand?'

'Of course.' Daisy understood the directness, the honesty. She looked again at Amy and said, 'She's got quite a mixed pot of genes, hasn't she?'

The girl laughed. 'I guess she has! You should meet my family.' She relaxed and said seriously, 'Toby says you and Miss Thorpe are very close. Almost telepathic.'

'Not almost.' Daisy smiled, proud that Toby had seen and understood. She said, 'Are you a model?' She took the plunge. 'A friend of mine is going to be a fashion guru. She made this skirt actually. She is looking for a model. We have to do a presentation of our work at the end of this term and . . .' she finished lamely, 'she's looking for a model.'

The girl blushed. 'Gosh. No one has ever – I'd love it. Actually, I restore paintings and artefacts. Dull stuff.'

Daisy said, 'Dull? You're a sort of detective. Like us really. May says everyone who researches stuff is a detective. And if you preserve that stuff, well . . .'

'I work in the same department?'

'Of course.' They both laughed. Daisy urged her towards Marcus. 'Little May will be OK with Zack. He's got two sisters and he's missing them. But he goes home next weekend, so . . .'

May watched them all; thought of Jack, Walter, Norman, Arthur; felt no pain, simply thankfulness. She had broken her promise to her mother and Arthur had helped her to discover other truths; truths that were still terrible but less so. And Arthur had told her of the Dresden he remembered; and she had seen, as he had seen, the ghastly emptiness of revenge.

She caught his eye above the crouching Zack as he offered little May a chocolate Bourbon, and they exchanged a look, a moment of complete understanding. He nodded once. She nodded back. Nothing was ever wasted, nothing ever lost. If only she could transfer that understanding to Daisy. Perhaps she already knew . . . May switched her gaze to the elfin girl talking so naturally to a perfect stranger. She nodded again and found Toby by her side.

'May?' He sounded untypically diffident. 'How are you now?'

She patted his hand maternally. 'I get a little stronger every day. One of the double flats will become available in June – the tenants are moving to the south coast. I think I'll be able to enjoy planning carpets and furniture. The sort of thing young brides do, you know.'

She laughed and he smiled but said seriously, 'A lot of catching up then.'

'Exactly.'

He said, 'You will let us in. Won't you?'

'Oh Toby. You don't need my permission. You have a master key.'

'You know precisely what I mean. Evie and I need a grandmother. So do our girls. And that's what you are, May Thorpe.'

'Then that's all right. Isn't it?' She looked at him. 'I'll let you in this much. Because of you, I cannot regret any of the things that happened. Not even Dad and Jack. I have always felt I was responsible for their deaths and it has been a terrible burden. But now . . . they have taken it on themselves – the burden, I mean. Jack might never have been able to live properly – he was injured and no one could see a wound so he could not be helped. And Dad . . . Dad knew exactly what he was doing. And I cannot blame my mother any more for making me promise to keep such secrets. It was a different world. I wouldn't be here now if I had spoken of it then.'

He said quietly, 'I don't know about your mother, May. But if you hadn't done what you did, I would not be here.' He picked up her hand and held it to his face. 'I want to be here, May. I want to come and see you and Arthur get married. Zoe and Philip too. Is that all right?'

She gave a chuckle. 'It will do for a start.'

Arthur went to the kitchen and returned with a cardboard wine carrier containing four bottles of champagne. Zoe and Philip went for glasses and were rather a long time about it.

Daisy said to Marcus, 'After this, I want to go home, Marc. Don't feel you have to come.'

'I want to come.' He looked into her dark eyes. 'What's up?'

'Nothing. Hormone trouble.'

'How long does this sort of thing go on for?'

'As long as it lasts, I suppose.'

'Oh Lord.'

'Precisely.'

Glasses were raised high to toast May and Arthur, Zoe and Philip. Zack pretended to chase little May around the other tables, the beautiful Evie disappeared into the kitchen to feed Amy and Daisy went to say goodbye to May.

'Will you come to see me when I am upstairs in the double flat?' May hung on to Daisy's hand, not wanting her to leave.

'Of course. Will you ask Arthur to drive you round to see our parents?'

'Of course.' They weren't quite at ease with one another. May said suddenly, 'When that happens again – that dread, that fear – remind yourself that the past is more than a burden, it's a treasure too.'

'How did you know . . . I mean, you were drinking the champagne and I was the other side of the pram. How could you know exactly how I was feeling, just for a moment?'

'I don't know. It happens sometimes.'

'For me too.' Daisy's wide smile shone forth. 'It's so bloody exciting, May! We could do a mind-reading act on the telly!'

'It might be a burden then. Let's just enjoy it and make it a treasure.'

'OK. A treasure-burden. Right?'

'Right.' May revealed her dimples. 'Give my love and congratulations to your parents. Same to your mother, Marcus.'

'Congratulations?' he queried.

May glanced at Daisy and she crowed delightedly, 'For being treasures as well as bloody great burdens!' She turned to May. 'Listen, if ever you're really short of cash we *could* cook up a turn for the telly! Don't forget!'

May watched the two of them go towards the door to the hall. Zack said a quick farewell to little May and Miss

Thorpe and joined them hurriedly. And Miss Thorpe said under her breath, 'Dear Daisy, how could I forget. Actually, I think I've stopped forgetting anything. I'm almost sure I can remember the whole world.'

She waited until the champagne ran out, which was not long, and then stood up and used her wonderful walking aid to go back to the lifts. People spoke, called their con-gratulations, peeled off to other things. Arthur was by her side. They lay on her bed as they had lain together in the hospital, so close they became one form, one whole.

May thought fleetingly of Toby Marsh, who looked so like his great-uncle. She turned into Arthur's shoulder and his arm came around her.

'Arthur. Isn't it marvellous that you and I are – are – are . . .'

'Sort of, like . . . what?'

'Sort of, like . . . real. Three-dimensional. I'm not just the batty old pedantic woman on Level Two. And you're not the fussy ancient buffer who lives down the corridor and still thinks he should have his *Times* ironed every morning.'

'I'm not sure about the old buffer. But the pedantic woman . . . she's such a scorcher. Those dimples. And the curls – better than Shirley Temple any day. And of course, she might seem goody-goody but she's wicked.'

'Arthur, be serious. You can look at me and see the frightened – terrified – child and the lonely, isolated young woman. And I can look at you, my darling, and see the gallant pilot officer, crouching over his knees, hating what he had to do. And he is my hero. My final hero.'

He was silent for so long, she thought he might have gone to sleep; and that would have been all right too. But he was not asleep and after a while he said thoughtfully, 'May . . .

can we also be young again but somewhere else? Can we be blackberrying perhaps? Can we stain each other's lips with juice? Can our names change too so that I am Edward and you are Amy?'

She whispered, 'Oh Arthur. I love you so much. We are universal lovers. How marvellous. This September we will go to Berkeley and pick blackberries. Yes?'

'Yes.' He put his cheek on top of her curls. 'How about a trip to Mablethorpe?'

She chuckled. 'You made a joke, Arthur!'

He said, 'Did I? Oh, I see . . . Ah . . . Dearest May, my whole life has been a journey to Mabel Thorpe.'

She smiled and he could just see her dimples. 'Oh, Arthur,' she whispered.

They slept entwined, both smiling. There was the past and this glorious present. And there was a future too.

They looked forward to it.

Daisy and Marcus were in the big kitchen looking through Daisy's portfolio and planning work for her interview at Bristol University for her art foundation course, which was soon. Their conversation was random, as usual. Daisy was wondering how Zack would get on back with his family. Marcus reminded her that his attackers had not been granted bail so he would probably be fairly relaxed. He said, 'His family must have missed him. I bet he's lovely with his sisters.'

She turned a page of her sketchbook and was confronted with sketches of a rocking crib, caps and bonnets, smocks and pattens.

'May said something once. That you were my friend, my brother . . .'

He said, 'And? Was there something else?'

'Yes.'

'Come on. I agree with the first two. What is the third?'

She kept her eyes on the sketchbook.

'I'm going to do a picture. A girl in a high-waisted muslin dress, slightly stained with blackberry juice. And a boy – a man, a young man – in cambric shirt and rough breeches . . .' She looked at him. 'May said we were friends, then brother and sister, then . . . lovers.'

He took her hands. They kissed for the third time. Above them, the television music crescendoed and they could hear Zack laughing his high laugh and Nerrie Patek's bass version. Downstairs they laughed too. And Daisy wondered whether she could hear other echoes . . . Mrs Ballinger and her rather outrageous Philip? Edward and Amy Jenner? May and Arthur Wentworth? She closed her eyes and listened with her whole being. Yes . . . she was fairly certain that the curious chiming laugh belonged to Aunty Alison.

Marcus said, not one bit unhappily, 'My ma and pa used to laugh like this.'

She held his hands tightly. 'I know. I do know, Marc. Honestly.'

He nodded and smiled and leaned forward to kiss her again.